SUICIDE
EXCEPTED

SUICIDE
EXCEPTED

CYRIL HARE

HarperPerennial
A Division of HarperCollinsPublishers

A hardcover edition of this book was originally published by Faber and Faber, London, England, in 1939 and is fully protected by copyright under the terms of the International Copyright Union. It is here reprinted by arrangement.

SUICIDE EXCEPTED. All rights reserved. Printed in the United States of America. No part of this book may be used or reproduced in any manner whatsoever without written permission except in the case of brief quotations embodied in critical articles and reviews. For information address HarperCollins Publishers, 10 East 53rd Street, New York, N.Y. 10022.

First Perennial Library edition published 1983. First HarperPerennial edition published 1991.

ISBN 0-06-080636-2

91 92 93 94 95 WB/OPM 10 9 8 7 6 5 4 3 2 1

To
H.H.G.C.
In gratitude, and with
apologies

SUICIDE
EXCEPTED

1

The Snail and His Trail

As you come over the brow of Pendlebury Hill, just beyond the milestone that reads "London, 42 miles," you see Pendlebury Old Hall below you. It lies a little way back from the road, a seemly brick-built Georgian house, looking from above like a rose-pink pearl on the green velvet cushion of the broad lawns surrounding it. You will probably think, if you are the type who has any leisure to think at all at the wheel of a car, that the owner of the Hall is a man to be greatly envied; and you must be very much pressed for time indeed if you do not slow down as you pass the wide entrance gates at the bottom of the hill to glance up the broad beech avenue at the simple and dignified façade of the house. At this point you will notice that over the entrance a board in lettering of impeccable taste announces "PENDLEBURY OLD HALL HOTEL," and below, in smaller but still chaster type: "Fully Licensed, Open to Non-Residents." Charmed by the sober beauty of the house, fascinated by the seclusion of its setting, your refined taste tickled by the good manners of the notice-board, you will decide that here at last is the country hotel of your dreams, where good cheer and comfort await the truly discriminating traveller. And that is where, English country hotels being what they are, you will be wrong.

Inspector Mallett of the C.I.D., sitting in the lounge of the hotel, wondered for the twentieth time, as he put down his coffee-cup with an expression of disgust, why he had ever been fool enough to enter the place. He was, he told himself, too old a hand to be caught in this way. He might have known—he should have known—from the moment that he set his foot inside the door, that it would be just like any other wayside motoring hotel, only more so, where the soup came out of a tin, and the fish had been too long on the ice, and far too long off it, where the entrée was yesterday's joint with something horrible added to it, and the joint was just about fit to make tomorrow's entrée, where tough little cubes of pineapple and tasteless rounds of banana joined to compose the fruit salad, where fresh dessert was non-existent—in the heart of the country, in mid-August! but then it was forty-two miles from Covent Garden—where bottles of sauce stood unashamed on every table, and where the coffee—he looked down again at his half empty cup, and felt for a cigarette to take away the taste.

"Did you enjoy your dinner?" said a voice at his elbow.

Mallett looked round. He saw a sallow, wrinkled face peering up into his with rheumy grey eyes which seemed to hold in them an earnest, almost desperate, expression of inquiry, quite out of keeping with the triviality of the words. Mallett recognized the symptoms at a glance— the craving for companionship of any kind, the determination to talk to somebody, no matter who, provided he would but listen—and his heart sank as he realized that to cap everything, he had fallen, bound hand and foot, into the power of an hotel bore.

"No, I did not." The inspector answered the question shortly. He did not really expect to choke the fellow off so easily, but one could but try.

"I thought not," said the other. He spoke in the muffled half-whisper habitually employed by the English in the public rooms of hotels. "But *they* didn't seem to mind it, did they?" He nodded towards the other guests in the room.

Mallett was roused in spite of himself to reply. The stranger had touched upon one of his favourite subjects.

"That's the whole trouble," he said. "So long as the public eat this kind of food without complaint, one can't expect to get anything different. It's no good blaming the hotels. I suppose these people would really feel cheated if they were given two good courses for dinner instead of five nasty ones. As it is—"

"Ah, that's just it!" the stranger broke in. "*And*, of course, with the best will in the world, you can't serve five good courses every day, lunch and dinner, in this place. For the simple reason, my dear sir, that the kitchen isn't large enough. If they had the capital to modernize it, it might be a different story, but they haven't. And so they have to resort to the wretched apologies for dishes which we've had tonight. Every time I come here it gets worse and worse. It's sad."

And looking at him, the inspector saw to his astonishment that he genuinely looked very sad indeed.

"You seem to know the place pretty well," he observed. "Have you been here often before?"

"I was born here," he answered simply, and for a space was silent.

He was a man of sixty years of age or thereabouts, perhaps more, Mallett decided. Very clean, with thin grey

3

hair and a shapeless moustache stained yellow with nico-
tine, he was an unattractive figure, but at the same time
queerly pathetic. Mallett was surprised to find himself
becoming interested in his acquaintance, and felt quite
disappointed that he seemed indisposed to say more. He
did not, however, care to break in upon thoughts that
were evidently painful.

Presently the stranger roused himself from his reverie,
and produced from his pocket a much-worn Ordnance
Survey map of the district. From another pocket he took
a mapping pen and a bottle of Indian ink. Then he
unfolded a square of the map and began to trace upon
it with great care a zigzag course.

"My day's journey," he explained. "I always keep a
record."

Looking over his shoulder, the inspector noted that
the line which he had just completed was only one
of many, several of them faded with age, and that
all of them appeared to centre upon, or radiate from,
Pendlebury Old Hall. For want of anything better to
say, he remarked:

"You are on a walking tour, I take it?"

"Yes—or rather I was. This is my last port of call. It
always is, you see." He indicated the network of lines
upon the map. "For many years I've spent my holidays
walking in this part of the world—it's wonderful country, it really is, when you know it well." He seemed anxious to forestall any possible criticism. "And since I—
h'm—since I retired, you know," he lowered his voice,
as though the fact of his retirement was in some way
shameful, "I have more leisure, can start from farther
afield. Why, one year, sir, I walked here all the way
from Shrewsbury!"

"Indeed!"

"Can't do so much now as I should like to, though.

4

My doctor tells me—but it doesn't do to pay too much attention to doctors, does it? But wherever I go, I always end—*here*."

He contemplated the map with affection.

"Wonderful how the lines all centre on this place!" he murmured.

Mallett was tempted to comment that there was nothing really wonderful in the fact, considering that he had made them all himself, but the pathetic earnestness of the man kept him silent.

"I often think," he went on, putting the map away again, "that if we left a trail behind us in all our wanderings like—like snails, if you follow me, mine would be found to be concentrated on this place. It begins here—for the first twenty years of my life it was here and hereabouts more than anywhere else—and now I've reached a time of life when I ask myself more and more often, where will it end?"

It was a thoroughly embarrassing moment for an undemonstrative man such as the inspector was. He could think of no better comment than to clear his throat loudly.

"Of course," the stranger pursued, still in the same hushed undertone, "we have this advantage over the snail—we can make our trail end when and where we wish."

"My dear sir!" said Mallett, thoroughly shocked, as he realized the full implication of the words.

"But, after all, why not? Take my own case, for example. No, not for example, I'm not interested in other cases—take my own case, for its own sake. I'm an elderly man, I've lived my life, such as it is, and believe me, I've had enough of it to know that the best of it is behind me. When my trail ends, I shall leave my family well provided for—I've seen to that, anyway. . . ."

5

"You have a family, then?" Mallett put in. "Then surely—"

"Oh, I know what you are going to say," he answered wearily. "But I don't flatter myself that they will miss me. They may think now that they will, but they won't. They have their own trails too, and theirs and mine take different directions. My fault, I dare say. I'm not complaining, I'm just facing the facts. I shouldn't have married a woman fifteen years younger than myself. She—"

He broke off suddenly, as some one walked behind Mallet's chair and down the room away from them.

"Hullo!" he said. "Why that's—no, I must have been mistaken. Thought it was somebody I knew, but it couldn't have been. Those back views are deceptive sometimes. As I was saying—my daughter is very fond of me, in her way, and I'm very fond of her, in my way, but they're not the same ways, so what's the good of pretending that we are necessary to each other? I don't like her—her friends, for instance, and that means a lot at her age."

Mallett had begun to lose interest again. The fellow seemed to be merely rambling. The way in which after a casual interruption he had suddenly introduced the subject of his daughter, who had not been previously mentioned, when he had been in the full flood of discussing his wife, indicated an ominous lack of grip on his train of thought. But suddenly he jerked himself alive again, and said in a quite new, determined tone of voice: "I'm going to have a liqueur brandy. My doctor doesn't allow it, but damn the doctor! We can only die once. And you are going to have one with me. Yes! I insist! There's still some of the old stuff in the cellar that was here when my father was alive. You'll like it. It will help to digest some of that horrible food you've just been eating."

The inspector allowed himself to be persuaded. He

6

felt that he deserved some recompense for having listened so patiently. When the drinks were brought, the stranger said:

"I like to know who I'm drinking with, and I expect you do too."

He extended a card. Mallett read: "Mr. Leonard Dickinson," followed by an address in Hampstead. He replied by giving his name, but concealed his rank and profession, which experience told him was apt to produce either an embarrassing constraint or a troublesome access of curiosity.

"Your very good health, Mr. Mallett!" said Dickinson.

The evening seemed likely to end on a mellower note than that on which it had begun. But when the glasses were empty, Dickinson reverted to the same subject.

"That was good!" he said. "It takes me back for a moment or two to the old days. To my family, Mr. Mallett, this is merely a third-rate hotel. To me, it is a place of memories—the only place where I have ever been in any degree happy."

He paused, holding the empty glass between cupped hands, savouring the bouquet that still rose from it.

"That is why," he added with quiet emphasis, "since my trail must end somewhere, I should like—I feel sure that it will end—here."

He got up. "Good night, sir," he said. "You are staying the night here, I suppose?"

"Yes," said Mallett. "My holiday ends tomorrow, and I am making the most of it. I shall see you at breakfast?"

Dickinson allowed this innocent question to remain unanswered for quite a considerable time. Then he said softly, "Perhaps!" and turned away.

Mallett watched him walk with the gait of a tired man down the length of the lounge, saw him stop and say something to the girl at the reception desk, and then make his way slowly upstairs. He shivered slightly. The old man's conversation had been too depressing. He felt as though a goose had walked over his grave. It was high time he too went to bed, but before he did so, he consumed another liqueur brandy.

2

The Trail Ends

Monday, August 14th

Hotels in England, however bad, seldom go very far wrong with breakfast, and Mallett, fortified by a good night's rest, for which, perhaps, he owed more to the admirable brandy of the previous evening than to the somewhat stony comfort of his bed, attacked his imported eggs and bacon next morning with his usual appetite. As he did so, his mind reverted more than once to his curious encounter with Mr. Dickinson. A garrulous, peevish old man, he reflected, with a bee in his bonnet about the hotel, and probably, if one could have got him to talk on any other subject, about everything else as well. If his conversation ran on the same gloomy lines at home, it was not very surprising that his family didn't altogether love him. At the same time, Mallett could not but feel a certain sympathy for him. He gave the impression of a man unjustly treated by fate. It seemed wrong for any one to be so depressed as to have to confide in a chance acquaintance in the way that he had done. And when the confidence amounted almost to a threat of suicide . . . ! He shrugged his shoulders. People who contemplated such things didn't confide their intentions, whether to chance acquaintances or to anybody else, he told himself. But at the same time, he could not altogether rid his mind of a persistent feeling of uneasiness with regard to Mr. Dickinson. The man seemed in some way haunted. Mallett's whole training rendered him averse from relying on, or even recognizing, any suspicion that was not founded on tangible facts. Nevertheless, he had to admit to himself that his companion of the night before had left him in a vaguely disturbed frame of mind. He seemed to carry an aura of calamity about him. And Mallett, who was hardened enough to calamities of all kinds, did not like auras.

As he finished his meal, the inspector glanced round the room. The hotel was evidently not very full, for only a bare half-dozen of the tables were occupied. He looked round for Mr. Dickinson, and looked in vain. For an instant the ominous "Perhaps!" on which they had parted flashed into his mind. Then his common sense reasserted itself. The old gentleman was having his breakfast in bed, most probably—at his age he was quite entitled to it, particularly at the end of a strenuous walking tour. In any case, it was none of his business. There would be plenty of genuine problems awaiting his solution at New Scotland Yard that afternoon.

Some five minutes later, he was walking across the lounge to the reception desk with the intention of paying his bill, when he saw a white-faced chambermaid hurry down the stairs and run to the desk in front of him. There was a hasty colloquy between her and the girl clerk. The latter spoke into the house telephone, and after a few moments, during which the maid hung miserably about the lounge, looking sadly out of place (which indeed she was, at that time of the morning), the manager, swart, flabby, and irascible, came on the scene.

10

He had a few angry words with the girl, who seemed on the verge of tears, and the pair of them disappeared up the stairs together. The clerk applied herself to the telephone, and seemed to be speaking with some urgency.

When she had finished, Mallett asked for his bill. It was some time in being prepared. The clerk seemed preoccupied and nervous. Obviously, something was not as it should be in the hotel, and once again the inspector felt an unreasoning qualm at the pit of his stomach. Once again, he told himself that whatever it was it did not concern him. Accordingly, without comment or inquiry, he settled his account, asked the hall porter (whom he found, quite irregularly, gossiping with someone from the kitchen regions) to fetch his bag down from his room, and went out to the garage for his car.

When he drove round to the front door to pick up his bag, there were two cars there that had not been there before. From the second of these, as Mallett drew up, there alighted a man in uniform. He turned to say something over his shoulder to another who was following him, looked up, and his eyes met the inspector's. Recognition was mutual. The man in uniform was the sergeant of police in charge at the local market town. Mallett had met him a year or two before in connexion with some inquiries which had resulted in the conviction of an important "fence," specializing in the produce of country-house burglaries. He had liked the man at the time, but just now, as he smiled and nodded, he could have wished him in Jericho.

"Mr. Mallett!" exclaimed the sergeant, coming across to him. "This is a coincidence, and no mistake! Are you here on business, sir?"

"I am here on holiday," said the inspector, firmly. "That is, I was here. Just now I'm on my way back to London."

11

The sergeant looked disappointed.

"Pity," he said. "It would have been a comfort to have you around, sir, just in case there did turn out to be anything in this job. Not that there ever is, in this part of the world."

"And even if there was, Sergeant," returned Mallett, "I am on holiday, and so remain until I report at the Yard at three o'clock this afternoon."

"Quite so, sir. Well, I'm very glad to have seen you again, sir, in any case. I must go and attend to my business now. It'll be quite a sensation in the neighbourhood, I expect, seeing that it's old Mr. Dickinson."

"Oh, it *is* Mr. Dickinson, is it?" exclaimed the inspector, taken off his guard for once.

The sergeant paused, one foot on the doorstep of the hotel, and looked at him with renewed interest.

"So you knew Mr. Dickinson, sir?" he said.

"I met him last night for the first time in my life. What has happened to him?"

"Found dead in bed this morning. An overdose of something or other, so far as I can understand. The doctor's up there now."

"Poor chap!" said Mallett. Then, conscious of the sergeant's curious gaze upon him, he added: "Look here, Sergeant, I had rather a curious talk with Mr. Dickinson last night. There's just a possibility I might be a useful witness at the inquest. I'd better give you a statement before I go, and meanwhile—do you mind very much if I come upstairs with you, purely as a witness, mind?"

Leonard Dickinson's room was at the end of the long corridor which ran the length of the hotel's first floor. Facing south and east, it was now flooded with the mellow August sun. On the large, old-fashioned bed lay the body, the angularities of the wizened features softened

12

in death, the lines of anxiety smoothed away. Mallett, looking down on the still countenance, reflected that he looked happier now than he had in life. The last line had been traced on the map, and the end was where he had desired.

The map, appropriately enough, lay on the table beside the bed, open at the section where the Hall marked the centre of the spider's web of tracks. Also on the table, he observed, was a bottle of small white tablets, and another, similar bottle, which was empty.

The doctor was just putting away his instruments when they entered. He was young, brisk, and cocksure.

"Overdose of a sedative drug," he remarked. "I suppose you'll have to have those things analysed." He nodded at the table. "But I can tell you what's in them." He muttered some scientific polysyllables and added: "Analyse him, too; you'll find he's full of it. It's apt to be a bit dangerous, that kind of stuff. You take your dose—it doesn't work properly—you wake up in the night, feeling a bit stupid—think, Good Lord, I never took my dose—take another—wake up again perhaps, if you've had a drink too much—take two or three more for luck, and you're in a coma before you know anything about it. Easy as winking."

Something white protruding from beneath the map caught the sergeant's eye. It was a small card, bearing on it some writing in a firm, clear hand. Without speaking, he drew it out, read it, and held it up for Mallett to see.

The words were: *We are in the power of no calamity, while Death is in our own.*

Mallett nodded silently. After the doctor had gone, he said, *"That's* why I thought I might be wanted as a witness."

He glanced round the room, and then, reminding himself that this was not his case, left the sergeant to

13

carry on until he was free to take a statement from him in due form.

When the time came for this, the sergeant, who could not bring himself to forego the rare opportunity of cross examining so great a man, had a few supplementary questions to ask. Mallett answered them good-humouredly enough. Having seen the statement completed to the other's satisfaction, he had a question of his own to ask.

"I don't want to waste your time, Sergeant," he said, "but I can't help being a bit interested in old Mr. Dickinson. He seemed rather an odd fish, to judge by the little I saw of him."

"He was, and all that," the other agreed heartily.

"I wish you could tell me a little about him. He said something to me last night about having been born in this place."

"You didn't mention that in your statement," said the sergeant severely.

"I'm afraid not. I thought it was hardly relevant."

"Well, perhaps it wasn't. In any case, sir, we hardly needed your evidence for that. It's what you might call common knowledge in these parts."

"He was a well-known character, then?"

"Lord bless you, yes, sir! You see, the Dickinsons had this place ever since it was built, and that was near on two hundred years ago, they say."

"But they got rid of it some time ago, surely?"

"Thirty years ago come Michaelmas—when old Mr. Dickinson died, that was."

Mallett laughed.

"I see that memories are long in the country," he said.

"T'isn't that exactly, sir," the sergeant explained. "Mr. Leonard—the deceased, I suppose I should call him—he couldn't bear to leave the house. He's been here and hereabouts off and on ever since. Quite potty about the place, he was."

"So I gathered from what he said to me."

"Funny, wasn't it, sir? None of the rest of the family felt that way about it. Mr. Arthur—that was his brother—made a pile of money in London and could have bought the old place back several times over, but he never bothered to. But Mr. Leonard, for all he had a wife and family of his own, couldn't keep away from it. Well," the sergeant concluded pointedly, "I mustn't keep you any longer, sir."

It was not often that Inspector Mallett had to be reminded that he was wasting his own time or anybody else's. He was quite ashamed to discover how interested he had allowed himself to become in what was, on the face of it, the commonplace suicide of a commonplace, if eccentric, elderly gentleman. He pulled himself together, thanked the sergeant for his kindness, and left the hotel. Then he turned his car in the direction of London, and put the tragedy of poor Mr. Dickinson firmly out of his mind.

3

Family Post-mortem

Friday, August 18th

"Typical of Leonard to want to be buried at Pendlebury! No consideration for anybody's convenience. Typical!"

The speaker was George Dickinson, the eldest surviving brother of the deceased; the occasion was, as will have been gathered, the funeral of Leonard, and the remarks were uttered as George was climbing heavily into his car after the ceremony. He had been a stout man when his morning-coat had been made for him, ten years before. In the interval he had added an inch and a quarter to his girth, and the resulting discomfort, accentuated by the heat of the day, had put him into what was for him an unusually bad temper. His temper, it may be added, was normally a bad one. What was for him an unusually bad temper was something quite beyond the range of the average adult. It belonged rather to the type of the ungovernable rages of the three-year-old. Unfortunately, it could not be dealt with in the same way.

"In August, too! It's really too much!" added George,

sitting down heavily in the back seat, and mopping his forehead where the top hat had creased it.

"Yes, George," said a thin submissive voice at his side.

Lucy Dickinson had been saying, "Yes, George," for close on thirty years. If she had got tired of saying it during that time, she kept her own counsel on the subject. It was certainly the easiest thing to say, and by confining her observations to those two monosyllables she did, as she had found by experience, contrive to save a good deal of trouble. At the present moment, for example, she would have been justified in pointing out that George himself had stipulated in his will that he too should be buried in the family vault, that at the present moment he was badly crushing her new black silk dress, and that it would have been more becoming, to say the least of it, to wait until they were out of sight of the churchyard gates before lighting one of the cigars which he was now, with immense efforts, fishing out of his tail-pocket. But to have mentioned any of these things would quite certainly have meant trouble. And trouble, after thirty years of marriage to such as George, is a thing that one learns the value of avoiding.

"Well! What are you hanging about for? Drive on, man, can't you? We don't want to be here all day!" was George's next observation, directed to the chauffeur, who was still standing at the door of the car.

The car, unfortunately, was a hired one, and the driver was a young man who showed no particular reverence for his temporary employer. Servants who depended on George for their livelihood soon learned the necessity of an eager obsequiousness which in George's language was called "knowing their place." This one merely stared with interest at the empurpled face confronting him, and remarked, "You haven't told me where to go to yet."

"Hampstead," barked George. "Sixty-seven, Plane

Street, Hampstead. Go down the High Street till you get to—"

"O.K.," the chauffeur said. "I know it." And he cut off further conversation by shutting the door rather louder than was necessary.

"Impertinent young swine," fumed George. "They're all like that nowadays. And what on earth made you tell Eleanor that we would go back there after the service?" he went on, rounding on Lucy. "Confound nuisance! God knows when we shall get home." He lit his cigar as the car moved forward.

Lucy's voice came faintly through the cloud of tobacco smoke. The smell of a cigar in a confined space always made her feel faint, but that was one of the things that dear George was apt to forget, and this was emphatically not an occasion to remind him of it.

"She asked me if we wouldn't come, dear," she said. "It was really rather difficult to say no. She wants all the help she can get just now, you know. I thought it was the least we could do."

George grunted. The cigar was beginning to have its customary mollifying effect on him, and his rage with the world at large was declining to a merely average crossness.

"Well, I hope she gives us dinner, that's all," he said. "It's the least *she* could do."

Lucy said nothing. She had not the smallest expectation that Leonard's widow would wish them to stay to dinner, but it would be wiser to let George discover this for himself in due course.

"But why did she pick on us?" George grumbled on. "Couldn't she have asked any of the others?"

If Lucy had been a woman of spirit she would have retorted that the reason that Mrs. Dickinson had asked them was that she happened to be extremely fond of her,

Lucy, and that George was included merely as a disagreeable but necessary appendage to her. But the wives of the Georges of this world are not women of spirit, or if they are they do not remain wives for long.

"She has asked some of the others, dear," she said mildly. "Edward is going back with her—"

"That smarmy parson? Why on earth—"

"Well, after all, George, he is her brother. Then I think some of the nephews wished to come, too, and of course, Martin."

"Martin?"

"Anne's fiancé, dear. You remember, you met him at dinner when we—"

"Yes! Yes! Of course I remember perfectly well," said George testily. "You needn't treat me as a complete child."

Lucy, who had done very little else for thirty years, was heroically silent. The mention of Martin presently sent George off on another tack.

"Positively indecent, those children not being at the funeral," he said.

"Anne and Stephen, you mean?"

"Of course I mean Anne and Stephen. They're the only children Leonard ever had, so far as I'm aware."

"But George, they couldn't be there. They are abroad. Eleanor wrote to us and explained—"

"Then they ought to have been got back again. It's indecent, I tell you. I can't see myself, if my father had died—"

But the words had suddenly jerked back to George's mind a recollection of what had really happened when his father died, and of the nasty, unforgivable scene that he had made with his mother on the very day of the funeral. And with that memory embittering even the flavour of his admirable cigar, he was silent.

"They are in Switzerland, climbing somewhere," Lucy went on, unaware of the reason for her husband's abrupt silence. "Stephen only went out to join Anne there just before Leonard died. Eleanor wired and wrote, of course, but she hasn't had any answer. You know what Stephen is on his holidays. He'll go off for days at a time, staying in huts and places. They may not even have heard about it yet. I'm sure they would have come back at once if they had."

"Silly young fools. I shouldn't wonder if they'd broken their necks."

After this charitable observation, no more was said upon the subject, and for the rest of the way to London George contented himself with explaining at great length the measures he had taken, in his own words, "to squash the newspaper snoopers" who had approached him for information about his brother's life and sudden death, and with reviling the Press with the paucity and inadequacy of the obituary notices. That there could be any connexion between the two facts naturally did not occur to him.

Just as they were approaching Hampstead, a thought struck him.

"By the way," he said, "d'you think Leonard left Eleanor very badly off?"

"I don't know, George, I'm sure."

"I was thinking, that will of Arthur's you know. She may be a bit hard hit. You're sure she didn't say anything to you about it?"

"No, I'm quite certain she did not."

"Um!" said George, turning over in his mind the disagreeable possibility that he was going to be asked for help. He decided that it would probably be best not to stay for dinner, after all.

*   *   *

It was certainly a full-blown family assembly. George, with his new-born fear strong within him, took as little part in it as possible, leaving it to Lucy to say the proper things to the various people who seemed to crowd the little room. These included a number of dim cousins, who had not been able to get to the funeral. Exactly what they were doing there it was difficult to say. They seemed a little uncertain on the point themselves. Martin Johnson, Anne's fiancé, hung rather miserably about the outskirts of the family group. In the absence of Anne, his position was an awkward one. The engagement had never been made public, and officially even the dimmest of the cousins had a better right to be there than he. Mrs. Dickinson's parson brother, Edward, on the other hand, seemed to be quite in his element. His guiding principle in life was one which he himself had happily described as "Looking on the Right Side of Things," and his round red face shone with unction—if that is the proper word for clerical perspiration—as he exploited the situation to the full. His one regret appeared to be the unavoidable absence of his wife, laid low by a recurrence of her chronic asthma. It was a regret shared by none who knew her. Aunt Elizabeth, to her numerous nephews and nieces, was The Holy Terror—a title which was on the whole well deserved.

Mrs. Dickinson, meanwhile, sat, the melancholy queen bee in the centre of the family hive, looking at least every inch a widow. George eyed her with interest. Lucy, he supposed, would look like that some day. After all, she was younger than he was, and a better life. What would she feel like? He averted his mind from the thought and concentrated upon Eleanor. What, in her heart of hearts, did she really think of it all? It could have been no joke being married to Leonard. He felt pretty sure that Lucy would—no, damn it! we are thinking

21

about Eleanor!—he felt morally certain that Eleanor's widowhood was a relief to her, even if she didn't know it yet. At the moment, she was everything that one could expect—calm, subdued, and appealingly helpless.

Presently sherry began lugubriously to circulate, accompanied by small, dusty-tasting sandwiches. Little by little conversation began to be more animated. There were even faint approximations to laughter in one corner of the room, where some of the less responsible of the cousins had forgathered. But, on the whole, the decencies were preserved, and talk remained at a low pitch, so that the sound of a taxi being driven up to the door was distinctly heard by every one in the room.

"Now, I wonder who—" said Edward, who happened to be nearest the window, peering out anxiously. "I only hope it's not—Bless my soul, but it's the children!"

A moment later Stephen and Anne Dickinson came into the room. They looked very much out of place in that funeral company. Except for the ice-axes and rucksacks which they had presumably just deposited in the hall, they were equipped as though Plane Street, Hampstead, were a glacier and No. 67 an Alpine refuge. Their huge iron-shot boots grated uneasily on the parquet floor, and when Anne bent to kiss her mother it became only too apparent that her breeches had been lavishly patched in the seat with some rock-resisting but alien material. From the cousins' corner came something very like a titter.

"The children," as Edward to their extreme annoyance persisted in calling them, were respectively twenty-six and twenty-four, Stephen being the elder. They were both tall, slim, and loose-limbed, but in other respects there was not much likeness between them. Stephen had light brown hair and a skin that was ordinarily pale. At the present moment his whole face was a fiery red, and

22

his rather prominent nose was beginning to peel in a markedly unbecoming fashion. Anne had been more fortunate, or more circumspect, in her encounter with the sun of high altitudes and rarified atmosphere. Her face and throat were burned a deep mahogany which blended pleasingly with her dark hair and brown eyes. It was a striking face, handsome rather than pretty, with a firm, rather too square chin that was at variance with her *retroussé*, essentially feminine nose. The chin, one felt, would have been better suited to her brother, whose intelligent brow and eyes were betrayed by a jaw that lacked character. Stephen had the carriage and expression of the fluent talker, easily making himself at home in any society in which he might find himself. In comparison, Anne's quiet and reserved manner seemed almost gauche. At the moment, it was certainly fortunate that he was present to carry off a situation that was sufficiently awkward.

"I must apologize for our clothes," he said. "We simply came straight away in what we stood up in. I hope they're sending on our luggage from Klosters." He looked round at the black-clad group. "I suppose the funeral was today?"

"You should have let us know you were coming," said his mother gently. "Of course, we should have put it off for you, if we had known where you were."

"Didn't you get my telegram? I gave a couple of francs to a porter at Davos to send one for me, but the fellow must have pocketed it and the cash for the wire as well. Too bad! You see, we knew nothing about this till the day before yesterday, and then it was only a pure fluke that I happened to see *The Times*."

"It may not be any affair of mine," put in George, in a tone that made it quite clear that he was satisfied that it was very much his affair, "but do you think it is quite

23

decent to come home in this way, in those clothes, on an occasion like this?"

Stephen very ostentatiously did not answer him.

"You see, Mother," he explained, "I actually got to Klosters the afternoon of the very day it must all have happened. There were the guides and Anne and everyone waiting, and I made them start out that very night. I suppose if we'd waited we'd have heard next morning. It was all my fault, really, but I couldn't have told, could I? We were absolutely out of touch with everything for three days until we came down into Guarda, where I picked up an old paper someone had left and saw the announcement. There was just time to get down to the station to catch the train. Stopping at Klosters for clothes and things would have simply wasted a day."

"Of course dear, I understand. Give yourself some sherry. You must be tired. It is good to have you back again."

Anne meanwhile had quickly gravitated towards Martin, who from the moment of her arrival had ceased to feel or to appear like an ownerless dog in the family pack. Stephen, watching them together, wondered not for the first time what his sister could see in the squat, sandy, short-sighted young man.

"I have asked Martin to stay to dinner," said Mrs. Dickinson, thereby tactfully indicating to the company in general that Martin was now to be regarded as one of the family, and to Anne that she would have plenty of opportunity of monopolizing him later.

"This business has been a step-up for Martin, at any rate," said Stephen to himself. "Mother always had a soft place for that little squirt. I wonder why."

He was wondering how he could contrive to say a few words to Aunt Lucy without involving himself with Uncle George when he was accosted by the least dim of the cousins, one Robert, who explained that he had been managing what he described as "the solicitor's end of the affair," pending his, Stephen's, arrival. Pinning him firmly in a corner, he produced sheafs of documents and began pouring out a flood of detail concerning matters that would require attention. Stephen was somewhat overcome by the mass of work which had to be done. He had entirely forgotten what a complex legal and financial operation dying is apt to be, particularly when it is carried out at short notice.

He tore himself away from Cousin Robert at last, and began to do his duty as host with the sherry and sandwiches.

"A pity you weren't back for the funeral," said his spinster cousin Mabel acidly, as he handed her a glass. Her tone seemed to imply that he had kept away deliberately.

He felt inclined to point out that he could hardly be blamed for it, but contented himself with saying mildly:

"Yes, Cousin Mabel, it was unfortunate."

"I was in favour of holding it up, but your mother wouldn't listen to reason. You'll go and see the grave as soon as you can, I suppose?"

"Oh, yes, Cousin Mabel."

"You mustn't let the inquest verdict distress you, my dear boy," said Uncle Edward, squeezing his arm affectionately as he pushed past him to get at the decanter.

"The verdict? I haven't heard anything about it. There was nothing in the only paper I saw."

"Suicide," said Uncle George with all the relish of the bearer of evil tidings. "While of unsound mind. 'Pon my soul, if I'd ever imagined that poor old Leonard would—"

"No, no!" Uncle Edward corrected him. "While the

Balance of his Mind was Disturbed. Not at all the same thing, I assure you, George."

"Same thing absolutely. Difference in wording, that's all. Why on earth the silly asses—"

"No," persisted Uncle Edward. "You must pardon me, George, but it is *not* the same thing. No Stigma, you follow me, no Stigma for the family. That makes all the difference in the world."

The argument, once under way, showed no signs of ever coming to an end, but an interjection from Anne stopped it abruptly.

"Suicide!" she exclaimed. "Do you mean to say that they actually think Father killed himself?"

"While the Balance of his Mind—" Uncle Edward began again, in his suavest tones.

"I don't believe it! Mother, Stephen, you don't any of you really think that? Why, it's—it's too horrible for words!"

"But I assure you there's no Stigma—"

"You were not at the inquest, Anne," said her mother quietly.

"No, of course I wasn't. All I've seen was the little obituary in *The Times*, the one that had the notice on the front page. It said something about an overdose of medicine. We took it for granted there had been some horrible accident, didn't we, Stephen? Why shouldn't it have been an accident? Nobody's going to persuade me that Father—"

She seemed on the brink of tears. Everybody began to talk at once.

"But Anne, dear, your father was always a little—"

"The detective fellow made it perfectly clear—"

"When a man leaves a message behind like that—"

"He couldn't have opened two bottles by accident—"

"I've got a complete record of all the evidence—"

26

Anne, her eyes swimming, her ears deafened with the sudden babel of noise, turned to her brother for support.

"Stephen," she said, "you don't believe this, do you? There's been a horrible mistake somewhere. You've got to put it right."

For the first time Stephen saw himself as the head of the family, the ultimate Court of Appeal in what concerned himself, his mother and sister, with whose decisions the uncles and cousins might disagree if they pleased, but dared not interfere. He squared his shoulders involuntarily beneath the weight of authority which had descended upon them.

"Obviously it was an accident," he said. "That is, I don't actually know anything more about the affair than you do. But I'll make it my business to find out." He turned to the dimmest of all the cousins, who had spoken last. "Did you say that you had a record of all the evidence at the inquest?"

"Yes. In the local paper. It's practically verbatim. They've spelled some of the names wrong, but you can check that from the other papers. I've got them all. I keep a press-cutting book, you know."

"All right. Will you let me have all you've got? As soon as you can?"

"Oh, rather. I'll send it round tonight."

"Thanks."

"You'll let me have it back again, won't you?"

"Certainly, if it's any use to you."

"Oh, rather. I mean, there's not much in my book yet, and—"

"I quite understand."

"I don't want to butt in, my boy," said Uncle George, who spent most of his life butting in, with frequently disastrous results, "but is it going to make a ha'porth of difference to anyone whether it was suicide or accident?"

"Not the smallest, *I* should say," remarked Cousin Mabel.

Uncle Edward's lips were to be seen silently forming the word "stigma."

"Probably not, I dare say," said Stephen wearily. "It isn't a bit what I expected, that's all." What did it matter what he said to these people? It was no concern of theirs.

"It makes a lot of difference to *us*," said Anne. Her glance included her mother, who sat, her hands in her lap, listening and saying nothing.

As if recalled to her surroundings by the words and the look that accompanied it, Mrs. Dickinson rose from her chair.

"If you will excuse me, I shall go and lie down for a little before dinner," she said. "Anne, I think you had better do the same. You have had a long journey. Stephen, will you show Martin where to wash his hands?"

The rest of the party took the hint and left the house in a noisy, chattering body, each with a private disappointment that he or she had not also been invited to stay for dinner. Only George, as he climbed once more into the hired car, with the cheerful prospect of soon getting into comfortable clothes again, was relieved that at all events the dreaded question of financial support for his sister-in-law was postponed for that evening.

4

Uncle Arthur's Will

Dinner proved to be a good deal more enjoyable than might have been expected, if only for the absence of the relations. Mrs. Dickinson strove with a surprising degree of success to make the occasion as much like a normal family party as possible. Now that she was no longer coping with the irritability of George, or being exhorted to be cheerful by Edward, her naturally sunny, equable temperament reasserted itself, and she contrived to keep the conversation going throughout the meal without once touching on the subject that hung like a black curtain in the background of the minds of each of them. Stephen and Anne felt that they were seeing a new side to their mother's character, and to each the same thought came, unbidden: that dinner at home was, regrettably but unmistakably, pleasanter for the absence of the querulous, contradictory figure who, as far back as they could remember anything, had sat at the head of the table.

But in the drawing-room, after dinner, Mrs. Dickinson's manner changed. Her face from being serious

29

became solemn, and she appeared to be nervously awaiting the moment when the door closed behind the maid who brought in the coffee. Then she drew a deep breath, patted her hair into place—a sure sign, in the family, that she was worried—and said:

"Stephen, I have something important to discuss with you. No, don't go, Martin. It concerns us all, and I count you as one of the family now. I have had a letter from Jelks, your father's solicitor, which I don't at all understand, and which rather disturbs me. I haven't shown it to Robert, as I didn't think it concerned him. You must deal with it, Stephen."

She fetched a letter from her desk, but did not immediately hand it over to Stephen. Instead, she continued to talk, holding it in her hand.

"I must explain, first of all," she said. "You all know, of course, about the very odd and improper will that your Uncle Arthur made?"

"Yes, of course," said Stephen and Anne together.

"Do you know what I am talking about, Martin?"

Martin looked at Anne.

"Do I?" he said. To Stephen, he appeared more oafish at that moment than he had ever done before, which was saying a good deal.

"Perhaps you don't," said Anne patiently. "I meant to tell you, but I don't think I did. Uncle Arthur—"

"Perhaps I had better explain," said her mother. "Arthur Dickinson, who was my husband's eldest brother, and the only wealthy member of the family, died last year. He was a bachelor, and he left a considerable amount of money, which he divided equally between his brothers, Leonard and George, and the children of Tom and of his sister Mary. Those are the cousins who were here this evening, some of them. We are rather a

30

large family, I'm afraid, but I expect Anne has told you all about us."

"Oh, yes," said Martin, squinting rather doubtfully through his thick glasses at Anne once more.

"Very well. As I have said, he left his money equally divided, as to the amount, that is. But in the way in which he left it, he did not deal fairly so far as we were concerned. Although he was always on perfectly friendly terms with my husband, he had or pretended to have some grievance against *us*, I mean against myself and Anne and Stephen. I need not go into how it all originated—it's an old story, and rather a painful one, I am afraid—but it seems to have worked upon his mind to such an extent . . ." She began to be a little flustered, and lost the thread of the story. "Of course, he was an old man, and not perhaps altogether—at all events, I have never felt it right to blame him, because he cannot really have been himself at the time—"

"The long and the short of it is, he cut us all out of his will," said Stephen impatiently.

Martin absorbed the information slowly.

"Cut you out? I see," he said. Then turning to Anne he said reproachfully: "I'm quite sure you didn't tell me anything about that. That was rather a rotten thing to do," he added solemnly. "What made him do a thing like that?"

There was a pause, long enough to make even as thick-skinned a man as Martin aware that he had said the wrong thing. Mrs. Dickinson pursed her lips, Anne flushed, and Stephen looked savagely angry.

"That's neither here nor there," he said. "The point is what he did, and that's what I'm trying to tell you. He left Father the interest on fifty thousand pounds—that was his share—for life only. Everybody else had their bit absolutely, to do what they liked with. But on Father's death the capital of his little lot was to go to some beastly charity or another, I forget what. Do you remember, Mother?"

"No. It doesn't matter what charity it was, does it? But as a matter of fact, only half of it was for the charity. The rest goes to somebody else—a woman," Mrs. Dickinson explained, lowering her voice. "I'm afraid rather a disreputable person, altogether."

Martin, to Stephen's disgust, showed a tendency to snigger at this point. That is to say, while keeping a perfectly straight face, he gave the impression that he was only doing so with difficulty.

"My husband was of course very much upset at the injustice of the will," Mrs. Dickinson went on, "and he decided to do what he could to provide for his family."

"He insured his life, I suppose," said Martin at once.

Stephen looked up in some surprise. The man was not altogether such a fool as he had thought. It was difficult to tell what went on behind those thick glasses. Had he been underrating him?

"Exactly. For twenty-five thousand pounds. The premium was very high, I understand, in view of his age. In fact, I do not think it left very much out of the income Arthur had left him. But as most of his other means consisted of his pension from the Civil Service, which would of course die with him, he thought it well worth while."

"I see."

"And now that we've had all this ancient history over again for Martin's benefit," said Stephen, "can we get to the point?"

His voice was impatient, and more than impatient. It seemed to contain a hint of anxiety, almost of nervousness.

Martin took off his glasses, polished them and blinked upwards at the light.

"I think that what Mrs. Dickinson is going to tell us is this," he said. "Since your Uncle Arthur died only a year ago, I presume that the insurance policy is less than a year old. Most insurance companies have a thing they call a suicide clause in their policies. What company is this one, Mrs. Dickinson?"

"The British Imperial."

"H'm, yes, just so," said Martin, replacing his spectacles. "They would be quite certain to have a suicide clause, and a very strictly drawn one too. It's a most unfortunate position altogether."

Looking extremely pleased with himself, he pulled from his pocket a foul-looking pipe, blew through it, and began to fill it. Stephen looked at him with feelings of disgust. He was disgusted with Martin for presuming to smoke a pipe in the drawing-room without asking permission, and still more disgusted with himself for having allowed this interloper to take possession of the discussion. Before he could say anything, however, Anne intervened.

"Martin!" she said sharply. "Put that beastly pipe of yours away, and explain things properly. What is a suicide clause, and how does it work?"

Martin blushed and put his pipe in his pocket with a mumbled "Sorry!" Then he said: "It simply means that if you insure your life and commit suicide within a certain time—usually a year—you don't recover anything on the policy. That's all."

"You mean," cried Anne, "that there won't be any money for us? Although Father insured himself?"

Martin nodded, took out his pipe again with an automatic gesture, looked at it, and put it back.

There was a shocked silence in the room for a moment

or two. Then Stephen, trying to keep his voice steady, said:

"And now, Mother, may I see Jelks's letter?"

The letter was quite short, and only too explicit. It ran:

DEAR MRS. DICKINSON,

I have been in communication with the Claims Manager of the British Imperial Insurance Company in connexion with your late husband's policy. He writes to me as follows:

"In reply to your letter of yesterday's date with regard to Life Policy No. 582/31647. In view of the finding of the coroner's jury, and of the fact that this policy has only been in force for eight months, it seems clear that Clause 4 (i) (a) of the policy applies. I am therefore instructed formally to repudiate liability on behalf of the Company. At the same time, I am to inform you that the Company would be prepared to consider the possibility of making some ex gratia payment to the widow and dependents of the assured, provided, of course, that all claims under the policy were explicitly withdrawn. Perhaps you will let me know when it would be convenient for a representative of the Company to call on Mrs. Dickinson in order to discuss this matter."

I should be glad of your instructions as to what attitude I should take in the matter. It would be advisable, in my opinion, for you to agree to see the Company's representative, without, of course, committing yourself in any way. But bearing in mind that your husband by his will left half his estate between your son and daughter and the other half to you during widowhood with remainder to them, it would, I think, be only proper for you to discuss the position

with them before coming to a decision. I should, of
of course, myself desire to be present at the interview,
to safeguard the interests of the estate.

Yours faithfully,

H. H. JELKS

Stephen read the letter through twice, once to himself
and then aloud.

"Well!" said Martin, when he had finished. "That
sounds pretty definite."

"How many halfpennies are there in twenty-five thousand pounds?" asked Anne.

"I don't altogether follow you," said her fiancé
stiffly.

"I do," said Stephen. "Uncle George said: 'Is it going
to make a ha'porth of difference to anyone, whether it's
suicide or not?' Well, we can tell him now."

"Father didn't kill himself," said Anne obstinately.

"How do you know?" said Stephen in a tone of despair. "How does anybody know?"

"I know *because* I know," Anne persisted. "He just
wasn't that sort of person. Nobody's going to persuade
me that Father did a thing like that, not if he came and
told me that he saw him do it. *Nobody*," she repeated.
"Mother, you feel like that, don't you?"

Mrs. Dickinson shook her head slowly.

"I never understood your father," she said simply.
"So far as I'm concerned, I'm afraid I feel like George
about it. I have lost him, and it doesn't seem to matter
very much to me how people say it happened. To you
children, obviously, it makes a great deal of difference.
That's why I asked your advice."

"But Mother, it makes just as much difference to you
as to any of us!" Anne protested.

"My dear, I was badly off before I married your father,

35

and I suppose I can bear to be badly off again afterwards. Don't let's say any more about that. But tell me, please, Stephen, what are we going to do? How am I going to reply to Mr. Jelks?"

"I'll deal with that," said Stephen, rousing himself abruptly from the stupor into which he had fallen since reading the letter. "You needn't bother your head about it any more, Mother. We'll see this insurance animal and tell him just where he gets off. As for abandoning the claim to the money, of course that's all nonsense."

"Then you do agree with me?" said Anne eagerly. "You think I'm right, that Father wouldn't have killed himself?"

"Obviously you've got to be right, if we don't all mean to be paupers."

"But that's not the same thing at all!" she protested.

Stephen assumed his most superior and infuriating attitude.

"My dear Anne," he said, "your sentiments do you credit, but they are not going to cut much ice with an insurance company. Our job—my job, perhaps I should say—is to prove to their satisfaction that they are legally bound to pay up. When we've done that we can afford to be highfalutin about it."

"That's absolutely the wrong way to look at it. It makes the whole business so sordid, so money-grubbing—"

"Money," Martin intervened in his flat, platitudinous voice, "can come in very handy sometimes. You shouldn't turn your nose up at it, Annie."

"Annie!" Stephen shuddered. This codfish called his sister "Annie," and she liked it!

"But what I don't quite see at present," Martin droned on, "is how you are going to set about proving all this. Insurance companies," he wagged his head sagely, "take a bit of satisfying, y'know."

36

Stephen was ready with his answer.

"All that the company has done is to take what the coroner's jury said as gospel," he said. "Well, we don't. We start from scratch. And to begin with, we can go over the same ground that they did, only a good deal more carefully."

"D'you mean, interview all the witnesses all over again, and get 'em to say something different?"

"We may have to do something like that before we're through. But to start with, there's the evidence that was actually given at the inquest. I don't know the first thing about that yet. My little cousin is lending me the reports of everything that was said. I mean to go through that with—with—"

"With a small-tooth comb," Martin prompted.

"With the greatest care," said Stephen, glaring at him. "Then I shall see what we're up against, at any rate. After that, we can set to work to build up our own case."

"Well," said Martin, "I wish you luck, I'm sure."

"You're in with us on this, Martin," said Anne. "It makes a bit of difference to us, you know."

Martin turned on Anne a look that might have been a tender one, if his spectacles had not deprived it of all expression.

"All right, Annie," he said rather thickly, "I'm with you."

And as if ashamed at this display of emotion, he shortly afterwards took his departure, lingering in the hall only long enough to kiss her perfunctorily and light his pipe.

5

Two Ways of Looking at It

The cousin with the taste for Press cuttings was as good as his word. Before he went to bed that night, Stephen was in possession of a thick, untidy volume, full of irregularly pasted extracts from publications of every kind. They began with snippets from school magazines, commemorating such earth-shaking events as that "Dickinson, mi., was a bad third" in the Junior Hundred Yards, and continued for a few pages to record the rare occasions when the doings of the owner or his family had escaped into print. "The short and simple annals of the obscure," was Stephen's comment as he fluttered the pages. It was not long before he came to the account of the tragedy at Pendlebury Old Hall, which absorbed more than twice as much space as the rest of the contents put together. With ghoulish assiduity the compiler had preserved every scrap of newsprint that contained any reference to the matter. Headlines and photographs, paragraphs short and long, all were fish for his net. The death of Mr. Dickinson, a respectable but not particularly noteworthy figure, had not, in fact, created much stir in the world, or occupied much room in the newspapers of the country, and most of the references were brief, although, when collected, they looked impressive enough. But it had evidently been an event of the first magnitude in the immediate neighbourhood of Pendlebury, and, as the owner of the book had said, the local Press had dealt with it thoroughly. By the time that he had finished reading its report of the proceedings, Stephen was confident that he knew as much about the affair as if he had been present at the inquest.

Stephen went up to his room very late that night. He had had a tiring day, and his researches had taken him a considerable time. None the less, he seemed even now strangely disinclined to go to bed. After wandering up and down the room for a short time, he sat down on a chair and lit a cigarette, frowning in an attempt at concentration. Had any observer been present, he would have seen a very different Stephen from the cocksure young man who over the coffee-cups had so blithely announced his intention of putting the insurance company in its place. This Stephen was anything but cocksure. On the contrary he was obviously acutely anxious, the observer might have even added nervous, at the prospect of the task which he now saw before him. At the same time, here was evidently a young man firmly determined in his mind on what he had to do. If he was different, he was certainly a more formidable person altogether.

The cigarette finished, he at last began to undress. He had propped the book of Press cuttings upon the chest of drawers, open at the report, and from time to time broke off his undressing to consult it again, as a fresh thought struck him. He was still half clad, poring over the book, when the door opened quietly. He looked up.

"Anne!" he exclaimed. "Why aren't you in bed? Do you know what time it is?"

"I couldn't sleep," she said. "I heard you moving about, so I knew you were still up."

She came in and sat on his bed, swinging her pyjamaed legs meditatively backwards and forwards. Looking at her, Stephen wondered, not for the first time, whether Martin really knew just how lucky he was.

"Give me a cigarette," she said.

He did so, and lit it for her in silence. The cigarette was half finished before she spoke again.

"Stephen."

"Yes?"

"Look here, you meant what you said in the drawing-room after dinner, didn't you?"

"Yes, of course."

"You still mean it?"

"Of course I do. Why shouldn't I?"

"I dunno. You look so worried, that's all."

"Not surprising. I am worried. Hellishly."

"Because of that?" She pointed to the open book upon the chest of drawers.

He nodded.

"But the verdict was wrong, wasn't it?" she persisted.

"Yes. As wrong as wrong. We start from that, don't we? But all the same, I'm damned if I can see what else they could have done on the evidence. Look here, for instance—"

"No, I don't want to hear about it, not now. I shall have to some time, I suppose, if I'm to be any use to you. Only, Stephen, I wanted to be sure that you weren't—weren't weakening about it, that's all."

"Weakening? I like that! Not on your life!"

"That's all right then." She grinned suddenly. "You look quite the strong man, even in those awful pink underclothes of yours. So long as you've made up your mind that it's worth going through with it—"

"I should damn' well think it was! Do you realize just how badly off we are going to be if we don't?"

"Oh, the money, yes! I wasn't thinking about that."

"Well, you can be pretty sure I was."

"You always were keen on money, weren't you, Stephen? Ever since we were tiny. That's not what's worrying me. It's simply that I can't stand the idea of people saying about Father—"

"What Uncle Edward calls the Stigma?"

"If you like—but it's more than that, really. Oh, I can't put it into words, but what I feel is that the poor old parent had a pretty rotten deal while he was alive, and it would help to make up a bit if we can stop people telling a lot of nasty lies about him now he's dead. Make up to him, I mean. Does that sound awful rot to you?"

"Yes."

"Well, I can't help it if it does. I never thought you would understand. You see, I was really fond of Father, only he never gave me the chance of showing it, and you really hated him, and never had the smallest difficulty in showing it. That's just the difference between us."

"I don't agree with you," said Stephen. "So far as my hating the old man is concerned, I mean. You've no right to say that."

"I'm sorry, Stephen. I didn't mean to hurt your feelings."

"I've got no feelings in the matter, one way or the other. I didn't get on with Father, I agree, but no more did you. We don't exactly seem to have a knack of getting on with our seniors. Look at Uncle Arthur, for example."

"Uncle Arthur doesn't count. He was a maniac. His will proves that. But Father was different. He did try to do his best for us, but always as if it went against the grain, somehow. And it wasn't just us, either. He seemed to have a sort of grievance against life."

"Exactly. That's what the jury found, wasn't it?"

"But he never ran away from life—that's the point. And the less we succeeded in making him happy while he was alive, the greater our duty to—to—"

"To make him happy now he's dead?" suggested Stephen with a yawn. "I'm sorry, Anne, but your doctrine of posthumous reparation does not appeal to me. Personally, I think that if he is conscious of anything at all, Father is probably rather glad to be dead, however in fact he came to die. Luckily, it doesn't matter very much which of us is right."

"No. I suppose it doesn't. I wish we looked at things in the same way, though. It might make things easier."

"My good girl, do be practical for once. We want the same thing, don't we?"

"Yes. With me bent on clearing Father's memory, and you with both eyes firmly fixed on the main chance, we ought to make a pretty strong team. Not to mention Martin."

"Yes, of course," said Stephen carelessly. "I was forgetting him."

"Well, please don't forget him in future, that's all." Anne's voice had suddenly taken on a dangerously hard quality. "I've no doubt you'd like to if you could."

Stephen knew perfectly well that the one way to precipitate a quarrel with his sister was to cast any aspersions on the man upon whom she had chosen, for reasons which he could not understand, to fix her affections. He was, moreover, desperately sleepy and longing for bed. He had, therefore, every reason to make some soothing reply and get Anne out of the room as quickly as possible. But some imp of perversity made him reply, instead:

"I'm not likely to have much chance with you about, am I?"

The mischief was done. Anne's slumberous brown eyes lit up for battle, her cheeks glowed, her chin was thrust forward.

"Why," she began, "why are you always so perfectly beastly about Martin?"

Too late, Stephen saw his danger.

"I'm not, really I'm not," he protested feebly.

"Yes, you are, always. If you're not, why don't you sometimes tell me you like him?"

"But I do like him. I can't always keep saying it can I? I—I admire him in lots of ways. Only . . ."

Fatal word.

" 'Only!' That's just it. That's always it where Martin's concerned. 'Only' what, may I ask?"

Stephen's temper took command.

"Only that I don't happen to think he's the right sort of man to make you happy, that's all."

"For God's sake don't talk like a good brother in a Victorian novel! It doesn't suit you in the least. Why can't you say what you mean?"

"I've said exactly what I mean, so far as I am aware."

"No, you haven't. You've simply hinted at it. What you mean is that you think Martin is a—what's your choice word for it?—a womanizer."

"Since you insist on introducing the subject, I do."

"Well, please understand once for all that Martin and I have absolutely no secrets from each other on that subject or any others. I don't care what his murky past may have been. If you're such a beastly little puritan as to object to someone for having sown a few wild oats, I'm not."

Stephen's fatal weakness for scoring a verbal point betrayed him once more.

"The trouble with these people who sow their wild oats," he said in his most aggravating manner, "is that

43

they're apt to have a grain or two left in odd corners of the sack when you think it's empty. As you may discover in due time."

"I suppose I'm to consider that witty," retorted Anne. "But if you imagine . . ."

From this point the quarrel degenerated into a mere schoolroom brawl, in which nothing was too sacred, nothing too trivial, to be snatched up as a weapon in the fight. The armoury of old grudges and grievances that every family keeps stored away somewhere was ruthlessly exploited by both sides. At one point Stephen was pointing out to Anne that she had hopelessly lost her nerve the year before during the descent of the Rimpfischorn, and was being reminded in turn how he had been caught cheating at cards at a children's party twelve years ago. At another, Anne got in a vicious blow by recalling the fatal misconduct by which her brother had finally alienated the affections of Uncle Arthur, and Stephen, white with rage at the mention of the unmentionable, retorted by disinterring her appalling *faux pas* at her coming out party. And on and on the battle raged, with the name of Martin recurring again and again to provide fresh fuel for fury when the flames showed signs of being exhausted.

"As I happen to be in love with Martin, and he with me—"

"How do you know he is in love with you, and not simply the money he thought you'd get?"

"Simply because you're incapable of loving anything except money, you imagine that everybody's like you!"

"Well, if he's as fond of you as all that, why did he shirk coming out to Switzerland with us? Or was he afraid of climbing?"

"You know as well as I do that he'd have come if he could. It was simply that he couldn't get away."

"Very likely! I wonder how he was amusing himself—and who with?"

"I'm not going to answer your beastly insinuations. For that matter, why did you come out three days later than you said you would, and leave me hanging about at the hotel by myself after Joyce had had to go home? A lot you cared!"

"I've explained to you already that I couldn't help it. My firm asked me to go specially to Birmingham because their accountant was ill and—"

"Yes, you've explained it already. I'm sick of your filthy accountant at Birmingham, if there is one. Then why couldn't you have come by air instead of wasting time in a train?"

"If you think I'm going to waste money on aeroplanes to suit your convenience . . ."

And so on.

"Anyhow," Anne said some time later, "Martin is in this with us, whether you like it or not. And you can just lump it!"

"Of course he's in it. He knows which side his bread is buttered. Has it occurred to you, in all your highfalutin reflections, that our collecting the boodle may make quite a difference to your chances of getting married?"

"Yes, it has occurred to me. I'm not quite a fool."

"You relieve my mind. Perhaps you remember also that one of the few things Father and I agreed on was that he couldn't stand the idea of Martin as a son-in-law at any price?"

"I dare say it was. But it's not the least good your thinking you can play the heavy father with me, because it won't work."

"I'm not going to. All I say is, that putting those two things together, namely, that Father wouldn't help you to marry while he was alive and that you can't afford to marry unless you collect your share of the insurance money, it seems to me a nauseating hypocrisy for you to pretend not (*a*) that you lament his death as a terrible blow, and (*b*) that your only interest in upsetting this verdict is . . ."

But Anne did not wait for the end of her brother's carefully polished period. Getting off the bed she stalked to the door with as much dignity as her dressing-gown allowed.

"You make me sick," she observed crisply, as she went out.

Thereafter these two highly intelligent, deeply affectionate, grown-up young persons went at last to bed, to wake next morning feeling more than a little ashamed of themselves.

6

A Visitor at Scotland Yard

Stephen was down late to breakfast next morning. Mrs. Dickinson, following the custom by which the privileges of invalids are always extended to the recently bereaved, was breakfasting in bed. Anne had already finished her meal some time before, but was still in the dining-room. Stephen came in just as she was jabbing the stub of her third cigarette into an ashtray. She had an air of impatient exasperation.

"Well?" she fired at him at once.

Stephen did not reply. He went over to the sideboard and helped himself to coffee.

"Stone-cold," he remarked. "And the milk has a disgusting skin on it. What a filthy stink you have made in here. It's the first time I've ever seen you smoking in the dining-room after breakfast."

"Go on! Say it!" said Anne. "If Father was alive I shouldn't be doing it. That's what you mean, isn't it?"

"Well, there's no harm in looking on the bright side, is there? You're very pugnacious this morning, Anne."

47

"I'm very impatient, if you like. I thought you were never coming down."

"Impatient?" said Stephen, buttering a piece of toast with great deliberation. "What about?"

"About everything, of course. Are you getting on to Jelks today? When are we going to see the insurance person? What are we going to do first? There are scores of things I want to discuss with you. And then you ask what I'm impatient about!"

"The first thing I'm going to do," said Stephen, "is to have my breakfast, and I wish I could feel that it was more than a forlorn hope that I should have it in comparative peace and quiet. After that—"

"Yes?"

"After that, I am not going to discuss matters with Jelks, or the insurance people, or, for the matter of that, with Martin. I am going to make a few quiet inquiries on my own. Now don't start making a fuss," he went on quickly before she could speak. "I know quite well what you are going to say. But I've thought this out, and I've made up my mind. I've read the evidence and you haven't. There's just one chance for us, as far as I can see, and I'm going to test it, and see if there's a reasonable prospect of its coming off. If there is, we go right ahead. If not—"

"You mean that you're looking for an excuse to back out. It's just the sort of thing I might have expected!"

"Need we go into all this again?" said Stephen wearily. "I am not anxious to back out, as I think I explained to you last night. But you don't understand the position at all. If," he went on with a maddening assumption of superiority, "you had had the decency to let me eat my breakfast in peace, I dare say I should have explained it to you. As it is, I'm afraid you'll have to wait."

Anne got up and went to the door. With her hand on the latch she turned and said:

"Stephen, this is all very ridiculous. I'm sorry about last night, if that's what you want me to say. Why on earth should this horrible thing have made us squabble like two children?"

"Because we look at it from two different angles, I suppose. Not that I admit for a moment that there is anything in the least childish in my behaviour, at any rate. So far as you are concerned—"

"Oh, very well!" Anne exclaimed, and flounced out of the room. A moment later she opened the door again, and did her best to repair the anti-climax by the sarcastic tone in which she asked: "Will your lordship be good enough to indicate where he is going to prosecute his inquiries, and whether he expects to be home to lunch?"

Bowing gravely over his boiled egg, Stephen replied: "I shall not be in to lunch. And I see no objection to informing you that I am going to Scotland Yard."

Going to Scotland Yard was simple enough; doing anything when there turned out to be a difficult matter. The polite but inquisitive policeman at the entrance made that clear to Stephen. So he wished to see Inspector Mallett, did he? Precisely. In connection with what case was it? Oh, a private matter? Just so. Had he an appointment, perhaps? No? That was unfortunate. Stephen, feeling uncomfortably warm with embarrassment and with a growing sensation that his collar was a size too small for him, agreed that it was unfortunate. No, he did not desire to state his business to any other officer. Yes, he quite understood that the inspector was a busy man, but the matter was urgent and would not detain the inspector long. Yes, here was his card. By all means he would wait. No, he really would prefer not to explain the position to the sergeant. No, not at all. . . .Oh, certainly. . . .Yes, rather. . . . Thanks,

if you don't mind. . . . I quite understand. . . . Yes. . . .
No. . . .

These preliminaries occupied about half an hour, and
the sojourn in the waiting-room that succeeded them
some twenty minutes more. At the end of that time,
Stephen was informed that the inspector was in conference with the Assistant Commissioner, and that when
the conference was over he would be at his lunch. The
tone in which this latter piece of information was delivered indicated that Inspector Mallett's lunch was not a
function to be treated lightly. After his lunch, if he was
not otherwise engaged, the card of this importunate visitor would be put before him, and he might consent to
receive him—if he thought fit. The officer obviously did
not think it likely that the inspector would so think, but
he indicated that there would be no harm in trying, and
Stephen, by now thoroughly cowed, promised to return
at two o'clock.

He lunched miserably in the neighbourhood and
soon after Big Ben had struck the three-quarters was
back again in the dirty brick quadrangle which seemed
by now depressingly familiar. Resigned to another long
period of unprofitable waiting, he was agreeably surprised
to be met by the news that the inspector's conference had
finished earlier than was expected, that the inspector had
had his lunch all right (this was a most important point,
evidently), that the inspector had seen Stephen's card,
and that the inspector was free and would see him now,
and would he come this way please?

Somewhat dazed, Stephen suffered himself to be led
along many passages and up many flights of stairs, and
finally found himself in a small airy room which overlooked the Thames, and which at first sight seemed to
him to be distinctly overcrowded. The impression of
overcrowding, he soon decided, was largely contrib-

uted to by the great bulk of the man who was its only occupant, and who now sat behind his desk regarding him with an expression that was at once genial and inquiring.

"Mr. Stephen Dickinson?" said Mallett in a voice surprisingly quiet and gentle for one of his large frame. "Won't you sit down?"

Stephen did so, and opened his mouth to explain himself, but the inspector went on: "Are you the son of the late Mr. Leonard Dickinson?"

"Yes. In fact I—"

"I thought so. You are rather like him in some ways."

The young man flushed.

"Oh, do you think so?" he said, in a tone of some annoyance. "I never thought there was much likeness myself."

Inspector Mallett chuckled.

"One of my grandmother's rules of conduct," he observed, "was: 'Never see a likeness.' She had a theory that it was rude. I'm afraid manners were never my strong point, though. I joined the Force before the days of courtesy cops. But there is a likeness, all the same," he added.

Recollecting the late Mr. Dickinson's unattractive elderliness, he was not in the least surprised that his son should repudiate the suggestion so curtly. It was in any case, he reflected, a likeness of expression rather than of feature. It was difficult to pin down, as family resemblances so often are, but the fact remained that with his first glance at Stephen, his mind had gone back at once to old Mr. Dickinson. Oddly enough, he had been reminded of the dead man's face, not as he had seen it pressed close to his own in garrulous confidences after dinner, but as it had appeared the next morning, silent and still, the lines of worry and disillusionment smoothed out in death. Then the essential cast of countenance had been revealed with the removal of the accidental tricks that life had played with it. In Stephen's case, experience had not yet had time to spin its web of disguise. And the common factor was—he fumbled for a definition—that each was essentially the face of a man who was before all things self-centred. At bottom, he felt, the likeness between father and son was a good deal more than skin-deep, though one was a weary pessimist and the other obviously alert and self-confident to the point of bumptiousness. Had he known it, this parallel between himself and his parent would have annoyed Stephen considerably more than the discovery that they possessed a similar nose or chin could possibly have done.

Meanwhile Stephen was speaking.

"At all events," he said, "it was about my father that I came to see you."

"Yes?" Mallett was friendly, but showed no inclination to help him out.

"Yes." He hesitated for a moment, braced himself as though for a plunge into cold water, and then came out with: "I'm not satisfied with the verdict on my father's death."

Mallett raised his eyebrows.

"The coroner's jury was wrong," Stephen repeated.

"Yes," said Mallett slowly. "I appreciate that that was what you meant. But in that case, Mr. Dickinson, don't you think you ought to go and see the police about it? I mean," he went on, smiling at the puzzled expression on the young man's face, "the Markshire police. This is their affair, you know. My own connexion with it was purely accidental and unofficial. Perhaps if I were to give you a note to the local superintendent—"

"No," said Stephen firmly. "I quite understand what

52

you say, but that isn't what I want. I came to see you personally, because . . ." He hesitated.

"Yes?"

"Because you were the person largely responsible for things going wrong at the inquest."

It was a long time since Inspector Mallett had had a remark of this kind addressed to him, and he did not take it very kindly. For a moment he was tempted to deal very severely with this impertinent person, and it was perhaps fortunate for Stephen that he was still in a post-prandial mood of kindliness. His momentary look of annoyance, however, did not pass unnoticed, and Stephen was prompt to apologize.

"Please don't think—" he began.

"Never mind what I think," the inspector interrupted him. "It's what I did that is in question, isn't it? Let's keep to that. I was a witness at the inquest on your father— a witness of fact, purely and simply. I hope I was an accurate witness. I certainly tried to be."

"Exactly. And it was your evidence that caused all the trouble. Although it was accurate—because it was accurate—it resulted in the coroner and the jury being hopelessly misled."

Stephen sat back with the air of one who has delivered an ultimatum. But Mallett showed no sign of being impressed. He merely laid his broad hands flat upon the desk in front of him, pursed his lips, and looked into space about a foot above the top of Stephen's head.

"You know, I haven't the least idea what you are talking about," he murmured. "Now look here—" He suddenly brought his gaze down full upon the other's face. "Suppose we start at the beginning. It's much more satisfactory. Mr. Dickinson died from an overdose of Medinal. The medical evidence was conclusive on that point, to my mind at least. Are you disputing it?"

"No."

"Very well. On the evidence, of which mine was part, the coroner's jury came to the conclusion that he had taken his own life. That you say was wrong?"

"Exactly."

"Apart from my evidence, do you think that the verdict would have been different?"

"I think there was a very good chance of a finding of accidental death."

"I don't altogether agree with you. As I recollect the evidence—but we can discuss that later. Do you think that accidental death would have been a proper verdict?"

"I should have been perfectly satisfied with it."

"But do you think it would have been a proper verdict?"

"No. If by 'proper' you mean in accordance with the facts, I don't think it would."

A long pause followed these words. Mallett opened his mouth to say something, evidently thought better of it, and then said: "But you told me just now you would have been satisfied with that verdict?"

"That's not quite the same thing, is it?"

"You needn't tell me that," said Mallett with some asperity. He looked at Stephen quizzically for a moment in silence and then said: "Mr. Dickinson, I don't understand you in the least. You object to the verdict which was given because you think it was incorrect, but you would have been perfectly prepared to accept another, equally incorrect. Evidently you are not concerned about—abstract justice, shall we say? And at the same time you don't strike me as a person who would worry very much about any stigma attaching to a finding of suicide. Or am I wrong?"

"No," said Stephen. "I'm not very strong on abstractions. As to stigmas," he grinned reminiscently, "some of my family seem to have them on the brain. Personally, I don't care two hoots about them. But it so happens that a very large sum of money depends upon my establishing that my father did not kill himself."

The inspector could not suppress a smile.

"And therefore you have determined that the verdict was wrong?" he said.

Stephen frowned at the imputation.

"No!" he protested. "I knew that the verdict was wrong as soon as I heard it. So would you, if you had known as much about my father as I do. But the wrongness doesn't concern me; its consequences do. That is why I should have been content with a verdict of accidental death. And that is why, very much against my will, I find myself in the position of having to prove the truth, which for other reasons it would have been much better for all concerned not to have bothered about."

To himself Inspector Mallett murmured with satisfaction, "Self-centred!" Aloud he said, "And what precisely do you mean by the truth, Mr. Dickinson?"

"That my father was murdered."

The inspector tugged thoughtfully at the points of his fierce military moustache. If he was at all shocked at the suggestion, he gave no signs of it.

"Murdered?" he said softly. "Just so! Then in that case, don't you think my original suggestion was the correct one—that you should put the case before the appropriate authority, the Markshire County Police?"

"I don't know whether it was correct or not," retorted Stephen with some impatience. "I do know that it's no sort of use to me. For one thing, I have at the present moment no evidence whatever to put before the Markshire or any other police, and for another, I am not interested in proving that any particular person killed my father. I only want to show, to the satisfaction of the insurance company, or a court of law if necessary, that he was killed by somebody."

"I see," said Mallett. "You put the position very clearly. You can hardly expect a police officer to take the same rather—er—detached view of crime as you do, but I appreciate your position. I take it that your object now is to get what evidence you can in order to prove your case against the insurance company?"

"That is what I am here for."

Mallett made a little gesture of impatience.

"But my dear sir," he said, "we are back where we started from! How can I help you? Officially—"

"I am here quite unofficially."

"Very good, then. Unofficially, I am simply an individual who was called to give some evidence which was perfectly accurate, and which the jury believed and acted upon. If you ever bring any proceedings in which your father's death is in question, I should probably be called as a witness again, and should give the same evidence, which would presumably have the same effect on another jury. What can I do about it?"

To his surprise, Stephen replied airily, "Oh, I can dispose of your evidence easily enough."

"Indeed!"

"Certainly. I should probably have done so at the inquest, if I had been there, instead of in Switzerland all the time, out of reach of newspapers and letters. After all, what did it amount to? You had a talk to my father the night before he died, or rather, if I know anything of the matter, he did the talking and you just listened and wished you could get away from such a shocking old bore. You found him a gloomy old man—as who wouldn't?—full of complaints about life in general and his family in particular. That is the main effect of it, isn't it?"

"Yes," the inspector admitted. "But it went a good deal further than that."

"I bet it did. You didn't enter into very many details, but I expect I can supply a few for you. He told you that he had made a mistake marrying a woman so much younger than himself, didn't he? He said that he had been born at Pendlebury Old Hall and that it meant much more to him than his family could ever imagine, because it was the only place where he had been happy in the whole of his life. And finally, he said that he felt like a snail, dragging its trail about with him wherever it went, and wondered with an air of deep significance where the trail would end."

"But I never mentioned that in my evidence," said Mallett. "How did you know that he used that expression?"

"Because he was always using it, of course. You don't imagine that he invented it for your benefit, do you? In the home one could expect that sort of stuff to come up every month or so. The snail and his trail has been the theme song of my family for ages. In fact, I did actually write a song about it. It begins like this:

> *How doth the melancholy snail*
> *Invigorate his friends,*
> *By looking back upon his trail*
> *And wondering where it ends.*

"Not very high-class verse, I admit, but it proves my point, anyhow. So far as your talk with him is relied on as evidence of suicide, you can wash it out altogether."

"My evidence was not confined to my conversation of the night before," Mallett pointed out. "And I don't think that the coroner relied on that alone when he came to sum up to the jury."

"No, of course he didn't. What he relied on most of all was the silliest bit of evidence of the whole lot—not that I blame him, he couldn't have known. It was simply the most sickening piece of bad luck—a pure coincidence that nobody could have foreseen. I suppose, by the way, that we are talking about the same thing—I mean the inscription, motto, or whatever you like to call it, that was found by his body?"

Mallett nodded.

"We are in the power of no calamity, while Death is in our own," Stephen quoted. He laughed mirthlessly. "Gosh! Isn't it ridiculous! By the way, Inspector," he went on, "did you happen to notice what sort of paper it was written on?"

"Yes. It was on a small slip of white paper of good quality. The ink was dark, I remember, as though it had been written at least some hours before I saw it, possibly more. That would depend on the type of ink, you know. The handwriting, you may remember, was identified at the inquest by your mother."

"Oh, no question about the writing," said Stephen. "The silly thing is, it might just as likely been mine. That would have puzzled the coroner a bit, wouldn't it?"

"Yours, Mr. Dickinson? How could that be?"

Stephen did not answer the question directly.

"Do you ever read detective stories, Inspector?" he said. "There's a very good one of Chesterton's, in which a man is found with an apparent confession of suicide beside him, which is really a fragment from a novel he is writing. The murderer pinches the sheet he has just written, and snips off the edge of the paper which has the inverted commas on it."

"But this was a small slip of paper," was Mallett's practical comment. "Not a fragment of a book or anything else. And I'm quite certain none of the edges were snipped off."

"And you may add with equal truth, my father was not writing a novel. But I'll tell you what he was doing, he was compiling a calendar."

"A calendar?"

"Yes—a calendar of quotations, one for every day of the year. And being my father, it was, of all things, a calendar of pessimistic quotations. Incidentally, can you imagine a man who really contemplated suicide devoting years of his life to selecting and arranging the three hundred and sixty-five gloomiest observations on life that he could find?"

"This was a quotation, then?"

"Lord, yes! My father wasn't capable of producing a sentiment of that kind out of his own head. It was written by a gent named Sir Thomas Browne, about three hundred years ago. Father was fearfully pleased when he discovered it, or rather when I discovered it for him. I wrote it down for him a month or two ago, and evidently he thought it good enough to keep for his permanent collection, as he copied it out on one of his little slips. He had hundreds of them, you see, and was always shuffling them about and rejecting the ones that didn't come up to his standard of depression. He got some perverted pleasure out of it—I can't think what. That's why his calendar took such a long time to complete. I've brought some to show you the sort of thing."

From his pocket he took several small slips of paper. "Here's a good example," he said.

> *My Brother, my poor Brothers, it is thus;*
> *This life itself holds nothing good for us,*
> *But it ends soon and nevermore can be;*
> *And we knew nothing of it ere our birth,*

And shall know nothing when consigned to earth:
I ponder these thoughts and they comfort me.

"*The City of Dreadful Night*, you know. He got quite a number of his best quotes out of that. Then this one is rather amusing:

Howbeit, I do here most certainely assure you, there be many wayes to Peru.

"I don't quite know how he came by that. It's out of Hakluyt's *Voyages*. He seems to have thought that Peru was symbolical of the next world, or something of the kind, whereas as a matter of fact it's a perfectly straightforward piece of geographical information. Anyhow, he discarded it in favour of something grislier. Like this, for example—"

"I think that's enough to go on with," said Mallett, who was beginning to feel somewhat overwhelmed at this display of erudition. "You seem to have proved your point, Mr. Dickinson. But I don't understand why this particular passage should have been found by your father's bed after he was dead. Are you asking me to believe that someone else put it there, in order to give the effect of suicide?"

Stephen pondered for a moment before he answered.

"No," he said. "No, I've thought of that, and it doesn't hold water. For one thing how would he have known where to find it? The simple explanation is that my father took it out of his pocket when he undressed, along with his other things, and kept it by his bedside to gloat over. I know that sounds improbable to you, Inspector, and God knows how I should ever get a jury to believe it, but that happens to be the kind of odd fish my father was. He got a kick out of this sort of thing, just as old men of another kind get a kick out of indecent photographs. And like them, he enjoyed having his pet vice handy."

"It's possible," said Mallett slowly. "Yes, I suppose it's just possible."

"It's a dead certainty to me, knowing Father as I did."

"Well, assuming—just assuming—that you are right so far, and that your father did not in fact kill himself. You are still a long way from proving the rather startling theory which you advanced just now—that this is a case of murder."

"If he didn't kill himself, then someone else did," said Stephen with an air of finality.

"That's just the point I want to put to you. Your father died, as we agreed just now, from an overdose of Medinal, a drug which he was regularly taking on medical advice. If we exclude the possibility that he took the overdose deliberately, surely the inference is that he took it by accident?"

"Yes, it ought to be, but there again luck is against us. I've told you already I'm not in the least keen to prove that a murder has been committed, but I'm driven to it. I think the evidence quite clearly puts an accidental overdose outside the bounds of possibility."

Mallett reflected for a moment.

"I begin to remember," he said. "There were two bottles of tablets beside the bed, were there not? One nearly full, and the other completely empty."

"Exactly. Two bottles. Now one can understand a man, having taken his proper dose, forgetting that he had done so, and taking another one, out of the same bottle. You could easily get a jury to swallow that. But who on earth is going to believe that anyone in his senses should go and open a fresh bottle when the old one is staring him in the face, to prove that he had taken his proper dose already?"

"Yes. I remember that the coroner dealt with that question."

"And," Stephen added, to clinch the point, "there weren't enough tablets missing from the full bottle to constitute a lethal dose."

"He certainly died from the effects of a very large overdose indeed. The doctors were quite clear on that."

"Quite so. Therefore I should fail if I attempted to prove that my father died accidentally. If I am to dispose of the verdict of suicide, I must rely on the only other possible cause of death—namely, murder."

"I suppose," said Mallett ironically, "that you haven't considered such minor questions as who murdered your father, or how, or why?"

"Not yet," answered Stephen with irritating composure. "That will, of course, be the next stage in my inquiries. And remember, it is no part of my job to convict anybody. I'm only interested to show that my father's estate is entitled to collect the cash from the insurance company. That's where I want your help. You are interested in punishing crime, I suppose, so I presume you have no objection to giving it."

"I have already explained," said the inspector, "that this case is no affair of mine. Even if you are right in your suggestion, I can take no part in any inquiries unless and until I am called in."

"You misunderstand me. I'm not asking you to take any part in the inquiries. I am sorry to have taken so long to come to the point, but I had to explain the position first. What I'm after is this: If this was a case of murder—and I, at any rate, am satisfied that it was—there must have been something to indicate it. Something fishy—something a little out of the ordinary, at least. And if there was, you were the person to notice it at the time. Oh, I know you're going to tell me that you weren't there on business. I admit that. But after all, you're a detective by training. You can't get away from that, wherever you

62

are and whatever you happen to be doing. You can't help noticing things and remembering them afterwards, even if they don't seem of any significance at the time."

"If I had noticed anything in the least suspicious," Mallett pointed out, "I should have mentioned it at once to the local police."

"I didn't say suspicious. I'm after anything you saw that was in the least unusual. It may not convey anything to you, but it may be of value to me. Do you see what I mean? Take my father's room, for example. What did you observe in it?"

Mallett almost laughed out loud. It had so often been his experience in the past to put a question of this kind to witnesses that it tickled him to find the tables turned in this way.

"Your father's room," he repeated. "Let me see. The bed was on the right of the door as you went in, against the wall. By the bed was a little table. You'll find everything that was on the table set out in the evidence at the inquest. You have read that, I take it?"

Stephen nodded.

"Furniture," Mallett went on. "A wardrobe, closed. A chair with some clothes left on it. Two ugly china vases on the mantelpiece. Near the window, a dressing-table with drawers beneath it. On the dressing-table, your father's hair-brushes, shaving things, and so on. Also the contents of his pockets—small change, keys, a note-book. And—yes, this was unusual—a small plate. On the plate was an apple, with a folding silver knife beside it. That's all I saw. Of course, I wasn't in the room any length of time, and I may have missed something."

"Well done!" said Stephen softly. "I'm much obliged, Inspector."

"Have I told you anything useful?"

"You've knocked another nail into the coffin of the suicide verdict, anyway. The apple, I mean."

"How so?"

"Father believed in an apple a day. He used to eat one every morning before breakfast, and after shaving. He was a creature of habit, you see. If he went away anywhere for a week, he'd take seven apples with him, so as to make sure he wouldn't run short. He took the silver knife with him too, to cut the apples up with. Before he went to bed, he would put an apple out for next morning. That's what he'd done this time, obviously. Not a likely thing for a man to do if he knew he wasn't going to be alive to eat it, was it?"

"I'm only telling you what I saw, I'm expressing no opinion. But there was something that happened the night before which you may as well hear, though I expect there's nothing in it. Your father saw a man in the hotel whom he thought he recognized."

"What!" Stephen sat bolt upright in excitement. "Where was this? Upstairs, in the corridor outside his room?"

"No, no. In the lounge, while we were talking after dinner."

"In the lounge? Someone he knew? By Jove, Inspector, but this is really interesting. What was he like?"

"I didn't see him myself. He passed behind me. I got the impression of someone who wasn't very tall, from his shadow, that's all. But if you'll take my advice, you won't build on this. Your father thought he saw an acquaintance and then decided that he hadn't. That's all. Probably his second impression was the right one."

"Did he say he was wrong?" Stephen persisted, unwilling to give up the slender clue. "You don't remember his actual words, I suppose?"

"As it happens, I do. He said: '*I must have been mis-*

taken. Thought it was somebody I knew, but it couldn't have been.' Then he said something about the deceptiveness of back views and went on talking. The interruption made him change the subject, I recollect, without his realizing he had done so."

" '*Must* have been mistaken,' " said Stephen. "That's not the same thing, is it? He thought he *must* have made a mistake, that it *couldn't* have been the person he thought it was, because he didn't think it possible that person could have been there. You know, Inspector, my father was an awful old dunderhead in lots of ways, but he had eyes in his head, and he didn't often make a mistake of that kind. Suppose he wasn't mistaken, and the person who 'couldn't' have been there really was there? Suppose—"

"There are a great many suppositions in your case, I'm afraid," said Mallett, looking at his watch.

"I'm afraid there are. And I'm afraid, too, that I've wasted a great deal too much of your time, as you have just reminded me." He got up. "That is all you have to tell me, I suppose?"

"There is nothing else that I can think of at this moment, Mr. Dickinson."

"Then I will say goodbye and thank you. You've given me something to go on, anyhow. At breakfast this morning I was half inclined to chuck the whole thing up."

"I don't see that I have given you very much help," said the inspector.

"You've given me enough to see this thing through, anyhow," was the answer. And a moment or two later a very determined-looking young man walked out of New Scotland Yard.

Left alone, Mallett sat thinking for a few moments. He was conscious that he had shamelessly wasted quite a considerable amount of valuable official time discuss-

65

ing a theory that was probably entirely without foundation and was certainly no affair of his. A conscientious officer should have felt a good deal of regret at the fact. But Mallett, whom his worst enemies had never called anything but conscientious, did not feel a single qualm of regret. Instead, to his surprise, he felt pleasurably excited. Some sixth sense seemed to tell him that this was only the second chapter, and not the end, of the story which had begun at Pendlebury Old Hall. From a drawer in his desk, he pulled out an empty file. Smiling at his own folly as he did so, he solemnly entitled it "*Re* Dickinson," and returned it, still empty, to the drawer. Then he took a sheet of notepaper and wrote a personal letter, in very guarded terms, to his good friend the head of the plain-clothes force of the Markshire County Constabulary.

When all this had been done, Inspector Mallett plunged again into his proper work. Routine reigned once more in the little room overlooking the river.

7

Council of War

The front door of the Dickinsons' house in Plane Street closed softly behind the departing visitor. The parlourmaid who had let him out walked back through the hall to her own domain below stairs. When the sound of her footsteps could no longer be heard a perfect silence reigned for a moment or two throughout the house. Then the little group of people congregated in the drawing-room looked at one another, drew each a deep breath and felt free to talk once more.

"Well!" said Anne, with a yawn of sheer nervous exhaustion.

"Stephen," said her mother, "you—you have surprised me very much." She seemed conscious of the inadequacy of her words. "I mean that . . ." She gave it up. "Of course, I am sure you only said what you thought was right," she concluded.

"Extraordinary business altogether!" said Martin solemnly. "Don't know that I like the sound of it very much. You certainly gave us all a bit of a shock, Steve. Didn't he, Annie?"

67

Stephen Dickinson stood in the middle of the room, his face a little flushed, his hair a little disordered, his expression half triumphant, half bewildered. He looked rather as an amateur conjuror must look who has successfully produced a rabbit from his hat and is wondering where on earth to put the animal. Except for a momentary twinge of pain when he heard himself addressed as "Steve," he paid no attention to what the others had said. Instead he turned to the only person present who had not yet spoken and said:

"What are your views about it, Mr. Jelks?"

Mr. Herbert Horatio Jelks, of Jelks, Jelks, Dedman and Jelks, solicitors of Bedford Row, did not reply for a moment or two. He had a pale and placid face, of the type that gives confidence to clients, and his broad forehead, made broader by incipient baldness, gave him an air of wisdom and reliability. But baldness, like death, often strikes before its due time, and he was in fact a quite young and inexperienced lawyer, the junior partner in his firm and the third and last of the Jelkses reading from left to right. Just now behind his mask of expressionless sagacity was a distinctly troubled mind. The exigencies of the long vacation had left him the sole representative of his firm, and the load of responsibility was at this moment sitting heavily upon his shoulders.

"My views, Mr. Dickinson?" he said in the plummy baritone that went so well with his delusive aspect of maturity. "Well, really I—ahem! I think you are taking a great deal upon yourself, I do indeed."

Anne came quickly to her brother's rescue.

"Please don't think that any of us were going to listen to what that man said," she put in. "We were all quite agreed about that."

"I quite understand that you are all unanimous in refusing the Company's offer," Mr. Jelks began.

"I should hope so," Anne interjected.

"And yet it was a very reasonable one, to my mind, generous, even. The return of the premium plus four per cent—it is quite a considerable sum, substantially over thirteen hundred pounds." He let the figures linger lovingly on his lips as he pronounced them. "Thirteen, getting on for fourteen—hundred—pounds."

"The insurance was for twenty-five thousand," said Stephen shortly.

"Quite, quite. I appreciate that. And as I was saying, the offer was rejected. You were within your rights to do so, though of course that may have consequences, serious consequences. And I had already gathered that that was likely to be your attitude. What I had not appreciated, and I think it came as a surprise to everybody else in this room, was that Mr. Dickinson was about to make the allegation that his father was—that in fact—"

"That he was murdered," said Stephen, in a tone expressive of his contempt for a man who could not call a spade a spade.

"Precisely. I think I am right, my dear young lady, in saying that the suggestion came as a shock to you?"

There are, it may be presumed, girls who like being addressed as dear young ladies by pseudo-elderly solicitors. Anne was not one of them. She flushed and said awkwardly, "Yes, I suppose it did."

Mr. Jelks felt that he was getting on well. None of the other partners, he thought, neither his father nor uncle, not even that ferociously efficient fellow Dedman, could have handled the situation better.

"In that case," he went on, sawing the air impressively with one hand, "you will appreciate what I meant when I said just now that your brother had taken—"

"Yes, we all understand that," said Martin. "Point is, it seems to me, what do we do now?"

There was a pause in which Mr. Jelks struggled to find words. In the absence of any very definite thoughts, he found the search difficult.

"I mean to say," Martin went on in his thick, unattractive voice, "the insurance chappie who has just gone out was very positive that it couldn't be accident. Steve here, who's read all the evidence and we haven't, agreed with him. We thought he'd sold the pass—didn't we, Annie? Then he came out with murder and gave us all a bit of a jump. Can't say I like the idea very much myself. Suicide in the family's bad enough, but murder's a long sight worse. Personally, I'd be in favour of giving the whole show a miss. Yes, I would, Annie, honestly. And I'm sure Mrs. Dickinson doesn't like the notion either. But of course I see Steve's point of view. Since it can't be accident and it mustn't be suicide, it's got to be murder. That's how he looks at it, and of course I see his point. As I've said already."

The solicitor turned to Stephen.

"Does that fairly indicate your attitude?" he asked.

"More or less," was the reply. "And I know what you are going to say. 'The wish is father to the thought.' Well, perhaps it is. But the thought is there, just the same. You see, we none of us ever really believed that Father killed himself. Did we, Anne?"

"I didn't, anyhow," said his sister.

"Very good. Therefore, as Martin puts it, it's got to be murder."

Poor Mr. Jelks, whose practice had hitherto lain in the quiet reaches of conveyances and settlements, felt utterly at a loss.

"In that case—if you really think—" he stammered— "I should have thought the police—"

"The police are no good to us, at this stage at any rate. I've seen one policeman already, and I can tell you that. For that matter, we may never have to get so far as proving the case against anybody. I mean, criminal proof isn't the same thing as civil proof, is it?"

Mr. Jelks began to feel on firmer ground again.

"You put it inaccurately," he said, "but I see what you mean. If it should be necessary to sue the British Imperial Company on the policy—" Thank Heaven! he thought, Dedman is in charge of all the litigation in the office! "—the burden will be on the Company to prove that the case falls within the exception of the policy."

"I'm not sure that I understand," Mrs. Dickinson put in. "Do you mean that in any case we bring against them, it will be for them to prove my husband's suicide all over again, in spite of what the coroner's jury has already said?"

"Certainly. Though I must say that on the evidence so far I think they would succeed in doing so. But if, in some way that I confess I don't yet understand, you are able to cast doubt upon the inquest verdict, by setting up a *prima facie* case of—" again he boggled at the word "—of the other thing, then you might succeed."

"It makes a big difference," said Martin, "if we haven't got to pin the crime on anyone. Just show it could have been done, and so on. But how does one set about finding a primer whatd'ye call it of murder? That's what I want to know."

Mr. Jelks gave an embarrassed little laugh.

"Well! Really, you know, this is hardly in my line," he said. "What is it the books say? Means, Motive, Opportunity: those are the three factors, aren't they? I suppose you have to look about for some person or body of persons who had all three, and then try to—ah—implicate them. But you must beware of the law of defamation while you're about it, you know," he added hastily.

"Thanks," said Stephen. "That's very helpful indeed."

"Oh, not at all, not at all," answered Mr. Jelks, who was happily impervious to irony. "Well, Mrs. Dickinson, I think I should really be going now. If I can be of any further assistance—"

"I think you can," Stephen interrupted him. "If we are to get any further in this business than talking about it, we have got to start investigating those three factors you mentioned just now. So far as opportunity goes, it was obviously confined to the people who happened to be in the hotel at the time."

"Oh, obviously. I take it that this—this committee of detection, shall I say?"—his little witticism brought no answering gleam from any of the faces around him—"will begin by adjourning to Pendlebury Old Hall to inquire into the staff and residents there."

"That's just the trouble," said Stephen. "I've been thinking about that, and so far as I'm concerned there's every objection to my being seen nosing around Pendlebury. I don't expect for a moment that the hotel people will be particularly anxious to help us—this sort of publicity would obviously be bad for them—and as soon as I gave my name they'd guess what was up and would shut up like oysters. The same objection applies to Anne going. I suppose Martin could, but—"

"I shouldn't be any use," said Martin at once. "The hotel people were all at the funeral, and someone'd be sure to spot me. Anyhow," he added, "I don't know that I'm so keen on all this investigating business. If Steve thinks there's been a murder, can't he prove it out of the evidence he's got already?"

"No," said Stephen. "Quite obviously I can't. I can't even disprove suicide, which is what we really have to do, though I can throw some doubt on it. If we're going to do any good, there's a lot of hard work in front of us. That's why somebody must begin by going down to

Pendlebury, as Mr. Jelks says. In fact, that's where Mr. Jelks comes in."

"Where I—I beg your pardon, Mr. Dickinson, but it was only a suggestion of mine. You can't mean that I should—"

"I imagined this sort of thing was just in your line. Surely solicitors are always having to make inquiries at hotels and places, for divorce and so on?"

"Divorce?" said Mr. Jelks. "We never touch it! There are firms, of course, who specialize in that class of business."

"Then I suppose we shall have to put our affairs in the hands of one of the firms who do."

Mr. Jelks had horrid visions of his partners returning from their holidays to find that he had lost a client.

"That will not be necessary," he said, hastily. "I think what you want is a good inquiry agent. This is hardly a lawyer's business at all, you know. You couldn't expect *me* . . ."

Stephen, looking at him, privately agreed that he could not.

"You can find me a man of that sort—at once?"

"Oh, certainly, yes. I have the very man in mind. I'll tell him to ring you up and make an appointment."

Mr. Jelks had not the faintest acquaintance with any inquiry agent, good or bad; but he was fairly confident that one of the managing clerks in the office would know where to find one. At the moment he was anxious above all things to get away from this persistent young man, who, not content with propounding the most harebrained plot, was actually suggesting that he, Herbert Horatio Jelks, should help to put it into execution. The sooner he returned to the sweet sanities of Bedford Row, the better.

Before he went, he had one further thing to say.

"You will remember that the Company's offer, thanks, I may say, to my own intervention, remains open for fourteen days," he said. "I shall receive confirmation of that in writing, no doubt, but we may take it that you have fourteen days before you need finally decide to reject it."

"We have rejected it," said Stephen, tight-lipped. "I don't see what else there is to decide."

"Wait a bit, though," said Martin. "There is something in this, y'know. Fourteen days is quite a bit of time—long enough to find out if there is anything in Steve's idea. I vote we give ourselves that time to prove our case, and if we can't, then take the thirteen hundred quid and look grateful. What d'you say, Annie?"

Anne turned to Stephen.

"Do you really stand by what you said?" she asked. "You really think that someone killed Father?"

"Yes. I do."

She passed her hands before her eyes.

"We seem to go from one horror to another," she murmured. "I think Martin is right, Stephen. At least, we needn't make a definite choice until then."

"I must ask you to make up your own minds about it," said Mr. Jelks, in a hurry to be gone. "It is a point that you should bear in mind, that is all. I expect Mr. Dickinson thinks nothing of the task of laying bare a criminal in a fortnight."

And with this last and utterly ineffective witticism, he took his departure.

"Pompous ass!" was Stephen's comment, as he watched the solicitor's chubby form recede along the pavement outside the house. "I might have known he'd be no sort of use."

"Decent sort of fellow, I thought," said Martin. "Of

course, it was a bit of a shock to him; couldn't take it in at first; but no more could the rest of us. It *is* a tall order, y'know. Anyhow, I think the idea of a trial fortnight is a good one. After all, one can do a lot in a fortnight."

"What seems to have escaped your notice is that we've got to do a lot in a fortnight. I have four weeks holiday and nearly two weeks of it have gone already. After that, things aren't going to be so easy."

"Jove, yes! I'm lucky, I've still got three weeks to play with, so I'm all right. And now I suppose there's nothing we can do till the inquiry chappie has got to work. Not that I like this business of poking about in hotel registers. You never know what you might find." He blinked solemnly behind his spectacles. "I'm short of exercise," he announced. "Is anybody coming for a stroll on the Heath?"

Nobody else felt inclined to go with him, and he walked out alone. As soon as he was gone, Anne took Stephen on one side.

"There's something I want to say to you," she said.

"Oh?"

"Yes. It's just that I'm sorry."

"What about?"

"About that beastly row we had the other night."

"Good Lord! That! I'd forgotten all about it."

"Well, I hadn't. You see, it's only just occurred to me that you must have just made up your mind that moment about this horrible business."

"That Father's death wasn't accidental, you mean?"

"Yes. It was a pretty bad shock to me when you brought it out just now, and I can understand what it was for you when you tumbled to it all by yourself. Of course you were all on edge."

"Say no more, sister. We both said some pretty silly things. Let's forget them."

The telephone bell rang. Stephen answered it. It was Mr. Jelks speaking from his office.

"I have got the man you want," he said. "The name is Elderson. Will it suit you to go and see him tomorrow morning?" He added an address in Shaftesbury Avenue.

"Thank you," said Stephen. He put down the receiver and began to laugh.

"What on earth is the matter?" Anne said.

"I—I'm sorry," he said, struggling with gusts of uncontrollable giggling. "But it does seem a bub—bloody silly position, doesn't it?"

"I don't see anything funny about it at all."

"Perhaps you're right. I shall be sane tomorrow. Just now I—hoo, hoo, hoo!"

And so odd is the effect of overstrained nerves, that when Martin came in from his walk he found Anne also in the grip of mirthless laughter.

8

Two Sorts of Private Inquiry

"Jas. Elderson, Private Inquiry Agent," said the notice in dirty yellow lettering on the dirty brown door. Stephen, as he stood collecting his breath on the landing after his climb up the steep staircase, tried to picture what manner of man Jas. Elderson would prove to be. He had never consciously set eyes on a private inquiry agent, but he imagined that a man could hardly be engaged in such a calling without having something more or less sleuth-like in his appearance. A lean, ferrety face, a sensitive nose that quivered slightly at the tip, small, beady eyes and a generally sly, cunning demeanour made up his idea of what a free-lance detective ought to be. If he did not expect to find all the features of his ideal compounded in Mr. Elderson, he did at least look to see some vestige of what he took to be the insignia of the profession. He would probably have been extremely nettled to be told, as was the fact, that his mental image was merely a reincarnation of the illustrations to a serial in a schoolboy's magazine which he had devoured with gusto some fifteen years before.

77

The reality, as might have been expected, was a disappointment. Mr. Elderson proved to be a large, bluff individual with a loud voice and a self-confident manner. He had a good-looking face, slightly blurred in outline, and his general appearance vaguely suggested a policeman gone to seed. There was nothing particularly surprising in the latter fact, since it was only a few years ago that he had left the Force; whether the circumstances of his retirement were in any way connected with the faint aroma of whisky which made itself felt as soon as he began to speak was his own secret.

He greeted Stephen in tones that contrived to blend the obsequious with the hearty, and proceeded, as he put it, "to take Mr. Dickinson's instructions." Stephen found, however, somewhat to his annoyance, that Mr. Jelks had already told him in general terms what would be required of him, and the only instructions that he found it necessary to give were devoted to confining Elderson's already ambitious programme. The delight with which the fellow had welcomed an investigation into a case of suspected murder was ludicrous and even somewhat pathetic.

"This is something like, Mr. Dickinson," he repeated several times, rubbing his beefy hands together. "This is something like!"

He did not specify what it was like, but it was easily to be gathered that the attraction of the case to him lay precisely in the fact that it was utterly unlike the dreary round of private detective's ordinary activities.

"If there was anything fishy about the people at that hotel," he went on, "I can promise you I'm the man to find it for you. You've come to the right place, sir, I can tell you that! And when it comes to a question of following up inquiries, well, sir, you may not credit it to look at me, but I can make myself to all intents and purposes invisible—virtually, morally, in-vis-ible, sir!"

At various points in the monologue Stephen endeavored to interrupt, but always without success. At last, however, he contrived to interpose: "I'm not at all sure, Mr. Elderson, whether you understand exactly what I am instructing you to do for me."

"But surely," Elderson protested, "I'm to be allowed a free 'and in me plan to campaign? Believe me, sir, when you employ an expert it's the only thing to do—a free hand." (The aspirate emerged triumphantly this time in an aura of spirits.) "Subject, of course, to your approval in the matter of exes. And I'm always most careful on the question of exes, that I can assure you."

Exes? Stephen blinked once or twice before he realized what was meant.

"We can discuss the question of expenses later," he said. "The point is that I am only instructing you to do one specific thing, which for various reasons I can't undertake myself. The plan of campaign, if there is one after you have done it, is my own business."

"Very good, sir," said Elderson, crestfallen, "if you wish it, of course. Theirs not to reason why, as Shakespeare says. At the same time, I should have thought—"

"Please don't undervalue what I am asking you to do," said Stephen swiftly, determined not to relinquish his hardly won grip on the conversation. "Your work in the first place, Mr. Elderson—I can't answer for the future—will be confined to ascertaining who was in the hotel the night that my father died, under what names they stayed, the addresses they gave, what rooms they occupied, and anything else about them that can be found out. Also any useful observations you can make about the staff at the place. I shall want a report on these matters as soon as possible—"

"Time is of the essence, sir; yes, I quite appreciate that," said Elderson, smacking his lips over the phrase, which meant no more to him than it did to his client. "Of the essence—absolutely. I can start to-day. Now on this question of exes, sir . . ."

That all-important point having been discussed and satisfactorily settled, Stephen prepared to go. Before he left, however, he was subjected to one last appeal.

"I do 'ate working in the dark, sir. Don't you think you could let me in on this a leetle bit more? If you follow what I mean, sir?"

"We are all working in the dark. That's exactly why I have had to come to you."

"But couldn't you just give me a line, sir, on the way you want things to turn out? I mean, for instance, Motive. You've considered that point, no doubt, sir. I presoom there was some motive for somebody to do away with the gentleman. If you could let me have a wrinkle or two on what's in your mind, then I should know the sort of somebody I'm wanted to find, and save us both a lot of trouble."

Motive! It was impossible not to realize that Elderson had put his finger on the weak spot in the whole project. But if he was to be of any use, it was clearly inadvisable to make him a present of the fact.

"I can't say anything about that at the moment," Stephen said with his hand on the door. Then a sudden thought struck him. "One moment," he added. "There is another matter which I should like you to look into and deal with in your report. Please be very careful to find out whether anybody on the night in question, or thereabouts, changed his room."

The speed with which Elderson saw the relevance of the remark did a good deal to raise him in Stephen's estimation.

"I take your point, sir," he said. "I take your point. If there was anything of that kind going on, and if the room where the gentleman was put away the one that was changed, it does open up vistas, so to speak, doesn't it, sir?"

After which Stephen walked out into the street. Elderson had been confident that his report would be ready within three days. It seemed a short enough time for the work, unless the man was a good deal more efficient than he appeared, but long enough in all conscience to wait. He turned into the first cinema he came to, and spent the first half-hour of those three days aimlessly contemplating records of events which seemed almost as fantastic and unreal as the mission that had brought him to Shaftesbury Avenue.

The time passed more quickly and with less strain than any of the family might have feared. Stephen saw comparatively little of Anne and Martin, and this was on the whole just as well. Since the interview with the Insurance Company's representative, he had re-established a *modus vivendi* with his sister, and they had relapsed into the easy-going relationship which had characterized their lives hitherto. A union that dates from the nursery is not easily dissolved. It can survive quarrels and explosions calculated to wreck nine marriages out of ten, possibly if only because the parties to it can take so much more for granted and are so much more ready to recognize what is forbidden territory. So far as Anne was concerned, her relations with Martin were clearly labelled, "Trespassers will be Prosecuted," and while Stephen kept to his side of the fence no questions were asked. She had not forgotten his attitude towards his future brother-in-law—it was not in her nature to do so—but she was quite capable of putting the cause of dissent away at the back of her mind, and behaving thereafter as if it did not exist. She gave no indication whether she had ever so much as mentioned the subject to Martin (what they did talk about when they were alone together was one of the problems that Stephen could never resolve), and Martin's manner to him was no more and no less cordial than it had been before. At the same time, a state of peace that depends on ignoring the existence of a cardinal fact is at the best an insecure affair and it was natural enough that the persons concerned should have agreed by common consent not to endanger it by too close association. Whether at Anne's instigation or not, Martin had suddenly developed a passion for what he described as "jaunts" into the countryside. Every morning his squat, tubby two-seater, looking strangely characteristic of its owner, would carry her away from Plane Street, to deposit her there again late in the long August evening, tired but bright-eyed, and with a strong smell of pipe tobacco clinging to her clothes. It was an arrangement that solved the problem of filling in the period of waiting very satisfactorily for two out of the three.

Engaged couples, in any case, are never supposed to feel, or at all events to admit that they feel, any boredom so long as they are together. Stephen, who was not engaged or likely to be, had resigned himself to a period of more or less unrelieved idleness and depression. But on the day following his call on Mr. Elderson, he unexpectedly found an outlet for his energies. He was sitting after breakfast, gloomily running over the financial columns in the morning paper, when his mother came into the room.

"How are the stocks and shares this morning?" she asked.

"Pretty mouldy," he mumbled.

"Have you been gambling again?" The matter-of-fact

way in which the question was put robbed it of offence. Actually, Mrs. Dickinson disliked her son's habit, and the dislike was a matter of common knowledge to them both. They did not refer to it more than was necessary, and the present inquiry was recognized as a mere request for information.

"A bit, yes," he answered.

"Talking of gambles," she went on, "I rather wanted to talk over this question with you."

It was unnecessary for her to say which question she meant. Since the production of the letter from Mr. Jelks on the evening after the funeral there had been only one question in the family, overshadowing every other.

Stephen put down his paper reluctantly.

"Must you, Mother?" he said. "And what has it to do with gambling, in any case?"

"Well, it is a gamble, isn't it?" she answered good-humouredly. "A very big gamble indeed, with a lot of money at stake. I imagine that is why it appeals to you. But what I wanted to ask you in particular was this: Why do you think that anybody should have had any interest in murdering your father?"

Stephen groaned.

"That's what they all keep on saying! I think that— but look here, Mother, this isn't a question I feel like discussing with you, of all people."

"But after all, why not?" said his mother placidly. "If everybody is asking the question, why shouldn't I? You know, Stephen, you have started this hare, and you can't complain of anybody else chasing it. As I told you before I feel that all this concerns you much more than it does me, and that is why I have allowed you to take your own course in the matter of the Insurance Company. At the same time, I can't help being interested in what is going on, and I have been thinking over it a good deal, just as an abstract problem. I've been glad to have something to occupy my mind." She smiled at him, and added: "You mustn't be shocked at me. It's only natural."

"No, I'm not shocked exactly," said Stephen. "Only I—"

"Only you wish I wouldn't talk about it. It seems to me to come to very much the same thing. Well, I'm sorry, but I intend to talk about it. If I am to accept, even for the sake of argument, that somebody has murdered my husband, it is of some importance to me who that somebody is. You don't feel like enlightening me, Stephen?"

"It isn't that I don't feel like enlightening you, Mother, exactly. But at this stage, I am a bit in the dark myself."

"Are you, really?"

Something in his mother's voice made Stephen look up sharply. For a moment he suspected that she was laughing at him. But her face remained quite serious.

"In that case," she went on, "it might be rather helpful to talk it over with someone else. Now, for instance, taking a detached view of the matter, suppose this was a case of murder—a clear case of murder, I mean, with a verdict of 'person or persons unknown' at the inquest—who do you suppose the police would begin by suspecting?"

Stephen looked at her vaguely.

"I dunno," he muttered.

"Come, come, Stephen! Where are your wits?" She was speaking to him now in exactly the same tones that she had employed, years ago, when he was stumbling over his first reading lessons. "The first people the police always suspect in such cases are the family."

"But good heavens, Mother, you don't mean—"

"The family," she repeated. It was now, at least, clear that Mrs. Dickinson was giving her somewhat disconcerting sense of humour free rein. "Especially, of course, the widow. Seriously, Stephen, I can't help feeling a little glad that I was away at Bournemouth all the time. I, at all events, have a very satisfactory alibi."

"Mother, I hate to hear you talk like this!"

"Never mind," said Mrs. Dickinson heartlessly. "It's good for me. After the widow, I suppose, come the rest of the immediate relations. You and Anne are safe enough it seems, with Klosters doing duty for Bournemouth in your case. Then there's Martin. Is he provided with an alibi, too?"

"Really, I've no idea. I haven't asked him."

"Well, I'm not suggesting that you should. It might not make for good feeling in the family, and I'm old-fashioned enough to think that of more importance than quite a lot of money. But it is the kind of question the police would ask, isn't it? Then, I suppose, if Martin satisfied them, they'd go on to the rest of the family. I'm not so sure about that," she added doubtfully. "Do they include brothers and cousins?"

"Where they are like Uncle George or Robert, I should be in favor of including them every time. Not to mention Uncle Edward, *and* The Holy Terror. Would you like me to start round cross-examining them straight away?"

"Perhaps on the whole it would be wiser not to. Let's suppose, though, that the police have seen all these people, and asked all those questions, and found nothing. They are still looking for the person with the motive to commit the crime. Where do they look next?"

"That depends on the kind of man who was murdered, I should imagine."

"The kind of man—exactly! So they have to set to work to find out what kind of man he was. They may have a good deal of difficulty doing that—almost as much difficulty as you would have in asking inconvenient questions of your Uncle George. Perhaps we have an advantage over them there, though."

"What is all this leading up to?" asked Stephen, who was evidently now at last genuinely interested.

His mother, as always, still preferred the oblique approach.

"What kind of man would you say your father was?" she asked.

It was not a very easy question to answer.

"Well, I don't suppose anybody could call him a very friendly bloke," Stephen said at last.

"But you wouldn't have thought him the sort of person to have many enemies—mortal enemies?"

"No, certainly not, so far as I know."

"So far as you know," she echoed softly. "I suppose that's as much as any of us could say—so far as we know. Perhaps it's rather a reflection on our life as a family that we can't go further than that. But at all events one could hardly expect the police to know more than we do on that point, if as much. They would find that he was retired and living on his pension, so that there was no question of anybody wishing to remove him out of rivalry, or wanting his position, or anything of that kind. They would find no evidence of quarrels or disturbances—outside the family, and we have dealt with them—to make any one anxious to take his life, *so far as we know*— that is, so long as we have known him. That is right, is it not?"

"Yes."

"So our imaginary police," Mrs. Dickinson went on, "would have to go further and further back in their searches, if they had the means to. And that is where I say we have the advantage over them."

Mrs. Dickinson pursed her lips and her hand went up in the familiar automatic gesture to her hair.

"How much do you know about your father's early life?" she asked.

"Nothing at all. Except for a few reminiscences about Pendlebury, and they seemed to date mostly from his childhood, he never told me anything about it. That was one of the rather uncanny things about Father— he seemed to be so self-contained, so to speak. One felt he was living in a vacuum."

She nodded.

"Exactly. And do you know, Stephen, you may think me a strangely incurious person, but I knew hardly any more than you did."

"Oh!" said Stephen in disappointment. "I thought you were going to tell me something useful."

"I am. Something interesting, at any rate. How far it will be useful to you I don't know, but I fancy that the police we have been imagining would have thought it worth listening to. The point is, you see, that I know rather more about it now than I did when he was alive."

She rose and went to her desk. From a drawer she took out a thick bundle of letters, held together by elastic bands which had grown slack with age.

"I found these last night," she explained, "put away among your father's things."

Stephen glanced at them. He noticed that the letter at the top of the pile was still in its envelope, and that this bore a penny stamp with King Edward VII's head upon it.

"This looks like ancient history," he observed.

"Very ancient history, some of it. I told you we should have to go a long way back, didn't I? But if you take the trouble to go through it, as I have, you may find that it has some bearing on quite recent history. At any rate, it will be an occupation for you. I'm afraid you are finding the present rather a dull and anxious time."

87

"Have you been inventing all this just because you thought I wanted something to do?" he asked in some annoyance.

Mrs. Dickinson smiled.

"It *is* good for you to have something to do, you must admit," she said. "And at the same time these things may be of real help to you. I think, in any case, that they are matters that you ought to know about. When you have read them, come and talk them over with me, and I dare say I shall be able to explain anything in them which you don't understand."

Stephen took the letters away to what had been his father's study. He sat down at the ugly great desk which loomed over the ugly small room and began to read. He was still reading when the gong went for lunch.

"Well?" his mother asked when they met at table.

"I've read them nearly all."

"Yes?"

"And this afternoon I'm going to read them again. I think it's all rather horrible, but I suppose I must go through with it."

Mrs. Dickinson raised her eyebrows at her son's evident disgust, but did not allude to it.

"Do, dear," she said amiably, then changed the subject.

Late that afternoon she went into the study. Stephen was just putting the letters back again into the bands that had contained them. He looked up when she came in but said nothing.

"Well," she said, sitting down in the room's only armchair, "did you find the letters interesting?"

"Interesting?" Stephen made a face. "I thought them disgusting."

"Really, Stephen," said Mrs. Dickinson, "it is a pity that you are such a puritan. It makes you so—so

88

ungrown-up. This sort of thing is all perfectly natural, you know. I sometimes think if you were a little more normal in these ways you wouldn't gamble so much."

"If by normal," said Stephen loftily, "you mean behaving in a thoroughly beastly way—"

"No, of course I don't. I mean taking a reasonable interest in the other sex, which is just what you never do. The moment you see a girl becoming in the least friendly you drop her like a hot potato. There was that nice Downing girl, for example. However, that isn't what I came in here to say. Tell me what impression you got from your reading."

"Really, Mother, I'd much rather not discuss these things with you."

"Nonsense! Of course you must discuss them. If you're afraid to talk about it, I'm not. What do these letters amount to, in any case? Simply that your father as a young man had an intrigue with a young woman, that there was trouble about it with *his* father and that he threw her over at a rather awkward moment for her. Then she had a child, in the inconvenient way in which these women always do seem to have children, and your father duly paid up for him until he was sixteen—which I believe is as long as the law can compel anyone to pay in such circumstances." She laughed softly. "It was just like him, you know, to fulfil his strict legal liability and no more."

"It's a pretty disgraceful story," said Stephen hotly.

She shrugged her shoulders.

"Perhaps it is. It is certainly a very old one. The child—it was a boy, wasn't it?—must be about ten years older than you."

"That means that Father was still paying for him long after he married, without saying a word to you about it!"

"That was just as well, perhaps. I might not have been quite so philosophical about it then as I am now. But we've only told half the story so far. The letters start again quite recently, after a long interval, don't they?"

"Yes, and this time they are from somebody who calls himself, 'Your injured son, Richard.' "

"Your half-brother, Stephen."

"Please don't rub it in. I suppose those letters are the reason why you wanted me to read the whole bundle. They seem to be in the nature of threats to Father. Apparently he claims that he has only recently discovered his parentage, that he is down on his luck, and thinks that he has a right to some assistance from Father."

"Exactly. And he expresses himself somewhat violently when he finds that he is not going to get any."

"Well, I suppose it is just possible that all this might be of some use, except for two things. The injured son doesn't give an address, except a Post Office in London, and we don't know his name. He merely says, in one of the letters, 'I have taken my mother's name.' And her letters are signed, not very helpfully, 'Fanny.' "

"That was just where I thought I might be able to help you," said Mrs. Dickinson.

"Good Heavens, Mother! You don't mean to say that you know this woman?"

"Not exactly. But I have an idea who she is. Do you remember your Uncle Arthur's will?"

"Yes, of course I do. What has that got to do with it?"

"Simply this. The woman to whom half the money was to go after your father's death was named Frances Annie March."

"But why on earth should Uncle Arthur want to benefit Father's old mistress?"

"It sounds a peculiar thing to do, doesn't it? But then Arthur was rather a strange man—as most of the Dickinsons were, I'm afraid. He had so often said that he meant to keep the money he had made in the family, that I feel it would be quite like him, when he fell out with us, to see that it went to the illegitimate branch. He would feel that he was keeping his word and injuring us at the same time."

"But that's no more than guesswork. Just because the woman's called Fanny, it doesn't prove that she's the same one."

"No. But if you look at some of the earlier letters, the affectionate ones, you'll find that they are signed, not 'Fanny,' but 'Fannyanny'. If you've had the misfortune to be christened Frances Annie, 'Fannyanny' is just the kind of nickname you would acquire, don't you think?"

Stephen looked at his mother as if he were seeing her for the first time.

"You ought to have been a detective," he said.

"At all events, if the imaginary police we were discussing just now had found out what we have done, I think they would consider it a clue worth following up. So I can only suggest that while you are waiting for any information that that man in Shaftesbury Avenue can collect for you, you should do what you can to investigate the identity of Frances Annie March."

Stephen rubbed his chin thoughtfully.

"These letters establish the date of Richard's birth, more or less," he said. "I suppose Somerset House will do the rest. I'll go there first thing tomorrow. Meanwhile, we'll keep this to ourselves. We needn't say anything to the others unless there turns out to be something in it."

So it was that after all Stephen found plenty of business to occupy him during the ensuing two days.

9

Elderson Reports

The three days which Jas. Elderson had allowed himself to complete his inquiries at Pendlebury were past. The first post on the morning of the fourth brought only bills and circulars to Plane Street. Stephen and Anne looked at each other silently and disgustedly across the breakfast-table. There was no need for words. The fellow had let them down. The moment when they would be able to do something towards the investigation of the mystery was once more postponed, and for how long? Each of them realized for the first time how great the strain of waiting had been, and how insufferable was the prospect of bearing much more of it.

"Of course," said Anne, speaking for the first time that morning, "I always thought three days was rather a short time to allow himself. But if he found it wasn't enough, he ought to have given us an interim report—something to go on with, at least."

"Um," said Stephen, and said no more.

Immediately after breakfast he went out, asking Anne to await his return at the house. The weather had broken, and a gusty south-west wind was driving thin showers of rain before it. The skirts of his mackintosh wrapped themselves around his trouser legs in an embrace that became progressively damper and more affectionate as he walked. It was a depressing day, and even the warm synthetic air of the Underground was welcome in contrast to the outside world.

Stephen had to ring twice at the door of Jas. Elderson's office before receiving any answer. When at last the door was opened, he found himself looking into the large grey eyes of a totally unknown young woman. She was undeniably good-looking, tall above the average, and somewhat dauntingly self-possessed. For a moment, recollecting the uncouth and grimy office-boy who had received him on the last occasion, he wondered whether he had stopped at the wrong landing, and he endeavoured to look past her to reassure himself by reading the name upon the door. He was aware as he did so that she was observing his embarrassment with a certain calm amusement.

"Do you want anything?" she asked, just as he had made up his mind that he was right after all. Her voice, without being particularly cultured, was quiet and pleasing.

"Is Mr. Elderson in?" said Stephen.

"I'm afraid he's not available today," was the reply. "Monday, I expect. In fact, I'm sure he'll be available all Monday."

"I particularly wanted to see him today," Stephen persisted. "Do you know where I could get hold of him, perhaps?"

She shook her head.

"Not today," she repeated. "Perhaps I can help you. What name is it?"

"Dickinson."

Her face cleared.

"Oh, Mr. Dickinson! Have you come about the Pendlebury matter?"

"Yes. Mr. Elderson promised me his report this morning, and I haven't had it. He knew that it was extremely urgent, and I—"

"Will you come inside?" she said, and stood on one side to let him pass. She closed the door behind him and then said: "If you don't mind waiting here a moment, I'll see whether it is ready for you."

Stephen waited in the narrow little hall while she went through into the passage within. Presently she returned, with an odd expression on her face which he tried in vain to interpret.

"I'm afraid you'll have to come in here to help me," she observed, and led the way into the office.

Mr. Elderson was sitting at a table littered with sheets of paper. His arms were spread out in front of him and his head was pillowed on his arms. He was breathing deeply and from time to time uttering a loud snore. A completely empty whisky bottle was beside him and a glass lay broken on the floor. The stench of spirit and stale tobacco smoke lay heavy upon the air.

"You see," said the young woman, calmly, "the trouble is that he's sitting on a lot of the papers. And he's too heavy for me to move. If you wouldn't mind lifting him up a bit, I could slide the chair out from underneath him and get them, and then put it back again."

Under her tranquil influence it seemed the most ordinary operation in the world. With his left hand pressing on Mr. Elderson's back and his right hand heaving at Mr. Elderson's fleshy thighs, Stephen contrived to shift him upwards and forwards just enough to allow her dexterously to disengage the chair, sweep from it the warm and crumpled papers upon the seat and replace it before

Stephen's aching muscles gave under the strain. During this process, Mr. Elderson muttered a few inarticulate words of protest and as soon as it was completed was sound asleep once more.

"Thanks," she said. "I think I've got it all now." She gathered up the sheets from the table and added them to those recovered from the chair. "I'll just arrange them in order. Luckily he always numbers his pages. Shall I put them in an envelope for you?"

"Yes—please do," Stephen gasped. "But is it—I mean, how do you know—is it all right, I mean?"

She paused in the act of licking the flap of a large square envelope.

"All right?" she asked. "Oh, the report, you mean. Yes, that will be all in order, you'll find. He never starts on *that*"—she nodded towards the bottle on the table—"until he's finished the job. It's a kind of reaction, you see. The only trouble is that when he starts he never knows where to stop. That's why—" She shrugged her shoulders and left the sentence uncompleted. "He got back pretty late from Pendlebury yesterday and must have been working here nearly all night." She held out the envelope to him. "Here you are, Mr. Dickinson," she said, in a tone that seemed to indicate some haste to be rid of him. "I'm sorry you've had the trouble of coming down here."

Stephen took the envelope and stuffed it into the pocket of his mackintosh.

"Thank you," he said. "But"—he looked once more at the sprawling creature at the table—"are you going to stay on here alone? I can't get you any help or anything?"

Her mouth straightened into a hard, narrow line.

"No, thank you," she said. "I shall be quite all right. Let me show you out."

On the doorstep, Stephen said: "Well, goodbye, and thank you for helping me, Miss—er—Miss—"

"Elderson," she said sharply, and shut the door.

As he had expected, Stephen found Martin with Anne when he returned home. They were in the study, Martin deep in the arm-chair in a cloud of acrid smoke, while Anne crouched at his feet on a foot-stool in an attitude of adoration.

"Morning, Steve," said Martin without getting up. "Nuisance about this detective feller. Annie's just been telling me."

"Did you manage to see him?" Anne asked.

"Oh, yes. I saw him all right," said Stephen.

"What had he got to say for himself?"

"He hadn't exactly a great deal to say for himself. But I've got his report."

Martin, as Stephen feared he would do, greeted the news with "Good egg!" and added, "Does it amount to much?"

"That," said Stephen, "is what we are now going to see."

He produced the envelope, still sealed, and began to open it. To his extreme annoyance he found his fingers trembling as he did so and for a moment or two he fumbled helplessly with the flap.

"Yes," observed Martin, watching him. "It is rather an excitin' moment, isn't it?"

Stephen, once more caught unawares by his prospective brother-in-law's penetration and annoyed by finding himself its victim, frowned hideously and at last succeeded in tearing the envelope and removing the contents. Written in a large copper-plate hand that flowed generously over sheet after sheet of ruled foolscap paper, these proved at a glance that Miss Elderson's account of her father's habits was correct. There could be no doubt that they were the work of a man who, at the time of writing them, was stone-cold sober. He smoothed out the pages where they had been crumpled by the pressure of their author's large posterior, cleared his throat, and began to read.

The document was headed in the starchy official manner that was no doubt a relic of the author's police service: " 'To Stephen Dickinson, Esq. *From* Jas. Elderson, private inquiry agent. *Re* Occurrence at Pendlebury Old Hall Hotel, Markshire.' " It continued, in numbered paragraphs:

" '1. Pursuant to your instructions of the 22nd inst., I proceeded forthwith to Pendlebury Old Hall Hotel, arriving there at approximately 8.30 p.m. I registered in the name of Eaton, and, the hour being somewhat late to commence prosecuting inquiries, occupied myself during the evening with familiarizing myself with the hotel staff and ascertaining the geography of the place.' "

"Funny phrase, that," remarked Martin. "I don't suppose he means the same thing as we generally mean by it, eh, Steve?"

"Shut up, you ass," said Anne softly.

" '2. During the succeeding two days, I succeeded in interviewing all the members of the hotel staff who appeared likely to be of any assistance, in inspecting the hotel register and obtaining their comments upon the same. I prolonged my stay at the hotel for the purpose of taking a statement from one important witness, the waitress Susan Carter, who was on her holiday and only returned to work on the morning of the 25th inst. I found all the persons interviewed quite willing to give me all the information within their power. The explanation of this fact, which was contrary to my anticipation and to past experience in like matters, appeared to be due—'

"Lord! What English this blighter writes!" said Stephen, breaking off. "Damn all board schools!"

"Don't be a prig," said Anne. "Go on."

" '—appeared to be due to their mistaken belief that I was acting in the interests of the British Imperial Insurance Company. It transpired that a representative of that concern had already visited the Hotel and made inquiries with a view to possible litigation. By representing to the persons concerned that the interests of the establishment coincided with those of that Company in suppressing any further publicity attaching to the death of the late Mr. Dickinson, and, as I have reason to believe, by a lavish disbursement of funds, the representative had succeeded in securing their whole-hearted co-operation. I thought it wise not to undeceive the persons in question as to my identity and was accordingly able to secure the maximum of information with the minimum of outlay (as to which, see Exes sheet, forwarded to Messrs. Jelks & Co., pursuant to instructions).

" '3. The only other preliminary matter which I should mention is that on the last day of my residence at the Hotel an individual whom I have reason for thinking to be a plain-clothes detective of the local constabulary also arrived and commenced to make inquiries, which I was able to ascertain were related to the matter in question. In consequence of the facts set out in Para. 2, above, the personnel of the Hotel were unwilling to give the individual whom I have mentioned any assistance, but I am unable to state precisely what form his inquiries took or how far the same were successful.' "

"The insurance blokes haven't wasted much time, have they?" Martin observed. "But what are the police poking about for? I thought you said, Steve, that they wouldn't touch this thing with a barge-pole?"

"I hope I never said anything so banal," answered Stephen curtly, preparing to read on.

"But wait a bit," said Anne in some excitement. "This is important, isn't it? If the police are making inquiries, doesn't that look as if they weren't satisfied with the inquest verdict after all?"

"Whether it's important or not," said her brother crossly, "do you want to hear what this man has to say? Or shall I take it away and read it to myself?"

After which little display of temper, the reading continued without further interruption:

" '4. The hotel consists of three floors only, having been originally constructed as a private residence. The guests' bedrooms are all accommodated on the first floor, the ground floor rooms being sitting-rooms and the second or attic floor comprising the apartments of the chambermaids and waitresses. There is also an annexe for additional accommodation. I formed the impression that business at the establishment was not brisk, for the annexe was wholly unoccupied at the time in question, and of the eleven bedrooms in the main building two were vacant. I append a sketch-map showing the position of the various rooms, all of which, it will be observed, open off a central corridor, which runs the length of the house.

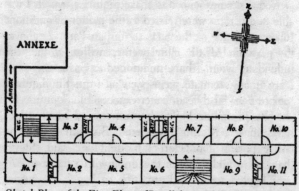

Sketch Plan of the First Floor of Pendlebury Old Hall, Markshire

" '5. On the night of the 13th August, to which I was directed to confine my attention, the following rooms were occupied, as under:

" 'No. 1. Mr. & Mrs. E. M. J. Carstairs, of 14 Ormidale Crescent, Brighton. Arrived on the 12th August by car; left on the 14th after lunch. A middle-aged couple. The only details that I was able to obtain concerning them were that Mr. Carstairs was interested in local antiquities, and delayed his departure in order to obtain a rubbing of the brasses in Pendlebury church.

" 'No. 2. Mrs. Howard-Blenkinsop, of The Grange, North Bentby, Lincs. Arrived on the 5th August; being met at the station by the hotel conveyance, left on the 19th August. An elderly lady, presumed to be a widow. Well known in the hotel, where she makes a habit of staying for a fortnight in each year, though not always at the same time of year. Mention of her name caused some amusement to the staff. I gathered that her character was in some degree peculiar, and the head housemaid went so far as to say that "she acted unusual for a lady." So far as I was able to determine, the imputation was that her behavior was not altogether consonant with her social status, but I could find nothing against her character.

" 'No. 3. Mr. P. Howard-Blenkinsop, of the same address. A young man, understood to be the son of the above. He seems to have been of a quiet and retiring disposition. The head waiter expressed the opinion that he was "a natural," which I ascertained to be a local expression, reflecting on his mental qualities and not on his legitimacy: I gathered that during his stay he did little or nothing all day, beyond keeping his mother company and reading light literature.

" 'No. 4. Mr. & Mrs. M. Jones, of 15 Parbury Gar-

101

dens, London, S.W. 7. Arrived on the evening of the 13th August by car; left on the morning of the 14th. A young couple. Opinion in the hotel seemed divided as to whether they were on their honeymoon or not married at all. It was agreed that their behaviour was "lover-like." The reception clerk recollected that the girl giggled a good deal while the register was being signed. I could not obtain any exact description of either, except that she was, in the words of the chambermaid, "a flash little thing" and he was "nothing much to look at, but acted like a gentleman." I formed the opinion that this referred to the size of her gratuity. I ascertained that they reached the hotel at about 8.30 p.m. while dinner was being served, and had some cold food sent up to their room on a tray about 9.0 p.m. The waitress who served them remembered the occasion particularly well, because of the extra trouble involved. She also recollected that they breakfasted in bed next morning, at about the time that the disturbance occasioned by the death of Mr. Dickinson was at its height.

" 'No. 5. Vacant.

" 'No. 6. Mr. J. S. Vanning. See as to this gentleman, remarks *re* Mr. Parsons, below.

" 'No. 7. Mr. J. Mallett. I am instructed that this individual is already known to you.

" 'No. 8. Vacant.

" 'No. 9. Mr. Robert C. Parsons. Arrived for tea on the 13th by cab from the station; left on the morning of the 14th. A middle-aged man. He is particularly well remembered by the office staff for the reasons following, viz.: He had reserved accommodation by letter, asking for a room with two beds and a single room, adjoining if possible. Room 9, which is a double room, and No. 11, next to it, had accordingly been reserved for him.

Some surprise was therefore expressed when he appeared by himself. He explained that he suffered very badly from insomnia, and had found that he could obtain some relief by changing from one bed to another during the course of the night; hence his desire for a double room. The other room, he said, was for a friend who would be joining him later. The reception clerk remembered that when she asked the name of the friend he was unable or unwilling to give it, but merely said that he would be mentioning his (Mr. Parsons') name. Mr. Parsons was shown his room and No. 11, adjoining, which is the best single room in the house. He expressed himself as pleased with them. A little later, however, Mr. Leonard Dickinson arrived at the hotel, on foot. He was of course well known to the management, having stayed there on numerous occasions. It was also understood that whenever he visited the hotel, room No. 11, if not occupied, should be kept for him. Indeed it had happened in the past that guests had been asked to change their rooms to suit Mr. Dickinson, who was, it is alleged, apt to make difficulties when crossed in any way. In this instance, No. 11 not being actually occupied, Mr. Dickinson was installed there, and on Mr. Parsons' guest arriving (by car, shortly before dinner), he was put into No. 6, being the only vacant single room. The guest registered in the name of J. S. Vanning, and the only address given was London. Mr. Parsons similarly gave no address, other than the town of Midchester. I was, however, able to get a sight of his letter reserving the rooms, and this was written on the note-paper of the Conservative Club of that city. There seems no doubt from what I was told that Mr. Parsons was in poor health. More than one witness remarked on his pallor and nervousness. As to Mr. Vanning, I could obtain no particulars whatever. He does not seem to have had any noticeable features at all. I should add that the two persons in question did not leave the hotel together. Mr. Vanning breakfasted early and left soon after 8 a.m. Mr. Parsons did not come down till later and seemed surprised and upset that his friend had already gone. It was pointed out to him, however, that Mr. Vanning had settled his own account. I was unable to ascertain whether this fact reassured him or not.

" 'No. 10. Mr. Stewart Davitt, of 42 Hawk Street, London, W.C. Arrived the 10th August, by train and hotel conveyance; left on the 14th by the same. This gentleman was described to me by one of the staff as "the mystery man." It appears that from the time of his arrival up to his departure he did not go outside the hotel, and, indeed, only rarely left his room. He is said to have explained that he was engaged upon work of a vitally important character and needed absolute rest and quiet. All his meals were served in his room. I was told that he was a "nice-looking young man," but could obtain no further particulars of his appearance. On the evening of the 13th, he asked for his account, and said that it would be necessary for him to catch the earliest fast train to London from Swanbury Junction, some eight miles away. This involved his leaving the hotel at approximately 6.30 a.m. the next morning, which he duly did, being driven to the station by the car attached to the hotel. In view of the decidedly unusual circumstances attending this person, I endeavoured to obtain further particulars concerning him, but without success. I was unable to ascertain anything *re* his work, about which, it seems, he was extremely reticent. It is to be presumed that it was of a literary nature.

" 'No. 11. Mr. Leonard Dickinson.

" '6. The above information comprises all that I was

able to ascertain *re* the matters to which my instructions were confined. I took the liberty, however, of pursuing my investigations somewhat further, with a view to discovering any matter which might throw light on the death of the deceased. I therefore venture to append the following.

" '7. The deceased retired to bed on the night of the 13th August, at approximately 10.45 p.m. Before doing so, he went to the reception office and asked (a) that a pot of china tea with a slice of lemon should be sent up to his room in about a quarter of an hour's time, and (b) that his breakfast should be served to him in bed the next morning at 9.0 a.m. (a) was duly performed; it was when he was called next morning prior to (b) that his death was discovered. Death was found to be due to the deceased having swallowed a quantity of Medinal overnight. These matters were, I am given to understand, investigated in the ordinary way at the inquest, the assumption being that the deceased took the fatal dose in the tea. This remained an assumption only, due to the fact that the teapot and cup had been removed and washed before the fact of death was discovered. It seemed to be a reasonable one, however, and I deemed it desirable to proceed upon the basis that it was correct, the question being whether anybody other than the deceased could have inserted the poison in the tea.

" '8. I accordingly proceeded to question the two persons who seemed most likely to assist on this question, viz. Miss Rosie Belling, chambermaid, and Miss Susan Carter, waitress (whom I have already mentioned, *supra*, Para. 2). Miss Belling was not very helpful. All that she could say was that at approximately 8.15 a.m. on the morning of the 14th August she went into room No. 11 and removed from it the tray with the teapot and cup upon it. Mr. Dickinson having given orders for breakfast in bed at 9.0 a.m., she would not normally have gone into his room at that hour, but for the fact that, several other guests having demanded tea in the morning, there was a shortage of tea-sets, following an accident on the staircase two mornings before. On this occasion, seeing the deceased apparently still asleep, she merely removed the tray and went out again without attempting to disturb him. On returning, shortly before 9.0 a.m., to inquire whether he was ready for breakfast, the fact of his death was ascertained, by which time the teapot and cup had been washed and used by another guest.

" '9. Miss. Carter's evidence at the inquest was confined to the fact that she took a tray up to the deceased's room on the night in question. In answer to my inquiries, however, she was able to describe her movements in very much more detail. It appears that this particular evening was an unusually busy one for her, so far as work upstairs was concerned. For besides taking the tea-tray to No. 11, she also had to take up dinner as usual to Mr. Davitt (No. 10), supper to Mr. and Mrs. Jones (No. 4) and hot water, sugar, lemon, and whisky to Mr. Vanning (No. 6). In fact, she had somewhat of a grievance *re* the amount of fetching and carrying that had to be done, especially in regard to No. 4, for it appears that these persons, having originally ordered a meal downstairs, changed their minds at the last moment. So far as I was able to ascertain, she visited the bedroom floor of the hotel four times during the course of the evening, as follows:

" '8.15 p.m. Taking dinner to No. 10.

" '9.0 p.m. Taking supper to No. 4, and removing dinner-tray from No. 10.

" '10.0 p.m. Removing supper-tray from No. 4.

106

" '11.0 p.m. Taking tea to No. 11 and hot water, etc. to No. 6.

" '10. I asked Miss Carter whether she had observed anything unusual in the manner of the deceased on bringing him his tea, and in reply she stated that on that occasion she had not seen him at all, but had only heard his voice. She explained that from her previous experience of the deceased, upon whom she had waited during several former visits of his to the hotel, she knew him to have a particular distaste to the presence of anybody, particularly any female, in his bedroom when he was, or might be, incompletely attired. Accordingly she merely knocked at the door, informed him of the fact that his tea was awaiting him and went away, leaving the tray in the corridor. Asked whether she had followed the same procedure in the case of Mr. Vanning she professed difficulty in recollecting the same, but finally stated that she was of opinion that on her knocking at his door he had himself opened it and taken the tray from her hand.

" '11. In view of the obvious significance of the facts stated in Para. 10 above, I deemed it advisable to inquire as to who of the residents in the hotel were in their rooms at the time when the tray was left outside No. 11. Miss Carter, having ascended to the first floor from the kitchen premises by the service staircase, was unable to state who was still in the lounge or smoking-room on the ground floor, and apart from Mr. Vanning, she saw nobody on the first floor at that time. One of the bathrooms was being used as she passed along the corridor, but she was unable to say which it was. The remainder of the staff were uncertain in their recollection on the point, but by collating all the evidence available, I was able to arrive at the conclusion that the following were at 11.0 p.m. almost certainly in their rooms:

Mr. Vanning.
Mr. Dickinson.
Mr. Davitt.
Mr. & Mrs. Jones.
Mr. Parsons.

" 'The following were in all probability in their rooms:

Mr. Howard-Blenkinsop.
Mrs. Carstairs.
Mr. Mallett.

" 'As to the remainder, Mrs. Howard-Blenkinsop
sat on in the lounge after her son had gone to
bed, endeavouring to finish a game of patience,
and Mr. Carstairs, after retiring at the same time as
Mrs. Carstairs, shortly returned again to the lounge,
where he gave some assistance to Mrs. Howard-
Blenkinsop in her game. I was able to ascertain
positively that the lights were extinguished before
midnight, and that these two individuals were the last
to retire.

" '12. With regard to the management and staff, I
was unsuccessful in obtaining any information to the
detriment of these. The deceased appears to have been
regarded as an asset to the establishment rather than
otherwise, and I could not find any evidence suggesting that a motive was present for procuring his
death so far as they were concerned. They appeared
to be a respectable body of individuals, though in
some respects deficient from the view-point of efficiency.

108

" '13. The above concludes my inquiries at Pendlebury Old Hall Hotel, and I await further instructions.

" '(Signed)
" 'JAS. ELDERSON.' "

10

Plan of Campaign

Saturday, August 26th

Stephen finished his reading and looked round at his audience. Anne, from her foot-stool, was regarding the carpet with an air of intense concentration. Martin was making notes with a stubby pencil on the back of an old envelope. He continued to do so for some moments after Stephen's voice had ceased, and then looked up.

"May I have a look at the blighter's plan of the course, Stevie, old son?" he asked.

Stephen handed him the plan, and Martin gave it a cursory glance through his thick spectacles.

"Thanks," he said, giving it back. "Well, we've got all the doings now, haven't we? I plump for Davitt, myself. Room next door and all, he'd have heard the girl knock on your guv'nor's door. Then all he had to do was to pop out and bung the stuff in the tea-pot. It's an open and shut case, *I* think. Don't you think so, Annie?"

Anne said, without looking up:

"There seem to have been a lot of odd people in that hotel. What about Vanning and Parsons? Parsons was a bad sleeper—he may very well have had Medinal with him. And then there are the Joneses—"

"Nothing odd about them. Just a couple out loose on the spree. It would have been much odder if there hadn't been a pair like that in a country hotel at the week-end. No, put your shirt on Davitt, the man of mystery, first favourite in the murderer's stakes. What do you say, Steve?"

"I think you will be making a great mistake if you start theorizing at this stage," said Stephen pedantically. "To begin with, you have got to consider all the evidence, and not simply what I have just read you."

"But that is all the evidence, ain't it?" said Martin.

"Not entirely. There are two other matters which may have some bearing on the problem. To begin with, here is a bit of ancient history which Mother told me the other day. Rather a nasty bit of history, I'm afraid."

He bit his lip and coloured slightly.

"Come on, Steve, don't be shy!" Martin guffawed. "Out with the old family skeleton!"

Stephen related, as briefly as he could, the gist of the letters which his mother had shown him two days before.

"I may add," he concluded, "that Mother's guess turned out to be perfectly right. I have been to Somerset House, and there is no doubt that the woman in question is this same Frances Annie March."

During the recital, Anne remained silent, still apparently in contemplation of some private problem of her own. Martin, however, was regrettably vocal. His appreciation of Mr. Dickinson's lapse was quite unrestrained in its expression.

"Who'd have thought the old man had so much blood in him?" was his final comment on the disclosure. "That's Shakespeare, or something like it. But seriously, Steve, does this get us any forrarder? Unless you're going to say that Frances Annie and the injured Richard are really Mrs. Whatnot-Blenkinsop and her son. Is that what you're after?"

"At the moment I'm merely after facts," said Stephen stiffly. "That happens to be one of them. Now here's another. Perhaps you'll think it more important. There was someone in the hotel that night whom Father thought he recognized."

He repeated what he had learned from the inspector of the man whose appearance had interrupted their conversation in the lounge. Martin showed little interest.

"That doesn't cut much ice with me," was his verdict. "Lots of chaps make mistakes like that. Only the other day I slapped a bloke on the back in the street, and it turned out I didn't know him from Adam. Most embarrassing. Besides, if this fellow was somebody staying in the hotel, why should your father have only seen him that once and not before or after? It was probably just a local who had blown in for a drink."

"Or," said Anne slowly, "or it was somebody who didn't want to be seen again. Somebody who had ordered a meal downstairs and changed his mind when he saw that Father was in the place. Mr. Jones, in fact."

"Um," said Martin, visibly impressed. "Um!" He relit his pipe and said no more for a moment or two. "All the same," he added, after reflection, "I still think Davitt is the man. With Jones as runner-up, perhaps. But I don't for the life of me see why a fellow should want to take a girl with him on a murdering expedition. I'm dam' sure I shouldn't—not even you, Annie."

"Perhaps—" Anne began, but Stephen interrupted her.

"This is getting us nowhere," he said impatiently. "We haven't a ha'porth of evidence to put before the Insurance Company to convince them that any of these people are guilty of the murder. All we have shown so far is that,

112

as Anne says, there were an odd lot of people in the hotel. Also that there was an opportunity for somebody to put an overdose of Medinal in the tea-pot before it reached Father. And that's not enough, by a long way."

"Perfectly right," said Martin. "No use wasting time gassing about these chaps. We've got to follow them up and try to find out something about them. This is where the sleuthing starts. Give us our marching orders, Steve."

"To begin with," said Stephen, "we've got some addresses to go on. Two of them are in London—Davitt and the Joneses. Then there are the Howard-Blenkinsops in Lincolnshire, and the Carstairs at Brighton. Vanning's address we don't know, except that he's somewhere in London, and Parsons is somewhere in Midchester. Presumably we could get at him through his club."

"If my club porter gave my address to a casual inquirer, I'd have his hide off," Martin observed parenthetically.

"When we find Parsons, we can find Vanning," Stephen went on. "If he is willing to help us, which he may very likely not be."

"Need we bother about these people?" Martin asked. "When we've got Davitt and Jones sticking out a mile? It seems to me obvious that these other chaps couldn't have had anything to do with it."

"It is anything but obvious," Stephen retorted. "I agree that we know nothing about them at all. That doesn't mean we ought to leave them out of account altogether. As for Parsons and Vanning, there is one very significant fact about them, which you seem to have overlooked."

"Meaning?"

"Simply this. Parsons booked both rooms. The room he booked for Vanning was the room that, as it turned out, Father slept in. It was next door to his own. Can we be sure that Parsons knew of the change? Father had something sent up to his room last thing at night. So did Vanning—do you remember the report says he was surprised to hear next morning that he had got up and had breakfast?—isn't it quite possible that he poisoned Father by mistake, thinking—"

"Thinking that a pot of tea was a bottle of whisky, I suppose," Martin interrupted with a horse laugh.

"If you're going to make a silly joke of the whole thing—" said Stephen crossly.

"I'm not, really, old man. I think it's all too frightfully subtle for words. Just exactly what you called getting us nowhere just now."

At which point the tension was mercifully relieved by the gong sounding for lunch.

In the afternoon the conference was resumed in a quieter mood.

"Obviously, we want to start with the nearest people," said Martin. "That is, Davitt and Jones. First question: Do we try our own hand or get Elderson to do the dirty work for us?"

"We employed Elderson only because I didn't want to be seen at Pendlebury," said Stephen. "So far as the start of our inquiry goes, I think we should keep it in our own hands. We can fall back on him if the business looks like getting beyond us."

"Right. Second question: What line exactly do we take? I mean, it's all very well to talk about making inquiries, following people up and so forth; but unless you're a bobby, you can't just go to a chap's house and say: 'Oh, Mr. So-and-so, I'm told you were staying at Pendlebury the other day. Did you by any chance happen to murder an old gentleman called Dickinson while you were there, because if so, I want your blood?' At least, I don't see myself doing it."

"I propose to use my own common sense in the matter,

and take whatever line seems best in the circumstances. I certainly don't intend to interview any of these people directly, until I have found out something about them, unless there's absolutely no other line of approach."

"I see—just nose around a bit, make oneself sweet to hall porters and landladies and so forth. Then get an interview by pretending you want to sell something, or that you're a long-lost brother from Fiji, or something of that sort. It ought to be rather a lark. Now, third and last question: Do we go out in a pack after the stuff, or do we split up, one lion to a Christian, so to speak?"

Anne broke her silence to say: "For goodness' sake, Martin, don't let you and Stephen go out on this business together. You know you'd simply be bickering the whole time."

"I think we had better see what we can do individually, to start with, at any rate," said Stephen. "We can join forces later if necessary."

"I dare say you're right. It'll save time, too. Then all we have to do now is to split up our quarry. Can I have first stab at Davitt? After all, I spotted him first."

"I'd rather thought of trying Davitt myself first," said Stephen at once.

"But hang it all, he was my selection! Look here, give me Davitt and you can have the Joneses, both of them."

"I think," Stephen answered very quietly, "that I'd better have Davitt, if you don't mind."

"Toss you for it!"

"You are a hopeless pair of idiots," said Anne wearily. "Look here, I've got it all worked out for you. Stephen will begin with Davitt and Martin with Jones. Then if neither of those leads to anything, Martin will drive me down to Lincolnshire and I shall see what can be done with Mrs. Howard-Blenkinsop. She sounds as if she might amuse me, and anyway that will be a woman's

115

job. While we are doing that, Stephen can go down to Brighton to find out what he can about Mr. and Mrs. Carstairs. We can leave Parsons to the last, because Midchester is such a long way off. Now for Heaven's sake go away and get on with it, and try not to make greater asses of yourselves than you can help."

"Thanks for these kind words," said Martin. "But what about you, Annie? Aren't you going to come along with me and help stir up the Joneses?"

"No, I am not. I've got other things to do here."

"What other things?"

"It doesn't seem to have occurred to either of you that the quickest way to find Vanning's address may be simply to look him up in the telephone directory. It's an out-of-the-way name, and it oughtn't to take long to make a list of all the Vannings. Then we can try them out and see if we can spot the right one."

"Not a bad idea, that," said Martin. He squinted at her for a moment and then added: "That's not all, Annie. You've got something else up your sleeve."

"I never said so."

"What is it?"

"Just something that occurred to me, that's all. Something very obvious, really, but not at all pleasant. I want to think it out."

"Well, you might give a fellow an idea—"

"Oh, why can't you let me alone!" she flashed out suddenly, and then, as suddenly, her anger evaporated. "I'm sorry, Martin, but this business has really got me down."

"Of course, old girl, I understand," Martin said. He patted her shoulder clumsily. "I vote we get going straight away," he said to Stephen.

"We'd better keep a record of what we're doing," Anne remarked.

She went to the desk and, taking a piece of paper, wrote down the list of names from Elderson's list, leaving a space opposite each which it was hoped would be filled by the details ferreted out by each investigator. When she had done so, she sat for a moment staring at her own work.

"Funny, that!" she murmured.

"What is funny?" asked Stephen.

"Nothing. Only . . ." She came out of her abstraction suddenly. "Oh, do get out, both of you!"

They went, Stephen silently shrugging his shoulders at his sister's moods and fancies, Martin apparently unimpressed, and humming under his breath what he conceived to be the tune of "We've Got to Keep Up with the Joneses."

II

First-Fruits

Anne had once, to her extreme discomfort, spent a Christmas holiday in a sporting household in the West of England, where, Sundays apart, non-hunting days were shooting days, and vice versa. She could not ride and had a violent dislike for shooting. Moreover, if while she was there the rain ever stopped for a single moment during the hours of daylight, it must have been when she was not looking. In consequence, while she had succeeded in forgetting most of that disastrous holiday, and in living down what could not be forgotten, one impression remained ineffaceable. It was the memory of long afternoons in the drawing-room, watching the rain splash against the windows, listening to the click of her hostess's knitting needles as they inexorably compiled yet another pair of sensible shooting-stockings, waiting for tea until the men came in.

She had an absurd sensation of being back in Devonshire just now, as she lay curled up on a sofa, trying to read a book. Despite the fact that there was no fire in the grate and that outside was full daylight instead of the

118

gloom of a winter afternoon, she could not rid herself of the feeling that she was once more "waiting for the men to come in" from the day's sport, and that at all costs, tea must be kept for them. They might be in at any moment now, their silly white breeches splashed all over with mud, and with a sickly certainty she foresaw that Johnny would be still utterly absorbed in that ghastly Bendish girl, discussing saddle-sores and overreaches, eternally, eternally, and never once noticing . . .

"Damn! Am I going quite off my head?" she said to herself, and sat up on the sofa. It is humiliating to find oneself so vividly remembering what has been so firmly forgotten. She was alone in the house, her mother having gone out soon after lunch. There was not the smallest reason to suppose that Stephen would be home before dinner, if then, and Martin might not choose to come back at all. Detection—if this absurd amateur business could be called that—didn't keep fixed hours like pheasant shooting or fox hunting, and it was ridiculous to imagine that anything worth speaking of could be done in an afternoon.

At all events, it was time to think of getting herself tea. She got up, and as she did so, noticed lying on the floor the paper recording the results of her investigations in the telephone directory. She picked it up, and reflected somewhat guiltily that it was not very much to show for an afternoon's work. She put it away with the list of suspects compiled at the end of the conference and then stood quite still for a full half-minute, thinking. That half-minute was the sum total of time given that day to the consideration of the matter which she had told Martin needed thinking out. When it had elapsed, the fact was still there, unchanged—perfectly obvious, perfectly inexplicable—a solid little chunk of reality lodged uncomfortably in her mind. And she remained as perversely determined as ever that for the present it should be shared by nobody else.

She was finishing her first cup of tea when a loud pounding on the door knocker made her start. So the men were back already, or rather one of them. Martin, of course. Stephen had his latchkey, and any other visitor would have rung the bell in the ordinary way. Martin preferred the knocker. Merely to put his finger on a bell push was too tame a method of announcing his presence. She ran to the door to let him in.

"Any tea left? Good!" were his first words, as he plumped down on the sofa beside her.

As she poured him out a cup, it was all that she could do not to ask him whether they had had a good day and where they had killed.

"You're back earlier than I expected," she said. "Have you—did you manage to find out anything, Martin?"

Martin popped a small scone into his mouth. He looked thoroughly self-satisfied.

"Depends what you mean by finding-out," he said with his mouth full. He chewed, swallowed, and then observed, "I've seen Mr. Jones, anyway."

"What?"

"Rather. Charming old gent with a beard. He was very friendly. Wanted me to stay to tea. But I thought I'd rather come back here."

"Martin, what on earth are you talking about?"

He laughed expansively.

"It was really rather fun," he said, "and as easy as falling off a log. I'll tell you exactly what happened. I beetled off to Parbury Gardens, and it turned out to be one of these big blocks of flats, with the names of all the tenants written up in the hall below, just to make things easy for the chap who tells the maid he's an old friend of the family and then when he's inside tries to insure your life—you know the sort of thing. Well, I looked at the list of names and the first thing that my eagle eye spotted was that the name opposite No. 15 wasn't Jones at all. It was Peabody—Mrs. Elizabeth Peabody. I always think there's something a bit bogus about any woman who calls herself Mrs. Elizabeth anybody, but that doesn't necessarily prove that she goes about in hotels under the name of Jones. Still, one never could tell, and there was always an odd chance that the Peabody might have let the place to Jones and nobody had bothered to alter the name. So I decided on a spot of finesse. I rang a bell marked 'Caretaker,' and after a longish time a small boy appeared. I asked him whether Mr. Jones lived at No. 15. He looked at me rather as if I was half-witted and said that Mrs. Peabody lived there. He didn't actually ask me whether I could read, but that was what he seemed to imply. I said, oh, I was sorry, but I thought Mr. Jones lived there. Then he seemed to take pity on my innocence and volunteered that a Mr. Jones lived at No. 34, on another staircase. I said Thank you so much and he said Not at all and that was that."

He devoted himself for a few moments to his tea. Anne poured him out a second cup and murmured, "Yes, darling?"

"Well," Martin went on, vigorously wiping crumbs off his face with his handkerchief, "there were still two possibilities, of course. (a) Mrs. Peabody might have been staying at Pendlebury as Mrs. Jones. (b) The detective fellow might have made a mistake in the number, and our Jones might be the one living at No. 34. (a) looked rather a stinker. I was loitering on the doorstep, wondering how I could lead the conversation round to Peabody, after all my interest so far had been in Jones, when I had a bit of luck. The boy was just going to slink back into his cubbyhole, after pointing out the way to No. 34, when a delivery van stopped at the door, and a fellow got out with a heavy-looking parcel in his arms. And it was addressed, very plainly, to Mrs. Peabody. Just for something to say, I remarked to the boy, 'Ah! A parcel for Mrs. Peabody!' It must have sounded a pretty imbecile remark to make, but it turned up trumps. He said, 'That'll be one of her books.' I said, 'It looks a jolly heavy book,' or words to that effect. Then he said, 'She has to have special sorts of books,' and suddenly I saw the light. 'Braille?' I said. 'That's right,' he said. 'Books for blind people, you know.' Just to make sure, I asked him, 'Is Mrs. Peabody blind?' and he said: "That's right. It's a shame, ain't it?' Well, I thought after that, I needn't worry about point (a) any more, so out I went."

"Darling, that was frightfully clever of you!"

"Well, it was luck as much as anything, of course," said Martin modestly.

He waited for her to contradict him, but with feminine perverseness she merely said: "Well, that left point (b). He turned out to be the old gentleman who asked you to stay to tea, I suppose?"

"Yes. It was all rather amusing. What happened was this . . ."

But Anne seemed indisposed to listen to further details.

"He wasn't even 'M. Jones' at all, I suppose?" she interrupted.

"As a matter of fact, he was T. P. M. Jones. I thought there was just a chance he might be the right chap, so I—"

"Anyhow, he obviously wasn't. And I don't expect Elderson would have made a mistake about the number."

"Oh, yes. So what we are left with is that the address in the book was a fake, and for all we know, the name, too. It's odd, though."

122

"I don't see anything odd about it. Just what I expected. Simply a couple out on the loose—"

"I know. That isn't what I meant. I've never done it, so I'm not sure, but do couples out on the loose usually put real addresses in the hotel book?"

"Of course not, silly! They put in a fake address, just as this one did."

"But that's just the point. It was a real address—not their own, of course, but somebody else's. It seems such a funny thing to do. Or perhaps I'm wrong. Tell me, Martin—you've had lots of experience. What used you to put in hotel registers?"

Martin had gone a warm pink.

"Oh, I dunno," he mumbled. "Just anything that came into my head, I suppose."

If Anne noticed his embarrassment, she was cruelly unfeeling about it.

"Anything that came into your head," she repeated. "Yes. I suppose that is what one would do. And the anything might be either a purely imaginary address or a real one. But if it was a real one, there must have been something to make it come into one's head—some association, don't you see, that made one think of that particular address rather than any other. So I can't help feeling that we haven't disposed of the Joneses just by finding out that they didn't live at 15 Parbury Gardens. If they didn't, one of them, at all events, probably had some reason for writing it down in the hotel register rather than—than Plane Street, Hampstead, for instance."

"This is all a bit deep for me," Martin observed.

"Oh, no, it isn't. You're quite sharp, really, and you know it."

"Anyhow, I don't see that we can do any more about the Joneses."

"Neither do I. But it's unsatisfactory, because of course

123

we haven't really eliminated them at all."

"Personally, I don't think they were ever worth troubling about. They were simply a couple out—"

"Yes, Martin darling, you've said that already. You do repeat yourself a lot, you know."

"Sorry, Annie. Let's forget them. Do you know, I can think of quite a lot of things I haven't repeated nearly enough lately."

And Martin proceeded to repeat them, with a warmth and variety that did him credit.

At the end of a quarter of an hour, a key was heard in the latch of the front door.

"That'll be Mother," said Anne, disengaging herself. "Martin, you've made my hair in a foul mess. And do go and wipe that powder off your coat."

But it was not Mrs. Dickinson, but Stephen. He came into the room looking bored and tired. From experience, Anne knew better than to start firing off questions at a man who had obviously not "had a good day."

"Would you like some tea?" she asked. "It won't take a minute to make a fresh pot."

Stephen shook his head.

"Is there any whisky in the house, d'you think?" he asked.

"There's half a decanter in the dining-room, if you haven't drunk it already. It's all there is, because I know Mother said she wasn't going to order any more till—"

"Till we touch the insurance money, I suppose. What a hope!"

"Well, why don't you order in some for yourself? After all, you're the only one who drinks it."

"Oh, yes, I can order it, all right. Only my credit happens to be a bit low just now."

"*I can call spirits from the vasty deep,*" remarked Martin unexpectedly. "*But will they come when you do call*

124

for them? I say! That really is rather neat, don't you think?"

Stephen gave him a disgusted look and went out of the room. He returned a moment or two later with a full glass. Sitting down, he drank off about half of it in silence. Then he said abruptly:

"Well, I've got rid of Davitt, anyhow."

"Got rid of him?" Anne asked.

"Eliminated him, expunged him, wiped him out. Do I make myself clear?"

"Don't say that, Stevie!" Martin protested. "Davitt, the man of mystery, my own selection! I can't bear to see him go!"

Stephen took no notice of him.

"So far as I can see the man is perfectly genuine and has no more to do with Father's death than—than the Archbishop of Canterbury."

He emptied his glass, and put it down beside him.

"How about Jones?" he said, turning to Martin.

Martin was opening his mouth to repeat his history, when Anne cut in.

"But Stephen, aren't you going to tell us about Davitt?"

"I've told you. He's a wash-out."

"But you can't leave it just like that. What did you do? How did you find out? You must tell us something!"

Stephen frowned in a bored manner which, in Anne's experienced eyes, concealed an excited awareness of the interest he was creating.

"Well, if you won't take my word for it," he said grudgingly, "here goes."

He leaned back in his chair, crossed his legs, and addressed the picture-rail on the opposite side of the room.

"Hawk Street is a depressing place. How anybody can contrive to live there I can't imagine. It's tucked

125

away behind Garmoyle Street, and that's tucked away behind Theobald's Road. It's all little two- and three-storied dirty brick houses with aspidistras and lace curtains in the ground floor windows. You know the sort of thing. Practically every house lets apartments, and a good proportion of the lodgers are foreigners, I should say—students, refugees, and so forth."

"Funny that a chap living in such a poor-class neighbourhood could afford to stay at Pendlebury," said Martin.

Stephen nodded.

"Just what occurred to me," he said. "Well, I found No. 42, and it was just like all the others, only perhaps a little dingier. It had the usual card in the window, impinging on the vegetation, to say that there were apartments, or at any rate an apartment, to let. That made it easy, of course. I rang the bell and an amiable old body came to the door. She was what I believe is known as 'motherly'—not my type, exactly, but I shouldn't be surprised if she was the answer to the lodger's prayer. I shall never know for certain, unfortunately. You see, I thought if the worst came to the worst, and Master Davitt seemed worth while investigating, I could take a room in the house and try a little sleuthing at close quarters. I asked the old dame if I could see her apartment and in I went. The room was pretty grisly, but I suppose it might have been worse. It was perfectly clean, anyway. Then I asked her if she hadn't a front room to let—the one she showed me looked out on the catrun at the back. No, the front room was let. I didn't ask her outright who it was let to, but she was the nice, gossipy sort of landlady—quite a good type for the learner-detective to practice on—and in next to no time she told me that the room had been occupied these last two years by a steady young man of the name of Davitt. From then on she proceeded to

126

disgorge without any prompting all that she knew of the said steady young man. Which was quite a lot."

Stephen paused dramatically. His air of boredom had disappeared and he was evidently enjoying his own recital.

"Disregarding inessential details, what it amounted to was this: He is a clerk in a big City firm—she is a bit vague about it, but they appear to be stockbrokers. He is all alone in the world, except for an aged mother in Glasgow, whom he goes to see every Christmas. Very quiet, very shy, no girl friends, and pays his rent regular. (That, of course, was the most important thing about him. There was a sort of Go Thou And Do Likewise look in her eyes when she said it that impressed me a lot.) The only thing that distresses her about him is that he never goes out anywhere in the evenings, but sits indoors all the time writing. And that is the clue to the whole of the great Davitt mystery. He's by way of being an author of genius. Whether his genius runs to epic poetry or plays or soap advertisements, she couldn't tell me. Personally, I think a man must have genius of a remarkable order if he can find anything to write about, sitting in a front room in Hawk Street and never poking his nose outside to see what the world is like. But that's by the way. Of course, his genius isn't recognized as yet, not completely recognized, I should say, because a month or two ago he did achieve a bit of recognition. He won a prize. Naturally, my thoughts turned at once to Football Pools, but it was nothing so banal. It was a prize offered by a literary magazine—quite a lot of money, she told me. I imagine it was ten or twenty pounds. And what did I think he did with it? By this time, I could have told her but it seemed more satisfactory to let her tell me."

"You mean he spent his prize money on staying at Pendlebury?" Anne asked.

"No less. It seems a pretty footling thing to do, doesn't it? His only use for what he had won by his writing, apparently, was to go away somewhere quiet and do yet more writing. He had a week or so of holiday due to him about then, and he couldn't do anything better with it than that. Rather pathetic, I thought. It seemed to me that he might just as well have saved his cash and stopped at Hawk Street all the time, but I forgot to mention among the charms of the neighbourhood that it's a favourite by-pass for heavy stuff going to and from the big railway stations, and I quite appreciate what she meant by his wanting somewhere quiet. So there he stayed, right up to the last minute of the last day of his holiday, and came back, I was not surprised to hear, looking as pale and tired as when he started."

"But why did he have to take all his meals in his room?" Anne asked.

"Same thing. He didn't want to be disturbed in his writing, or the meditations incidental to his writing. Time and again Mrs. Thing—I never found out her name—had to drag him downstairs by the scruff of his neck to his supper, he was that taken up by his work, you wouldn't believe. I suppose to have his meals—even Pendlebury meals—brought up to his room three times a day must have been the seventh heaven to him. Poor devil! I don't expect he's ever heard of *cacoethes scribendi*, but he's got it pretty badly."

He ended his story, and then added after a pause: "Well, that's all there is to it. I shook the dust of Hawk Street off my feet as soon as I could, once I'd got what I wanted. I said I'd let the old woman know about the back room. She'll have to wait a long time before she catches me down there again, though."

Nobody said anything for a moment or two, and then

Martin said: "You didn't get hold of the name of the stockbrokers, I think you said?"

"No. It didn't seem to matter much."

"I was just wondering. Suppose it turned out that Vanning was a stockbroker—"

"Well—" Stephen began, with a shrug that showed what he thought of the suggestion.

"He's not," Anne put in. "At any rate, if he is, he doesn't live in London, or anywhere near it."

"Lots of stockbrokers live at Brighton," Martin said.

"My good Martin," said Stephen, exasperated, "if you want to pursue this ridiculous hare, why don't you get hold of a list of members of the Stock Exchange and find out for yourself?"

"Quite right, Steve, I hadn't thought of that. Silly of me. Apologies and all that."

"And now," said Stephen, turning to his sister, "who is Vanning, what is he? I hope the Directory has been useful."

"It all depends what you call useful," said Anne. "This is what it says."

She fetched the little document which she had compiled and handed it to him. Stephen read:

Vanning, Alfred & Co., Ltd., Fruit Mrchts., Covt Gdn. W.C.2.

Vanning, Alfred E., Osokosi, Watling Way, Strthm.

Vanning, Chas. C., Grngrcr, 42 Victoria Ave., S.W.16.

Vanning, K. S. T., Barrister-at-Law, 2 Nisi Prius Row, Temple, E.C.4.

Vanning, K. S. T., 46 Exeter Mans., S.W.11.

Vanning, Mrs., 94b Grosvenor Sq., W.1.

Vanning, Peter, Artist, 3 Hogarth Studios, Kingfisher Walk, S.W.3.

Vanning, Thos. B., Grngrcr, 85 Brick St., N.1.

Vanning, Waldron & Smith, Chtrd Acctnts, 14 Gossip Lane, E.C.3.

"Quite amusing in its way," he remarked. "Observe how Alfred E., no doubt the big noise of the firm at Covent Garden, establishes his younglings in the retail trade to the north and south of him! Wait a bit, though— perhaps they're only nephews. He seeks higher things for his son, and sends him to the Bar."

"Where does the artist come in?" said Anne.

"Oh, he's obviously a sport from the parent stock, who sickened of the sight of whole oranges in crates, and went off to paint half ones on dishes instead. But I can't quite work in Mrs. Vanning. Grosvenor Square clashes rather with Osokosi, don't you think? Perhaps—"

"The point is, it seems to me," said Martin heavily, "does any of this help us to find J. S. Vanning?"

"Not in the least. I suppose we could solemnly go through everyone on the list and try to find if any of them is harboring a son or brother with the initials J. S., but it seems a waste of time when we've got another line on him through Parsons."

"Just what I thought. Well, the upshot of the day's work is, we've knocked Davitt off the list—subject to what I said about stockbrokers—and Vanning and Jones are left much where we found 'em."

"Jones!" said Stephen. "I forgot. You haven't told me about him yet."

And Martin did tell him, with all and more than all the elaboration with which he had already told Anne. Soon the two men were comparing notes on their experiences and arguing like old hands as to the merits of different methods of detective inquiry. To Anne, sitting bored and tired between them, it was all very reminiscent of after-tea

130

conversation in Devonshire. . . . "What you want to do, old man, is to drive the Long Wood first, and put three guns forward, with a stop in the hollow."—"It's no good, my dear chap, with the wind in the South—they simply break back over the boundary fence every time."—" 'f course, if you'd only taken my advice last year and cut another ride through the larch plantation. . . ." If it hadn't been for the consciousness of that nagging little fact, ever present at the back of her mind, she would have gone fast asleep.

12

Mrs. Howard-Blenkinsop

Sunday, August 27th

"That looks like the place," said Martin.

Anne peered through the window of the car.

It was a house of medium size, square and plain, standing back from the road, to which it was connected by a curving drive. There was nothing in the least remarkable about it—it was the type of house that might be found in almost any country district of England. One could guess that inside there were at most two bathrooms, rather antiquated, and that somewhere in the background was stabling for at least three hunters. But the very fact that it was so ordinary in appearance made it seem all the more daunting to one of the investigators at least. Anne's heart sank as she gazed at the somewhat shabby placidity of the Grange. These people, she reflected, had been there for years, probably for generations. They barely acknowledged the existence of anybody who had not lived in the neighbourhood for at least ten hunting seasons. As for visitors from London, unknown and unannounced, they would be regarded as no better than tramps. She smiled wryly as she remembered how simple the whole arrangement had seemed when she planned it in the study at

Hampstead. Only one thing remained to give her any hope of success—the brief description of Mrs. Howard-Blenkinsop's character in Elderson's report. Obviously the woman was an eccentric, and with eccentrics anything was possible.

She had said nothing, but Martin, as usual, seemed to divine her thoughts.

"I dare say things'll look a bit easier after a feed," he said.

"I vote we try the village pub. It's only just down the road."

They lunched alone in the front room of the Black Swan. The food was more than tolerable, and by the time they had finished their meal, Anne was disposed to take a more cheerful view of life, though she seemed no nearer to ascertaining anything about the owners of the Grange than before. She had made one or two efforts to get into conversation with the landlord's wife, who served them, only to find that she was both hard of hearing and incomprehensible of speech. A Sabbath calm brooded over the village, broken only by the hum of voices from the adjacent taproom and by the intermittent barking of dogs from the opposite side of the street. This latter sound attracted Martin's attention. Going across to the window, he stared out for some time, sucking noisily at his pipe, and then called Anne.

"Here's something worth trying," he remarked.

Anne saw that he was pointing at a notice which hung over a yard gate almost immediately opposite the inn. It read:

BENTBY KENNELS
PEDIGREE PUPS FOR SALE
SCOTTIES, CAIRNS, FOX-TERRIERS
Dogs Boarded   Expert attention

"I think a puppy would make rather a nice present for you," said Martin. "Would you like a Scottie or a Cairn?"

"Neither," said Anne. "I'm not very fond of dogs."

"You ought to be," said Martin, seriously. "There's something about a dog which you don't get in anything else." He puffed silently for a moment or two and then added: "Anyhow, you could always inquire about boarding a dog. That won't commit you to anything."

"What on earth are you talking about.?"

"About the Kennels, of course. It's the best place to try any snooping in we could find. To start with, it's the only place that's likely to be open on a Sunday, it's almost certain to be kept by a female—these places nearly always are—and with any luck it'll be a centre for gossip. I can look at the dogs, while you get to work on the woman-to-woman stuff. If you can get a line on the old lady up at the Grange, I can always amuse myself in the kennels while you are trying to break in there. I think it's rather a good spec, taken all round."

Anne had said from the first that interviewing Mrs. Howard-Blenkinsop was woman's work. Rather to her annoyance, Martin had taken her at her word, and resolutely refused to take any part in the job himself, except the highly enjoyable task of driving her to the scene of action. It was therefore quite an agreeable surprise to find him planning a campaign on her behalf.

"Of course," Martin went on meditatively, still staring out of the window, "it may take a bit of time to get hold of *la belle* Blenkinsop. It's rather a pity, in a way, we didn't allow ourselves a bit longer. If I was on my own, I should certainly want to spend the night here, and give myself a full day tomorrow, so as not to have to rush things. Of course, as it is, that's out of the question, I suppose—unless . . ."

He left the sentence unfinished, and looked over his shoulder at Anne with an air that was at once malicious and appealing.

"No," she answered. "I'm sorry, Martin, but I'm not going to sleep here tonight. In the first place, I have no intention of losing my virtue without so much as a tooth-brush to sustain me—"

"As a matter of fact," said Martin with an air of unabashed innocence, "I do happen to have a few odd things in the back of the car—including, as it happens, a new toothbrush."

"In the second place, I promised Mother I'd be home before she went to bed tonight."

"Oh, well—"

"And in the third place, my darling, I'm not allowing any liberties until I've got my marriage lines. Sorry and all that, but I'm funny that way."

"Righto!" said Martin, with the air of one who was used to taking such rebuffs in good part. "In that case, I'd better pay our bill, and then we'll see what is to be seen across the way."

A tall young woman, dressed in a dirty kennel coat and corduroy breeches was walking across the yard when they entered. A cigarette depended from her mouth, and her short black hair would have been the better for some expert attention. She put down the pail which she was carrying and slouched in their direction, a predatory gleam in her eye.

"Good afternoon," said Martin politely. "We wanted to look at the Kennels."

The girl nodded.

"That's what we're here for," she said. "What are you

135

interested in? Cairns? Scotties? We've got rather a nice litter of Dandies you might like to look at, but—Get down, Sheila!"

The last observation was directed to a fox-terrier bitch, in the last stages of pregnancy, which was fawning round her boots.

"Well, as a matter of fact we hadn't quite made up our minds," said Martin. "We just thought we'd have a look round first, didn't we, Annie?"

The girl's interest in them waned perceptibly.

"Oh, I see," she said. "Well, you'd better come along and see if there's anything you'd care for."

She led the way to a long range of kennels, the occupants of which set up a furious barking as they approached.

"Nice place you've got here," Martin observed. "I wonder whether—"

"Not bad. We're apt to have trouble about the water-supply, that's all. Now these Scotties might interest you—six months old, guaranteed through distemper. Dogs, eight guineas; bitches, seven and a half. The sire got two reserves at Crufts and the dam was by Champion Watmough of Wakerly. You can see the pedigree if you like."

"They look very sweet," remarked Anne, who felt that it was about time she said something.

"Jolly little chaps," chimed in Martin, with considerably more sincerity in his voice. "By the way, I suppose in this village—"

"Now these two are all that we've got left of Sheila's last litter. House-trained. Three and a half guineas, or you can have the pair for six. It's a bargain, really."

"Awfully jolly," said Martin. "I wanted to ask you, what is that house—"

"These are the Dandies I was telling you about," the

young woman went on remorselessly, and once more proper words of non-committal appreciation had to be found. Clearly it was not going to be a simple business to get any gossip from the Kennels. The whole affair began to seem to Anne more and more unreal and nightmarish as they trailed on from one noisy, bounding family to another. At last it seemed that they had reached the end of their tour. Only one compartment remained, and this was tenanted by a solitary red setter. He had a dejected appearance, and something about him made Anne, who did not care for dogs, feel that she had found a kindred spirit.

"What a darling fellow!" she exclaimed.

"Not one of ours," said her guide in a chilly tone. "Just a boarder. He's been convalescing after gastritis. His coat's pretty bad still, isn't it? I expect he'll be going home in a day or two."

"Has he far to go?" Anne asked, stifling a yawn. But her boredom vanished instantly at the reply.

"Oh, no. He's only going up to the Grange."

Trying not to seem too excited, Anne said: "Is this Mrs. Howard-Blenkinsop's dog, then?"

"Yes. Do you know her?"

"Yes—I mean, no—that is—"

"I expect she'll be down here directly to look at him. She looks in most afternoons."

Here was good fortune indeed! Hardly knowing what she was saying, Anne gasped out: "Really! How awfully nice!"

Her companion looked at her in surprise.

"Well, she's not a bad sort really," she said. "For all that she's my landlord."

Pulling herself together, Anne said: "I'd like to have another look at the Scotties, if you don't mind," and walked back to the kennel nearest the entrance to the yard, determined at all costs to keep within the precincts until her quarry should appear. Martin had left them. From the corner of her eye she saw him half hidden by an angle of the wall, apparently engaged in deep conversation with the two young fox-terriers. Anne cursed him bitterly in her heart and grimly prepared to talk dogs for the rest of the day, if need be.

Luck was with her. She had barely reached the litter of Scotties before somebody who could only have been Mrs. Howard-Blenkinsop appeared upon the scene. She was a fairly stout woman of early middle age, who looked as if she owned the earth she walked on—which in fact she did. Anne was rather taken by her face. It looked sensible. The same adjective might have been applied to everything about her. She wore sensible low-heeled brogue shoes, sensible thick stockings, and a tweed coat and skirt which could certainly only be justified by an appeal to reason, so rigorously had all the allurements of fashion been excluded. In one particular only did she show a certain lack of intelligence. She had elected to bring with her to the kennels a timid and elderly dachshund, who, evidently warned by previous experience, skulked miserably behind her skirts. This did not save him from repeated and savage assaults from Sheila, and conversation was continually being interrupted to placate or separate the unequal combatants.

"Good afternoon, Mary," Mrs. Howard-Blenkinsop began, as she hove in sight. "I came to see how my poor Rufus is getting on. (Now don't be silly, Fritz, you know she won't hurt you.)"

"Good afternoon," said the young woman. "Sheila! Come away from him! I'm so sorry, Mrs. Howard-Blenkinsop. I'm afraid she is rather a nuisance. Rufus is quite—*Sheila!* Come to heel!"

"Come along, Fritz! It's only that she knows he's frightened of her, you know. Of course, she's really—I'm so sorry, Mary, I shall have to ask you to take her away. I shouldn't have brought him with me, only he does miss his walkie-walks on Sundays, don't you, darling?"

Rather sulkily, Mary grabbed the bitch by the scruff of her neck and dragged her indoors. Fritz, relieved of his fears, sat down and began to scratch himself. His mistress bent down to reprove him and then looked up to see Anne for the first time.

"Oh!" she said. "I must apologize. I suppose you've come to buy something and I've interrupted the deal. I didn't see you were here."

Face to face with the object of her coming to Lincoln-shire, Anne found herself completely tongue-tied. Fortunately Mrs. Howard-Blenkinsop was evidently quite accustomed to finding younger women speechless in her presence, and proceeded to put her at her ease by doing all the talking herself.

"Fond of dogs?" she inquired, as she led the way towards where the red setter was barking a welcome in the distance. "But of course you are! Every nice person is, I think. Well"—she looked over her shoulder at Mary, who was following in their wake—"Mary's a very nice girl, though she can't always pay her rent, and I'm out to help her all I can. All the same, don't pay what she asks. You can always beat her down half a guinea or so! But don't tell her I said so! Well, Rufus, my pet! Here's your old missus come to see you! How's the poor old fellow! There's a poor mannie, then!" and she broke into a flood of the infantile endearments which the most intelligent people always seem to find necessary when conversing with the friend of man.

Martin appeared from nowhere and took Anne by the arm. He led her away a few paces and whispered, "Who is this?"

"Mrs. Howard-Blenkinsop," said Anne in surprise. Martin looked puzzled.

"Surely not," he said.

Anne stared at him for a moment before she guessed to what he was referring. Then she began to understand, and her bewilderment grew. There was no doubt that this woman was quite different to anything that Elderson's report had led them to expect. Without any pretence to fine airs or graces, she was obviously a woman of breeding. She was of the type that might cause some amusement in Hampstead, but in a country village she was perfectly in the picture. And nobody—least of all such keen judges of social distinctions as hotel servants—could possibly say of her that she "acted unusual for a lady."

"There must be some mistake," she said at last.

"This wasn't the woman at the hotel," said Martin positively. "It couldn't have been."

"Perhaps she's quite different when she's away from home," Anne suggested faintly.

But a moment later Mrs. Howard-Blenkinsop settled the question herself. She ended her colloquy with Rufus, dusted her skirt where his eager paws had marked it, and observed: "Well, I'm a silly old woman, I suppose, to make such a fuss about him. But I can tell you this, Mary: when you're my age and haven't any children of your own, you get to depend a lot on your dogs."

So that left the son also to be explained! thought Anne. She was burning with curiosity and at a loss as to how to set about satisfying it. And all the time the precious minutes were slipping away, as Mrs. Howard-Blenkinsop exchanged a few last morsels of canine gossip with Mary before leaving the Kennels. Anne would have given anything to scrape acquaintance with her, and had not the least idea how it should be done.

It was Martin, unexpectedly, who came to the rescue. Evidently the mystery had whetted his appetite also, for he entirely abandoned his declared policy of leaving the investigation to her. At precisely the right moment, he injected into the ladies' conversation a supremely shrewd piece of doggy knowledge—it was, he afterwards confessed to Anne, almost the only scrap of kennel-lore he possessed—and in next to no time he was one of the party. Mrs. Howard-Blenkinsop was delighted with him, and demanded his name and Anne's. The name of Dickinson evidently set her fumbling in her memory.

"Dickinson!" she repeated. "That reminds me of something—I heard the name lately—oh, of course!" She looked at Anne doubtfully. "Girls don't wear much mourning nowadays," she ventured.

"That was my father," said Anne.

"Dear, dear!" She clicked her tongue in sympathy. "Well, it's quite a good idea to buy a dog at a time like that. It takes your mind off things."

How Martin managed it, Anne did not precisely know, but ten minutes later they were walking up the village street towards the Grange with her, having somehow escaped from the Kennels without having committed themselves to a purchase. She proved to be good company, and before they had reached the gates of the house Anne had learned a considerable amount about the agricultural depression, the vagaries of the vicar and the idiosyncrasies of the late Colonel Howard-Blenkinsop. But of Pendlebury Old Hall, not a word.

They were invited to stay for tea in the shabby, comfortable old house, which was much as Anne had pictured it, except, quite unaccountably, for a fine collection of Whistler etchings, probably worth as much as the rest of the contents put together. After tea they were taken out to admire what little a hot summer had left of the herbaceous border. At this point, Anne felt that they were on sufficiently good terms for her to take the plunge.

"Excuse my asking you, Mrs. Howard-Blenkinsop," she said, "but were you ever at Pendlebury?"

"Where did you say, my dear? Pembury? Where's that?"

"No—Pendlebury. I mean Pendlebury Old Hall. It used to be in our family, but it's an hotel now. It's where my father—died."

"Oh, dear me, no! What makes you think that?"

"Well, you may think it very odd of me to ask, but you see, your name and address are in the visitor's book there."

"God bless my soul! My name? Are you quite sure?"

"Oh, yes; there's no doubt about it."

"But this is most extraordinary! When am I supposed to have stayed there?"

"About the beginning of this month—for a fortnight. You and a young man who was supposed to be your son."

"A young man!" Her face went purple. For a moment Anne thought she would have a fit. Then suddenly she cried: "A fortnight! The beginning of this month! Oh, my stars! But this is rich!"

And Mrs. Howard-Blenkinsop, throwing back her head, let out peal upon peal of laughter.

"The impertinence!" she exclaimed when she could speak again. "For sheer, cool impertinence! Oh, my dear," she went on, wiping her eyes with a man's-sized silk handkerchief, "how I wish now I hadn't quarrelled with the vicar! How he would have enjoyed it!"

She stuffed the handkerchief back into the pocket of the sensible coat, and said soberly: "Well, I'll be blowed! Now come indoors, both of you. You must have seen quite enough of the garden. I'll give you both a glass of sherry before you go, and tell you all about it."

"There's not much to tell, really," she said, when the sherry had been poured out. "And if you didn't know her, you wouldn't see the joke. That's why I regret the vicar so. But I must tell somebody. You see, I had a cook."

"Do you mean to say that your cook stayed at Pendlebury under your name?" said Anne.

Mrs. Howard-Blenkinsop nodded.

"That's all," she said. "It sounds very bald, put like that, doesn't it? But if you could only have seen her! Mrs. Howard-Blenkinsop, indeed! Really, I'm very cross about it. It's just as well she isn't here to get a bit of my mind. But"—she began to laugh again—"she *was* a character! I can just see her flaunting it in an hotel in her best clothes—old clothes of mine, incidentally! She always gave herself such tremendous airs, though I will say she was a good cook."

She sighed a tribute to the departed.

"When did she leave you?" Anne asked.

"Why, only a week ago, as soon as she came back from her holiday. It was really a most extraordinary—but I'm telling this very badly. Let me start at the beginning."

But instead of starting at the beginning, Mrs. Howard-Blenkinsop suddenly looked narrowly at her guests and said: "Really, this is a very odd situation! Why should I tell you all this? What business is it of yours?"

"Please, Mrs. Howard-Blenkinsop," said Anne. "Please tell us. It really is a matter of importance to us, though it would take much too long to explain."

"We've come here the whole way from London simply to ask you about this entry in the hotel books," Martin put in.

"What? I thought you came here to look at Mary's dogs!"

Martin shook his head.

"Simply a blind. I don't know much about them, and Anne here hates the sight of them."

Anne, who saw her hostess's brow darken ominously, hastily interjected: "Oh, that's not true, Martin. You know I simply fell in love with poor Rufus!"

"I really don't know whether I'm standing on my head or my heels," said Mrs. Howard-Blenkinsop. "What is all this about?"

"I can tell you this much," said Martin. "There's a great deal of money involved."

"Money? You don't mean Mrs. March's money, do you?"

"Mrs. *Who*?"

"Mrs. March—my cook. Of course, I forgot, you don't know her."

"Golly!" said Martin.

Mrs. Howard-Blenkinsop looked at him with an expression so dubious that Anne felt it was time for her to intervene.

"I'm sorry," she said, "but you really must tell us all about this Mrs. March. It seems awful cheek on our part, I know, but it is most frightfully important to us. We are—we're quite respectable people, honestly, but we're in a great difficulty and you are the only person who can help us."

Mrs. Howard-Blenkinsop looked her up and down. Then: "Help yourselves to some more sherry," she said. "You both look as if you needed it. I don't know what all this is about, but if you can take Mrs. March's money away, perhaps she'll come back as my cook again and that will be something. Now, what do you want to know?"

"Everything," said Martin, gulping his sherry.

"Well, then, Mrs. March has been my cook for the last ten years—ever since her husband died, in fact."

"Oh! Then March was her husband's name?" asked Anne.

"Certainly. He was a local man, a builder in a small way. There are a lot of Marches in these parts, you know."

"I see," said Anne disappointedly. "Then she wasn't . . ."

"You don't know her maiden name, I suppose?" Martin asked.

"Good gracious! Do you children want to go back into all that ancient history? She was a March too—she married her cousin."

Anne breathed again. "Please go on," she said.

"She had one son, who lived with her. She was devoted to him, but he was a little—you know, not quite right in the head. I used to give him odd jobs on the farm to do, but he was really not worth his keep. Doctors can say what they like, but cousins ought not to marry. Dogs are different, of course."

"Excuse me, but are you quite sure he was a child of the marriage?" Martin asked.

"Really, what a question! Certainly he was. She and her husband were always—And anyhow, Philip is a March all over, and the image of his father to look at."

"But there was another son, wasn't there?" Martin persisted.

"Now what on earth made you say that? I really didn't expect people from London to come down here and rake up our village scandals. It isn't even a village scandal, for that matter. The Marches kept very quiet about it and nobody here knew anything about it, except the vicar, and he very properly told me when I proposed taking her into my service. The child wasn't born here, you know.

145

Her parents had moved to Markshire, and then when this thing happened they sent her to live with her uncle and aunt because she couldn't face the people there any more. You know what they are like in villages, among the respectable classes. Then, later on, she married Fred March, who was a good deal older than she was, and a very good wife she made him."

"But the child?" Anne asked. "What became of him?"

"He was brought up somewhere—I never asked her any questions about it, though she knew I knew about him. The father paid something for his maintenance, and I rather fancy that old Fred, who was a broad-minded sort of man, contributed a little too. She used to go and see him sometimes, and I do know that in later life he caused her a lot of anxiety with his wild ways. That didn't prevent her making a terrible to-do when he died, though."

There was a pause, in which Anne heard herself echoing stupidly, "When he died?"

"Yes. About six months ago. I gave her two days off to go to the funeral, I remember. It was very inconvenient, because I had arranged a dinner-party just then."

Feeling a little dazed, Anne reached for her handbag.

"Thank you very much," she contrived to say. "I really think that is all we wanted to know."

"Wait a bit, though!" Martin broke in. "You haven't told us, why did Mrs. March leave you?"

"I should have told you a quarter of an hour ago, if you hadn't kept on interrupting," answered Mrs. Howard-Blenkinsop tartly. "She left because she had come into money. No notice—she even offered to pay me a month's wages. Me! Well, perhaps it wasn't quite as ridiculous as it sounds. I dare say she is a richer woman now than I am, though it was difficult to make head or tail of what she was saying."

146

"You mean, the money seemed to come as a surprise to her?" Martin suggested.

"A surprise? For a cook when she inherits a fortune? Think, my boy, think! I never saw a woman more flabbergasted in my life. It was a bit of a shock for me too, as you can imagine. Of course, she was always a bit better off than most women of her class. Old Fred didn't leave her penniless, and she used to give herself airs about it. But I think that most of that money went on her holidays. She had a fortnight every year, and used to take Philip away with her."

"Yes," said Anne. "You are reputed to have stayed at Pendlebury several years running."

"Tchah!" snorted Mrs. Howard-Blenkinsop. "Don't remind me of it! I suppose it tickled the old ruffian to go back there and pass as a lady, where she had been— But that reminds me. Of course! Pendlebury! Now I remember! My dear girl, why didn't you tell me before? It was at Pendlebury that—That's why I recognized your name. I had read about it in *The Times*, just a short paragraph, you know, it made no particular impression on me, and then when Mrs. March came back, in addition to all the excitement about her legacy—the lawyer's letter was waiting for her when she returned—she had some fantastic rigmarole that I couldn't fathom, which seemed to have something to do with it."

"Do please try to remember what it was," Anne urged her.

"Let me think, now. You know when you are suddenly losing a cook who has been with you ten years, you're in no state to pay much attention to anything else. . . . Yes—I think I've got it. It was something to the effect that an old friend—only she didn't put it quite like that, I forget the expression—an old friend had been staying in the same place, and she had never known it, he was so changed. And then he had killed himself, and she had been at his funeral, and now she had all this money—it was an inextricable jumble, you know, what one might expect from an uneducated woman. But that was the gist of it. Of course, I didn't understand then that it was he who had left her all this money. . . ."

She looked inquiringly at Martin and Anne, but they kept their own counsel.

"Ah, well!" she said at last. "If you do manage to upset the will, or whatever it is that you're after, it will be a consolation to me to have Mrs. March back, even if she did behave so badly on her holidays!"

After which, there was clearly nothing to be done but to thank her for her forbearance and drive back to London.

"Well," said Martin, as they got into the car, "that disposes of Fannyanny, anyway."

"Yes," said Anne. "And of Richard too. We seem to be getting through our suspects pretty quick."

"Parsons, Vanning, and Carstairs left. I wonder whether old Steve will have brought home the bacon from Brighton?"

"The Carstairs people seemed the most innocent of the lot, so far as I could gather. But don't forget, we haven't really disposed of the Joneses yet."

"Oh, them! They were nothing but a couple out on the—"

"Shut up!"

13

Sunday at the Seaside

Sunday, August 27th

Stephen walked out of Brighton station among a throng of holiday makers. He allowed them to carry him with them in the direction of the front. The beach was a mass of warm, untidy humanity, the sea scarcely audible above the clamour of thousands of chattering, laughing, screaming voices. To a philanthropist the spectacle would have been a pleasing one. It made Stephen feel slightly sick. He was reminded of pictures he had seen of a colony of nesting gannets. The same ridiculous herding instinct, the same insensate noise, the same abominable mess that would be left behind them when they were gone. The only difference was that their droppings were newspapers and cigarette cartons, and in that respect the advantage seemed to him all on the side of the birds. Guano was of some use, at all events. . . .

He remained for some time staring at the crowds. He told himself more than once that he was wasting his time—that he had not come down there to watch a crowd of fools enjoying themselves. None the less, a full quarter of an hour had gone by before he could bring himself to leave the front, and when he did so he walked away with lagging footsteps. He felt a very decided reluctance towards his task, not that he had any particular qualms at invading the privacy of strangers, but simply because he felt morally certain that this particular line of inquiry would prove fruitless. But it obviously had to be investigated, and his one hope now was that Mr. and Mrs. Carstairs would prove to be at home and amenable to his blandishments. Otherwise he might find himself faced with the necessity of spending a night away from home, and he grudged the expense.

As he went, he nervously fingered the little manual on medieval English brasses in his pocket. The one clue to Carstairs' interests or character was the chance reference in Elderson's report to the fact that he had delayed his departure from the hotel in order to obtain a rubbing from Pendlebury church. Stephen remembered a contemporary at school with a passion for this odd amusement. He was the only boy in the school to possess this interest, and, being unique, was naturally enough regarded as to that extent contemptible. His study was hung with long sheets of paper, bearing smudgy black figures, the fruit of long and solitary bicycle expeditions to distant churches. Stephen had never paid the smallest attention to them, except once, when an exceptionally acute phase of dislike for the young antiquarian had inspired him and half a dozen others to smash up the study furniture and destroy most of the rubbings. Having thus spurned the opportunity to acquire knowledge, he had now been reduced to mugging up the subject as best he could in the train. If Carstairs turned out to be a real expert, his ignorance would be exposed in no time.

Ormidale Crescent proved to be a street of respectable Regency houses, not very far from the sea, but a world away in spirit from the charabancs and trippers of the front. It was a positive shock to see a bathing-dress hanging out to dry on one of the elegant wrought-iron balustrades. The thing looked as much out of place there as a clothes line in Belgrave Square. No such incongruity defaced the narrow front of No. 14. On the other hand, the house hardly came up to the standard of its neighbours in the matter of cleanliness. Its windows were opaque with dirt, its doorstep was a sooty grey, and the condition of the door-knocker showed that the household's interest in brass did not extend to the secular work of the nineteenth century.

A sullen and slovenly maid came to the door after Stephen had rung the bell two or three times. Asked whether Mr. Carstairs lived there, she answered grudgingly that he did. Was he at home? No, was the reply, he was at the church. The tone in which this was said clearly implied that the questioner was a fool for expecting him to be anywhere else. When would he be back? The maid couldn't say for sure. As an afterthought she observed that he would not be home for his lunch. And Mrs. Carstairs? She was at church too. And the door slammed.

Stephen walked away up the Crescent feeling decidedly annoyed with himself. He had completely failed to take account of the fact that it was Sunday, and that there were still people who went to church on Sunday mornings. Now he would have to kill time until Mr. Carstairs should have come back from his lunch, whenever that might be. He had gone some way before the significance of something said by the maid struck his mind. He had noticed at the time that she had said, "Mr. Carstairs is at the church," and not "at church." There might be nothing in it, but it seemed an odd phrase to employ. It had an almost proprietary air. She had said it in just the same way that a stockbroker's servant would

151

have told him, "Mr. Smith is at the office." Was that the explanation? Was Mr. Carstairs at the church for the same reason that Mr. Smith would have been at the office—because it was his job? True, there was nothing in Elderson's report to indicate that he was a parson, but it remained a possibility.

At this point he passed a telephone kiosk, and it occurred to him to do what any moderately efficient detective would have done in the first place; namely, to turn up Mr. Carstairs' entry in the directory. Sure enough, it ran: "Carstairs, Rev. E. M. J." So that settled the point! Clergymen were comparatively approachable people, at all events, and if he could once get into touch with this one, he had little doubt that he would be able to make him talk. But he still cursed his luck in having to hang about until the afternoon before he could begin.

A little further on a pinched Gothic façade in grey stone broke the suave frontage of stucco. Was this "the" church? he wondered. It was worth trying, at all events. With a vague idea of assuming the rôle of an earnest inquirer in the vestry after the service, he made his way in. At the worst, it was as good a way of getting through the next half-hour as any other.

The service had been in progress some time. He entered just as a portly old gentleman was declaiming from the lectern, "Here Endeth the First Lesson." A verger emerged from somewhere in the shadows and propelled him into a seat as the congregation rose for the Psalms. He was placed well at the back of the church and was striving to get a view of the face attached to the surpliced figure at the other end, when he was aware that his arm was being squeezed by his neighbour in the pew. Glancing round, he found himself looking into the face of his Aunt Lucy.

152

"Stephen! What a surprise finding you here!" she whispered.

Stephen smiled, nodded and hastily fumbled for his place in the greasy Prayer Book which the verger had provided. Here was a complication! There was nothing particularly surprising about the meeting, now he came to think of it, for he recollected that Aunt Lucy had mentioned when they last met after the funeral that she and George were thinking of going for a few weeks to Brighton; and the chances of finding Aunt Lucy in church on a Sunday morning might be safely computed at odds on. Stephen's private opinion was that she went there to get away from Uncle George. And if he had to meet any of his family here she would certainly have been his first choice. But he had not come to Brighton to meet her, but Carstairs. Now there would have to be explanations, chatter, and more time wasted. And Uncle George would be certain to make a nuisance of himself if he possibly could. . . .

"Will you come back to lunch with us afterwards?" hissed Aunt Lucy as the doxology ended.

He shook his head.

"Sorry. I don't think I can manage it," he whispered back.

"Oh, do! You'll help me out with the Carstairs," was the astonishing rejoinder.

"Good Lord!" Stephen exclaimed almost out loud.

Aunt Lucy shot a reproachful glance at him as she sat back in her pew, while "Here Beginneth" boomed out from the lectern.

So it came about that after all his apprehensions Stephen found himself being introduced in a perfectly normal way to Mr. and Mrs. Carstairs. He had returned with his aunt after the service to their hotel. There they had found Uncle George, hot and peevish after an unsuccessful morning's golf. The account of his misfortunes and the catalogue of his partner's shortcomings sufficed to fill up the interval before the arrival of the guests, and Stephen was able without difficulty to stave off any inquiries as to the reason for his presence in Brighton.

The Reverend E. M. J. Carstairs proved to be a fleshy, beetle-browed man of middle age. He was not, Stephen learned from his aunt, the regular incumbent of the church which he had attended that morning, but was merely "taking duty" during the absence of the vicar on holiday. Aunt Lucy, with her passion for all things ecclesiastical, had collected him, as she always collected parsons, as naturally as a child picking wild flowers. He lived in Brighton, whither he had retired two or three years before on giving up a missionary post abroad. He was a fluent talker on many subjects, but principally about himself, and his tones were loud and self-important. Evidently in his own eyes he was a person of consequence. It was some time before Stephen so much as noticed Mrs. Carstairs. Beside him, she was not a particularly noticeable person. She was small, mousy and ill-dressed, with a thin little mouth and very bright eyes. But it soon became apparent that she was very far from being in awe of her husband. She gave a taste of her quality quite early in the proceedings.

"I've met you before, haven't I?" said Mr. Carstairs to Stephen as they sat down to lunch.

Stephen denied having ever had that pleasure.

"Seen you before, anyhow."

"I think not."

"My husband," observed Mrs. Carstairs to the table in general, "is always saying that sort of thing to perfect strangers. He has in fact a shocking memory for faces. It really used to be very awkward when we were living

154

out East, where one native looks exactly like another in any case. So you mustn't mind what he says, Mr. Dickinson."

Mr. Carstairs looked extremely uncomfortable and said no more. Aunt Lucy shot a look of admiration at the courageous wife, who continued to eat her lunch with perfect *sang-froid*.

By the time they had reached coffee she had twice corrected anecdotes of her husband's about his experiences in the missionary field, and once flatly contradicted Uncle George when he ventured on a generalization on the subject of China. Otherwise she had contributed little to the conversation. Mr. Carstairs was meekness itself under her corrections, while Uncle George was so astonished at her temerity that by the end of the meal he had become gloomily silent. Stephen derived a certain amusement from the spectacle, but apart from that it did not seem as if the afternoon was going to show much profit after all. The atmosphere, however, changed completely after lunch, when Aunt Lucy inveigled Mrs. Carstairs up to her room on some pretext or another. With undisguised relief Uncle George led the way to the smoking-room, cigars were produced, and the comfortable illusion of masculine predominance was re-established.

"What you'll never get people to understand about China—" said Uncle George, and proceeded to restate with emphasis the fallacy which Mrs. Carstairs had exposed ten minutes before.

"I absolutely agree with you," said Mr. Carstairs heartily.

The two he-men nodded their heads in concert, and the feast of reason proceeded harmoniously, to the complete exclusion of Stephen. Presently—

"Would you care for a liqueur, Carstairs?"

"Well—er—it's very good of you. I hardly care to, just at present." He fingered his clerical collar. "It was different the other day. I was in mufti then. Ha, Ha! As a matter of fact I never wear this unless I am actually—"

"Don't talk so much. Go on, a liqueur can't hurt you."

"Well, well . . ."

Over his liqueur Mr. Carstairs became quite confiding.

"My wife—" he said haltingly. "I don't think you've met my wife before today, Mr. Dickinson?"

"No," said Uncle George, his cigar clenched between his teeth, "I haven't."

"She's been in London all the week. I've been quite a grass widower down here. Ha, Ha!" For some incomprehensible reason this simple statement of fact was apparently expected to be regarded as humorous. "She's a very remarkable woman in many ways."

"I dare say." George's rudeness would have been obvious to anyone not gifted with an unusually thick skin.

"She is, I assure you. She doesn't spend her time in London amusing herself, I can tell you that! Ha, Ha!"

From the look on George's face it was apparent that he was quite prepared to believe it. He made no comment, and it was left for Stephen to keep the conversation going.

"What does she do, exactly?" he asked.

"She works," replied Mr. Carstairs complacently. "Work is the very breath of her nostrils. Naturally I miss her. A house without a woman's guiding hand is only half a home. But I am an old campaigner, and, though I say it, I make shift very well by myself."

Stephen remembered the dilapidated aspect of the house in Ormidale Crescent and shuddered.

"My own interests are mainly of a more scholarly character," the parson went on. "Since my retirement I have busied myself in antiquarian pursuits—of an ecclesiastical nature, of course. I don't know whether you are at all interested in our grand old medieval brasses, sir?"

He addressed George. But George, his cigar gone out, was dozing in his chair.

"As a matter of fact, I am rather interested—" Stephen began, but Mr. Carstairs was off again.

"But my wife remains heart and soul in her work," he went on. "Work that I am happy to say does not go unrewarded, in the material sense, I mean. And what splendid work it is! She is Organizing Secretary of the Society for the Relief of Distress amongst the Widows of Professional Men—the S.R.D.W.P.M. Rather a mouthful that, eh? We call it the R.D. for short. Perhaps the initials are more familiar to you in another connexion, my young friend? Ha, Ha!" (Stephen was furious to find himself flushing at this point. They were, indeed, sickeningly familiar.) "A wonderful organization, but ill-supported, alas! Indeed, had it not been for a fortunate windfall the other day, it might have—"

He stopped abruptly, and the sudden ceasing of the soothing flow of words awakened George, who opened his eyes and sat up.

"Where the devil's your aunt?" said George to Stephen, crossly, struggling stiffly to get up. "Time we went out to get up an appetite for tea."

"Dear me," said Mr. Carstairs, "it's getting quite late. I wonder where my wife has got to."

Fortunately the ladies appeared at this point, and the party broke up. Stephen took his leave as soon as he decently could, and made his way back to the station. He wondered as he went why the name of the Society for the Relief of Distress amongst the Widows of Professional Men seemed familiar. It was not until his train had nearly reached Victoria that he remembered.

On the whole, he reported to Anne when they met, the day had not been completely wasted.

14

Monday at Midchester

Martin and Stephen were having tea in the Palm Lounge of the Grand Hotel, Midchester. It was not, they agreed, a very exhilarating experience. Built in the spacious days of Queen Victoria, and redecorated in the yet more spacious days of the post-war boom, the Grand Hotel, like the rest of Midchester, had fallen on evil days. The decorations were cracked and faded, the big rooms, designed for the leisure hours of tired and prosperous business men, were an echoing emptiness. A couple of gloomy commercial travellers, evidently comparing notes on the impossibility of doing business in Midchester, were the only other occupants of the lounge.

"Rather a depressing place, don't you think?" said Martin.

It was the third time at least that he had said the same thing or words to the same effect, since they had driven into the town that afternoon, through acres of derelict factories. Stephen this time did not trouble to reply. He

159

was studying a local directory, and presently called for the waiter.

"Whereabouts is Chorlby Moor?" he asked him.

"About two miles south, out of town, sir," he was told. "What you might call a suburb, sir. A tram will take you there."

"Is that where this chap lives?" Martin asked.

"Apparently so. I can't find any business address for him in this book."

"We passed Chorlby Moor coming in. Just where the tramlines started. Didn't you notice it? Rather superior little houses with gardens and garages. You know, Steve, I don't somehow fancy bearding a chap in a suburb. They're not inclined to be matey. Think an Englishman's home is his castle and all that. Which," he added solemnly, "it ought to be, of course."

"No doubt. It's not a very suitable article of faith for detectives, unfortunately."

"But seriously, Steve, do you propose to go off and beard this chap?"

"I wish," said Stephen, irritably, "that you wouldn't use such perfectly foul expressions, or having used them, repeat them over and over again."

Martin took off his glasses and polished them thoughtfully.

"I know I'm a lowbrow," he observed. "All the same, I do want to know. Do you want to—do what I said?"

"I don't know," Stephen answered crossly.

"That's just it. Fact is, we've neither of us the least notion what to do or how to set about doing it. We've come up to this place, which, as I said just now, is distinctly depressing, because Annie told us to, really. And now we're here we don't really know what to do."

"As you've said once already."

"I will say this for you, Steve, you do listen to a fellow. You always seem to spot when I say anything, even if it's only once. Well, there we are. Short of bearding—I'm sorry, but what else can you call it?—short of that, I suppose we shall have to hang about Midchester and Chorlby Moor until we can scrape acquaintance with this Parsons person. It may take us ages. Of course, we had a great stroke of luck at Bentby yesterday, and you clicked in very quick time at Brighton, so perhaps our luck will hold, but you never can tell. Just chuck me that directory, would you?"

Stephen passed it to him.

"You won't find anything else about Parsons in it," he remarked. "But—I wanted to look at something else."

Martin turned the pages over, found the entry he wanted and closed the book.

"Think I'll go out and sniff the breeze for a bit," he observed.

"Do," said Stephen. "You'll find it very enjoyable. In spite of the depression, there are two or three tanneries still working here, I fancy."

Martin went out and Stephen was left to his own devices for nearly half an hour. He spent the time reading a guide to Midchester, published by the local Chamber of Commerce. It was two years out of date—he could well believe that they had lost heart trying to publicize that moribund town—but none the less it had some useful information. He had just come to the end of it when Martin returned, evidently highly elated about something.

"A snip, my boy, definitely a snip!" he exclaimed as soon as he entered.

"Where have you been?"

"At the Conservative Club—in Hay Street, just the other side of the Market-Place. You remember, Parsons wrote his letter to Pendlebury from there."

161

"Yes, of course I do."

"Well, I've found out something rather useful. He's the secretary of the City Conservative Association."

Nothing ever gave Stephen more pleasure than scoring off his brother-in-law elect, all the more so because the opportunity did not often arise. Nobody, however, could have divined the fact from the casual tone in which he now answered.

"Oh? Yes, I know. He's an alderman too, or was a couple of years ago."

Martin looked as disappointed as Stephen hoped he would.

"How did you find out?" he asked.

"It's all in this little book here," said Stephen indicating the guide. "Much better way of getting information, you know, Martin, than running about and calling attention to yourself by asking questions."

"Sorry and all that," said Martin. "But as a matter of fact, I didn't ask any questions. Anyhow, that isn't the real snip I meant to tell you about. The point is—there's a meeting at the Club to-night. I found out about Parsons from the advertisement of it hanging up outside."

"I don't quite see where what you describe as the snip comes in," Stephen said.

"Well, the meeting—it isn't a meeting exactly, but a Rally—d'you think there's much difference?—is being addressed by the Conservative candidate, and all are welcome. It occurs to me that all includes us."

"Do you really suggest that we should go to a political meeting?"

"Well, after all, why not? It's all in the day's work. You went to church yesterday, didn't you? This can't be half as dull—in fact it might be quite amusing. Besides, I'm a Conservative myself, anyway. Everybody ought to be, I think, if he cares for his country. But that's not the point. Don't you see, Parsons is bound to be there, as secretary of the blooming show, and we can get a good squint at him."

"There is something in that," Stephen admitted. "I don't see what good it's going to do us looking at the fellow at a public meeting, but it will be one way of spending an evening in this God-forsaken place, at all events. What time does it start?"

"Eight o'clock. It's a foul time, I know, but I expect the chaps in these parts mostly go in for high tea. I suppose there's quite a chance of our dropping in for a row at the meeting," he went on hopefully. "This place must be pretty red with all the unemployment there is about."

If Martin had looked forward to grappling with embattled Bolsheviks at the Conservative Club, he was disappointed. True, Midchester was "red," in the sense that it had returned a Labour member time out of mind, but this very fact made the majority less disposed to pay any attention to the activities of their opponents. If Sir Oswald Mosley himself had visited Midchester, he would have been greeted with not more than a few languid brickbats. The Conservative Rally proved to be a dull, decorous function. It was poorly attended, so that Stephen and Martin were able to pick seats with a good view of the platform. Evidently the good party men of the locality rated their chances of success as low as did the Socialists, and the proceedings opened with the reading of an impressive list of those who apologized for their absence. There was a sprinkling of unbelievers present, pale, shabby men in whom even the instinct of revolt had been all but extinguished by years of unemployment and what politicians have agreed to disguise beneath the polite word "malnutrition." Quite plainly, they did not believe a word of what was being said from the platform, but they were too listless to heckle, and even an incautious reference to the Government's work for the unemployed produced no more than a few sniggers, which were meant to be sarcastic, but sounded merely melancholy. It was difficult to understand why they should have troubled to attend a political meeting, except from sheer force of habit, so clear was it that nothing that could be said from any platform would ever raise them to hope or even credulity again.

By contrast, the men and women on the platform looked almost indecently well fed. The chairman was bald and pink and round—the eternal type of chairman all the world over. The candidate was a vigorous young man of obvious ability, who had been selected to contest this hopeless constituency on the excellent principle that reserves safe seats for those who can afford them. The others were a nondescript collection, bearing one and all the self-righteous look of those who are enduring boredom for the sake of duty. Stephen did not have to look at them long before he found the man he sought. One does not have to be an expert detective to recognize the honorary secretary at any sort of gathering.

To make sure, he said to his neighbour before the speeches began: "Is that the secretary, sitting on the chairman's left?"

"That's right, Mr. Parsons. And that's the agent he's talking to, Mr. Turner. A good sort, he is."

"He looks ill," Stephen remarked.

"Who, Turner?"

"No, Mr. Parsons."

"Oh, him! Yes, he does look queer, doesn't he? Sort of worried, he looks—has been some time. I don't know what *he's* got to worry him, considering . . ."

But at this point the chairman rose, not more than a quarter of an hour after the advertised time, and the proceedings began.

Stephen devoted most of the rest of the evening to studying Mr. Parsons. There was no doubt of his looking ill. His face was pale, as pale as those of the unemployed at the back of the hall, but it was a pallor of a different quality—the type that goes with too much work rather than with none at all. His forehead and cheeks were deeply creased and there were ugly dark patches beneath his eyes. But what was particularly striking about him was his restlessness. He seemed unable to control the movements of his hands, which were forever playing with his gold watch-chain or alternatively ruffling and smoothing his sparse grey hair, while his eyes wandered incessantly about the hall, scanning it from floor to ceiling and back again. Altogether, he appeared to be paying considerably less attention to the speeches than was becoming to the secretary of the association.

That he had his wits about him, none the less, became evident when, at the close of the candidate's speech, and a half-hearted sputter of irrelevant questions, he was called upon by the chairman to propose a vote of thanks. This he did briefly and wittily, in the manner of an experienced public speaker. It seemed however, to one observer at least, that his mind was hardly on the task which he was accomplishing with such ease; and the instant that he sat down he resumed his former air of abstraction.

Stephen made use of the occasion to observe to his neighbour as they were preparing to go out, "Good speech, that."

"Yes," the man replied. "He's not half a bad candidate."

"I meant Mr. Parsons' speech."

"Oh, yes, that was good enough. But after all, it's no wonder with all the practice he's had. Been in politics here a long time, y'know. Well, I must be going now. Good night."

And he took himself off, leaving Stephen's curiosity as to Mr. Parsons' business and position in life still unsatisfied.

Martin, meanwhile, had been following the proceedings of the meeting with every semblance of enthusiasm. He had clapped vigorously, "hear heared" loudly and shown a face of disgust and scorn at the rare interruptions from the dissidents. When the audience dispersed, Stephen found him eagerly talking to a man at the door who was distributing forms of enrolment in the Association.

"My good Martin, what on earth—" Stephen began in disgusted tones.

"Just a minute, old chap. I'm coming," Martin answered over his shoulder. He took two of the forms and a bundle of political pamphlets with one hand, while he warmly wrung the organizer's hand with the other. "I say, Steve," he went on as he rejoined his companion, "wasn't that a grand speech? I thought he fairly gave the Socialists hell, didn't you? Pity there wasn't a better audience."

"Really? I didn't listen to it myself."

"Great mistake," said Martin as they made their way out into the street. "You'd have learnt something if you had; you really would. I know I did, anyway."

"You seem to forget that we didn't go to the meeting to learn about politics. I flatter myself that I have learnt something this evening, rather more useful than the Tory propaganda you've been listening to."

"Oh, yes, of course." Martin's spectacles gleamed up in his direction, as if groping for enlightenment. "Did

166

you find out much? I spotted you trying to pump the fellow on the other side of you. Rather dangerous, I thought. Chap might have been a friend of the quarry's. Put him on his guard and all that."

"I took very good care to do nothing of the sort," said Stephen coldly. "In any event, one must take certain risks in an inquiry of this kind. I can't see that offering to join the Conservative Association is going to get us any further."

"Did you find out what sort of job Parsons has got?"

"No, as a matter of fact, I didn't manage to get so far, but—"

"That reminds me," Martin interrupted him. He stopped under a street lamp and held one of the papers in his hand close up to his nose.

"Damned small print," he muttered. Then: "I've got it! Central Buildings, Westgate Street."

"What are you talking about?"

"Parsons' business address. You see, I knew they'd be bound to have the secretary's address on the enrolment forms, or how would anyone know where to write to get enrolled? Then it was long odds that they'd put his business address, as chaps don't care to be bothered with letters about that sort of thing in the home. At least, I was secretary of a Rugger club once and I know I didn't. You can always sweat the office typist to do the donkey work, if you know how to manage her. So, you see, I—"

"I see. Now we might as well be going home."

"Wait a sec. Westgate Street ought to start somewhere about here. I thought I noticed it on the way to the meeting. Might as well go and have a squint at Central Buildings, don't you think?"

Stephen felt too humiliated to protest, and a few minutes later they found themselves opposite a tall, soot-blackened range of offices in what was evidently the business centre of the city.

"Classy-looking offices." Martin observed. "Wonder whose they are?"

They crossed the road and read the names outside the main entrance.

"An architect, a solicitor and the local income tax extortioner," Martin said. "All on the top floors. The rest of the palace seems to be the property of the Midchester and District Gas Company. Well, if friend Parsons is in that, he's presumably on a fairly good thing."

Stephen remembered the remark of his chance acquaintance at the meeting. "I don't know what *he's* got to worry about, considering . . ."

"I should think that is his job, in all probability," he said. "And in view of his public position in the town, he's probably fairly high up in it."

"Humph," said Martin as they made their way back to the hotel. "There's something done this evening, anyway. You had a good look at him, Steve. Tell me, do you think he's beardable, so to speak?"

"I shouldn't wonder," said Stephen, remembering Parsons's strained and nervous manner. "We'll sleep on it."

But the most important discovery of the day was still to be made. The were in the lounge of the hotel, drinking a last whisky and soda before going to bed. Martin had recurred once more to the arguments which had so impressed him at the meeting and was now regurgitating them with enthusiasm and emphasis. Stephen, thoroughly bored, was only prevented from being extremely rude to him by the reflection that if he insulted him, he could hardly in decency allow him to pay for the drinks. Finding the strain of listening to Martin's political views too much to bear, he compromised by picking up the first piece of reading matter at hand, which happened to be a copy of the *Midchester Evening Star*. Automatically, he turned to the City page, and was about to read the Stock Exchange closing prices when his eye caught something in an adjoining column of greater moment. He read it to the end, and then cut Martin's periods short with an excited exclamation.

"What's the matter?" asked Martin. "You know, Steve, I may be a lowbrow, but I do think about politics, and if you'd only listen to me, you might learn something. After all, nowadays—"

"Damn politics! Just look at this, you chump!" said Stephen, and thrust the paper under Martin's nose.

"Oh! Sorry! Is it anything important? Look here, Steve, you've been had. This paper's three days old."

"That doesn't matter in the least."

"Doesn't it? Oh, I see now what you're getting at, 'Annual General Meeting of the Midchester and District Gas Company.' M'm. Extraordinary time of the year to have an Annual General Meeting. Just shows what these chaps in the provinces will do, doesn't it?"

"What the hell does it matter? Read it!"

"Oh, Lord, have I got to read it all? It looks as dull as hell. I suppose I can skip a bit. . . . Aha! Parsons is the assistant manager, I see. Hell, that's worth knowing, I suppose. Anything else about him in this?"

"No. But just look down at the bottom of the column."

"What? That's the balance sheet. No good expecting me to understand figures, you know. Not got the head for them, somehow. I can't—Oh, wow; oh, wow; oh, wow! Steve, I apologize. This *is* a snip, and no mistake! I nearly missed it altogether. Right at the bottom of the page, as you said. 'Vanning, Maldron and Smith, Chartered Accountants.' Who'd have thought it?"

They were both silent for a moment.

"When the assistant manager of a firm in the Midlands," said Stephen slowly, "meets a partner in that firm's London accountants at a quiet hotel in Markshire on a Sunday just before the Annual General Meeting, what's the inference?"

"Dirty work," said Martin promptly, and drained his glass.

"The only question is," Stephen went on, "do we tackle Parsons now on what we've got or ought we to go back to London first and reconnoitre the Vanning end of the conspiracy?"

"One thing I can tell you," answered Martin. "You won't find Vanning if you do."

"Eh?"

"There's no such person—in the office of Vanning, Waldron and Smith, anyway."

"How do you know?"

"I looked 'em up in the official list. You remember when I suggested he might be a stockbroker, you told me I could find out by looking at the list of members. I took your tip and then thought it would do no harm if I checked up on the accountants as well. And there wasn't a Vanning in either of them. Not a solitary one. And so far as this crowd goes, the partners now are Waldron, Smith and some one called Cohen. I take it that Vanning has been gathered to his fathers and they keep the name on the door for old sake's sake."

"I see. Then why—Damn it all, Martin, it can't be simply a coincidence!"

"Not on your life! That'd be a bit too thick. Tell you another thing. Parsons couldn't give the hotel the name of his friend until he turned up. Reason—the blighter was travelling under an alias and Parsons didn't know what it would be. And he had the cheek to take the name of his firm's late senior partner. Pretty cool that, don't you think?"

"Lord, I'd forgotten that!" Stephen lit a cigarette and reflected for a moment or two before he went on. "Let's work this out properly," he said at last. "What is our theory about the whole affair?"

"Parsons has been monkeying with the Gas Company's accounts," Martin began. "The clerk or whatnot sent down to audit them smells a rat."

"Instead of showing him up," Stephen chimed in, "he keeps the knowledge to himself—"

"—And uses it to do a spot of blackmailing on the side."

"Which would explain the fact that Parsons has not been sleeping too well at nights lately."

"You bet your life it would! Then just before the accounts are due to be passed, the chap from Vanning's summons Parsons for a nice confidential little chat about how much he's to cough up and so on."

"They quarrel on that all-important point. I wonder, by the way, Martin, whether Parsons has been embezzling for some time?"

"And paying tribute to the blood-sucker in Gossip Lane? (Appropriate address that, by the way!) I shouldn't be surprised. Anyhow, a point comes when he tells him that he can't go on. No use trying to get blood out of a stone, you know."

"Yes, I expect that's just the sort of expression Parsons would use on that occasion."

"Is it? Well, I dare say you know. No offence meant, and all that. Where are we? Yes—they quarrel, as you said just now. Vanning—we'll have to call him that— goes up to bed first. Parsons comes up later feeling pretty murderous about him, sees the tray with the pot of tea outside what he thinks is his room—sorry I laughed at

171

your idea when you suggested it the other day, Steve, but I see there is something in it now—"

"Being a bad sleeper, he has some drugs with him," Stephen suggested. "For that matter, a man in his position might well have been contemplating suicide."

"Right you are! It's all working out beautifully. He says to himself: 'Why shouldn't this hellhound take the medicine instead of me?' So he pops the stuff into the tea-pot, and goes to bed feeling that he's made everything all serene so far as Vanning is concerned."

"And next morning—"

"Good Lord, yes! Next morning he gets a really nasty one in the eye when he finds that the corpse has quietly got up and had his breakfast and mizzled off. Steve, I really believe we've got to the bottom of this!"

"I wonder," said Stephen slowly. "Somehow, it looks almost too good to be true."

Martin rubbed his hands together gleefully.

"Rot, it looks good because it is true. What's the catch in it?"

"Well, there's one thing. How do we know that Parsons had any of this particular dope with him?"

"He must have. That was what your guv'nor died of, wasn't it?"

"But that's begging the whole question!"

"I don't see that. If he didn't do it, who did? Can you answer that one?"

"No, of course I can't."

"All right! Then so far as I can see the only question is, how do we deal with this thing tomorrow?"

"I think that's a question we had better decide tomorrow," said Stephen. "I don't know about you, but I feel distinctly tired."

"Same here. It's been a long day, but a good one. I only wish . . ."

"Yes?"

"I wish," said Martin regretfully, "there had been a bit of a row at that meeting."

15

"Something Attempted,
Something Done"

Tuesday, August 29th

"Are we all set?" said Martin.

Stephen said nothing, but nodded. His face was pale, his lips drawn in a thin, straight line. Martin, on the other hand, seemed no more than pleasantly excited. He chatted happily as they left the hotel and walked the short distance that separated them from Westgate Street.

"I think with a chap like this we can afford to do a bit of bluffing, don't you?" he said.

"Yes, I suppose so."

"I mean, in the state he's in already, he'll probably cave in all at once as soon as he sees that we know something."

"Perhaps he will."

"Do you think we could get him to write a confession? That'd floor the insurance blighters absolutely, wouldn't it?"

"It certainly would."

"Well, do you think he's the sort of chap who would make a confession?"

"I don't know."

174

"Mind you, Steve, I shall leave all the talking to you. You're a lot cleverer at that sort of thing than I am. I shall just sit around and weigh in where I think you want any support, and so forth, but by and large I shall leave all the talking to you."

"Then for God's sake stop talking now, and let me think in peace for a moment!" Stephen exclaimed, stung to sudden fury.

Martin apologized as amiably as ever, and contented himself with whistling loudly to himself, until Stephen was compelled to ask him to stop.

"I'm sorry," said Martin once more. "You see, the fact is, Steve, that I'm just as worried and excited about this show as you are, really, only it takes me differently. You go all sick inside, and pale outside, and I feel frightfully pepped up and go about feeling like one of those fellows in the advertisements. You know, the chaps who take whatever it is every morning."

"Yes, I do know. I read the papers too, as it happens."

And from then on Stephen gave up the attempt to silence him and let him express his excitement in his own way.

At the office Stephen asked for Mr. Parsons.

"Have you got an appointment, sir?" asked the clerk who received them.

"Yes."

After much discussion, Stephen and Martin had decided that it would be safer to telephone and make an appointment. The nominal excuse for their visit was "a matter arising out of the meeting last night," and this had proved sufficient to procure them an interview.

They were taken through a vast hall, loud with the clatter of typewriters, into a small waiting-room, and here, after a short delay, Mr. Parsons joined them. In the light of day his face did not look nearly so ghastly

175

as it had done under the crude glare of the lamps in the Conservative Club, and he seemed comparatively self-possessed.

"Good morning, gentlemen!" he began. "I understand that you wanted to see me?"

"Yes," said Stephen. His face was almost as pale as Mr. Parsons', and he seemed in some difficulty in finding words to open the conversation. "Er—I don't think you know my name," he went on. "My name is Dickinson—Stephen Dickinson."

"Yes?" Mr. Parsons smiled politely. If the name conveyed anything whatever to him, he was an uncommonly good actor.

"My friend and I wanted to ask you . . ." Stephen lost track of his sentence and stopped. Out of the tail of his eye he could see Martin drawing breath to speak, and he plunged on hastily: "I think, Mr. Parsons, you know the Pendlebury Old Hall Hotel?"

Mr. Parsons raised his eyebrows.

"Pendlebury Old Hall?" he said, in a voice that was perhaps a semitone higher than was usual for him. "Why, yes, certainly. I have stayed there."

"That's just the point," said Martin loudly and unexpectedly.

Mr. Parsons spun round and looked at him in a somewhat startled manner, and indeed, Martin's abrupt incursion into the conversation was enough to make any one jump.

"Really—" he began, but Stephen did not give him time to go on.

"As my friend says," he proceeded smoothly, "we are interested in the circumstances of your recent stay at Pendlebury. We are making inquiries—"

"One moment!" Mr. Parsons held up a hand which Stephen observed was now perfectly steady. "You tell me you are 'making inquiries.' Please let me ask you before you go any further, whether from that rather official phrasing I am to take it you are connected with the police?"

Martin was about to say something, but once more Stephen forestalled him.

"No," he said. "We are making private inquiries on behalf of—of an interested party."

Mr. Parsons smiled. There could be no doubt of it; he positively smiled!

"Then you may take it that I am not an interested party in your private inquiries into my private affairs," he said, and while he was speaking he pressed a bell.

Almost at once, a commissionaire opened the door of the room.

"Will you show these gentlemen out, please, Robertson?" said Mr. Parsons.

"But look here!" cried Martin. "How—"

"This way, gentlemen, if you please!" said the commissionaire. He was a very large commissionaire.

If Stephen had complained of Martin's talkativeness on the way from the Grand Hotel to Central Buildings, he would have given anything for him to have said something on the way back from Central Buildings to the Grand Hotel. As for uttering a word himself, it was out of the question. But Martin did not come to his aid. They trailed back through the loathly streets of Midchester in the silence of the utterly defeated, and though in the course of the morning some words of a sort did contrive to pass between them, it looked as if they were going to return the whole way to London without once mentioning the topic of Mr. Parsons.

It was lunch that restored them to comparative normality. Restored Martin, at all events, to the point that

177

he was suddenly enabled to discuss the whole incident with philosophic detachment.

"Y'know, Steve," he began abruptly, "it just shows how one can be mistaken about a chap. If ever I saw anybody who looked really beardable it was that one. And then . . ."

Stephen said nothing.

"Of course, I dare say it was a mistake trying it on in his office. My fault, I know and all that, but I didn't fancy Chorlby Moor somehow. All the same, there aren't any commissionaires in the suburbs."

Stephen still remained silent, and the monologue continued:

"Not but what I dare say he'd have been a pretty tough nut anywhere. That is, if there was ever anything to the whole business. . . . It's funny to think we never even got round to mentioning Vanning's name to him, when you come to think of it."

"Wouldn't have made any difference," Stephen muttered.

"P'raps not. Tell you what, though. If we'd bluffed a bit and said we were policemen when he asked us— I wanted to, you know—"

"I know you did. And if we had, he'd have had us both arrested straight away."

"Good Lord, d'you think so? Well, we're well out of that, anyhow. All the same, it's pretty sickening to think we've been all this way and taken all this trouble and then got absolutely nothing to show for it. . . ."

His voice trailed away. Clearly there was no more to be said.

To add to their miseries, when about twenty miles short of London the car choked, spluttered, recovered itself, spluttered again, and finally stopped. Stephen, who knew nothing whatever about the insides of motor-cars,

178

sat patiently inside while Martin did mysterious things to the engine with an adjustable spanner. It was quite a simple job, he explained, simply the old carburettor playing up again. He wouldn't be half a jiffy. He knew the old bus's tricks backwards.

In the end it took him nearly an hour and a half, and thereafter for the rest of the way their speed was reduced to a precarious fifteen miles an hour. It seemed to be the last touch necessary to make their failure complete. They had aimed at reaching home in time for tea, but it was nearly seven before they entered Hampstead High Street. Just before the turning to Plane Street, Martin pulled up with a jerk. Stephen, who had been dozing, opened his eyes and said irritably:

"What's the matter now?"

"Look!" said Martin, and pointed across the street.

Opposite, some newspaper-sellers had their pitch. It was a day of little news, as was evidenced by the fact that each placard bore a totally different legend. The first that Stephen noticed ran:

LIBYA TROOP
MOVEMENT
RUMOURS DENIED

Next to it was:

TWO GASSED
IN
SWANAGE
LOVE-NEST

Then a little farther down the street, in huge letters of black on yellow, he read:

179

Before Stephen had properly taken it in, Martin was out of the car and dodging among the omnibuses across the road.

He was back, waving a paper, long before the shops and houses had ceased to be a confused blur before Stephen's eyes. He climbed into the car, his face pink with excitement, threw the paper across to Stephen, shut the door, and engaged the gear.

"It's him all right," he said in a hushed voice, as if he were speaking in the very presence of the dead.

Stephen found voice to say: "Did he use Medinal, by any chance?"

"No. Shot himself. In the office."

"Oh!"

Shortly before they reached Mrs. Dickinson's door, Martin, looking straight in front of him, murmured, "Just as well we didn't give our names at the office, Steve."

"Yes."

"Funny I was complaining just now that we hadn't done anything on the trip."

"M'm."

At the house, Stephen got out and Martin remained in the car.

"Think I'll go straight home and turn in early," he said, apparently to the mascot on the radiator cap. "Feel a bit tired. Will you explain to Annie?"

"Right," said Stephen, looking at his boots. "Good night. Oh, and thanks for driving me up and all that."

"That's all right," answered Martin without shifting his gaze. "Good night."

In the hall, Stephen looked at the newspaper for the first time. He was still there when his mother came out of the drawing-room to greet him.

"Well, Stephen, what sort of day have you had?" she asked him.

He did not answer. He was reading:

"The deceased leaves a wife and three children. Interviewed today in the pretty drawing-room of her Chorlby Moor home, Mrs. Parsons told our representative . . ."

"What's the matter, Stephen? You look quite pale."

"Oh, I'm all right, Mother. A bit tired, that's all. It's been rather an exhausting day. Do you think there's any brandy in the house?"

16

Parbury Gardens

Tuesday, August 29th

On the second day of the absence of her brother and
fiancé at Midchester, Anne could stand inaction no
longer. Waiting for the men to come in was all very
well, but waiting prolonged over two days was too much
of a good thing, particularly when the strain of waiting
was aggravated by the presence of an obstinate something
at the back of her mind, which refused to be exorcised.
At first that something had seemed like a tiny grain of
solid matter lodged somewhere in the cogs of a well-oiled
machine, giving no evidence of its existence except now
and then, when there would be a faint jar in the process of
her thought. She could ignore it by turning her thoughts
elsewhere, by letting that part of the machine lie idle. But
now it had taken on a different aspect. She pictured it no
longer as an inert obstruction in her smoothly working
brain, but as a living, malignant growth, sending out its
ramifications in every direction, proliferating, breaking
down the resistances she had built against it. . . .

She went out on the Heath and walked about until
she was tired. For the first time, she envied all the

people who had dogs with them—quarrelsome, excitable dogs, disobedient, runaway dogs, dogs that were embarrassingly friendly with the dogs of other people, dogs that were incessantly requiring balls or sticks to be thrown for them—each one of them something that had to be called, to be whistled to, cursed, put on the lead, dragged away from somebody or something, or at least continually watched over and thought about. For the first and only time she yearned for a Scottie, six months old, guaranteed through distemper. There was, as Martin had said, something about a dog you didn't get anywhere else.

After lunch, her restlessness persisted. She went out again, and, too tired for any more walking, got on a bus. Any bus, she told herself, would have done. Since the particular one she was on had happened to come past, there was, after all, no reason why she should have taken it. But the fact remained that she had let two go by before she finally mounted this one.

The bus rattled her down the hill, down into the sticky heat of London. She bought a sixpenny ticket—there was no point in not having a long outing while she was about it. She might have tea somewhere, or go to a flick, or look up Ruth Downing, only she would be sure to be still away. And when the bus drew up at the fare stage opposite the corner of Parbury Gardens, she told herself that she was genuinely surprised to find herself there.

She alighted and crossed the road. After all, why not? There was nothing in the least disloyal in what she was doing. She was simply checking up. It was an obvious precaution. Martin would quite understand. In fact, she meant to tell him all about it when she got home. He would probably be rather amused. None the less, though she told herself all this, she felt her knees tremble ever so slightly as she walked up to the ugly brick block of flats.

What was so particularly absurd, as she admitted in her own mind, was that she had not really any idea what she expected to find. But this circumstance did not make her relief any the less genuine when, opposite number 15, she found in the narrow vestibule the name of Mrs. Elizabeth Peabody, precisely as Martin had said. With a lighter heart and a growing sense that she had been making herself ridiculous, she walked on to No. 34. There, sure enough, was Mr. T. P. M. Jones, and the sensation of reassurance at once deepened. She walked out into the sunlight, feeling that it was hardly worth while attempting to verify the fact that Mrs. Peabody was blind, or that Mr. Jones wore a beard.

Instead of walking away at once, however, she took a turn round the square of which Parbury Gardens formed one side. Under the plane-trees shading the little green patch in the middle of the square was a perambulator. In the perambulator, presumably was a baby, and beside it a cross-eyed nurse squatted on a stool and knitted. Anne paused in her walk and watched them vacantly. The baby belonged to one of the flats, she mused. Surprising that they hadn't sent it to the seaside at this time of the year. Perhaps they couldn't afford to. Curious, you'd have thought they were well enough off, though—it looked a fairly expensive kind of pram. Hire purchase, very likely. . . . All the same, if it was mine, I'd have found a way to . . . But that nurse! Surely it can't be good for a child to be looked after by any one with a squint as bad as that? I should be terrified of the baby picking it up. Of course, very likely the real nurse is on holiday and this one is only a temporary. . . .

She dragged herself away and resumed her walk. This won't do, my girl, she said to herself. You're a deal too scatter-brained, that's what's the matter with you. You didn't come down here to moon over babies but to investigate something. Think, girl, think! And I'm going to keep you walking round this blasted square until you've something to show for it!

Fifteen, Parbury Gardens, Anne repeated to herself as her feet dragged slowly along the pavement. Fifteen, Parbury Gardens. That was the address the Joneses gave at the hotel, and the Joneses weren't Joneses at all, but a couple out on the loose. So Martin said. Several times. And when you're a couple out on the loose, you don't put your real name and address in the book. Martin says so, and Martin knows. I suppose if I had spent the night at Bentby with Martin we'd have put . . . I wonder what sort of name and address we'd have put?

Her incorrigible mind wandered away into other paths for a moment until conscience, striding after, pulled it back with a jerk. You're as bad as those dogs on the Heath, conscience told mind severely. Meekly, mind took up the trail again, as Anne completed her first circuit of the square.

But if you have to put down a sham address on the spur of the moment, what you put down has probably some association with you. Martin said so. No, he didn't. I said so, and Martin just looked glum and pretended to be stupid, because he knew all about the technique of sham addresses. But he didn't contradict, anyway. If you invented an address that didn't exist, it might be different, though even then there would probably be some unconscious—subconscious? I never can remember the difference—some association, anyhow, which directed your mind in making that particular invention. But where you chose a real address, one that was sham only in the sense that it wasn't yours, the odds were that you had some reason for your choice.

185

And that's as far as I got three days ago, talking to Martin. And now that I am in Parbury Gardens, where do we go from here? Fifteen, Parbury Gardens *means something*. It's a kind of code which we haven't got the key to. And the key was in the mind of the Joneses, or one of them, when they wrote down those words in the book at Pendlebury Old Hall. Wait a bit. Try and picture them standing there, with the book open in front of them, and the reception clerk staring at them in that vacant superior way they always do. . . . Damn difficult to picture anyone when you don't know what their faces are like. But there is a picture all the same, an impression anyway. Now why?

Of course! Anne stopped suddenly in her stride as she came abreast of the cross-eyed nurse for the second time. Elderson's report said distinctly that the girl was giggling while the register was being signed. That was it! The address was a joke, then. Ha, Ha! Let's have a good laugh, even if we can't see it just yet. Fifteen, very funny. Parbury, an absolute scream. Gardens, we all roared! It's enough to make you drop a stitch, isn't it, nurse?

Anne's mind went once more to the Black Swan at Bentby, and this time conscience made no move. She tried to imagine herself in the smelly little hall there, standing behind Martin and sniggering at the name and address he was writing. The effort made her nearly sick, but she persisted. What sort of address could have made her snigger, if she had been the sniggering kind? Obviously, there was no joke in something that didn't mean anything to you at all. If you enjoyed cheap jokes—and *ex hypothesi* you did—there were two possible ones that might appeal to you. First, you put down somebody else's address, because to your dirty mind it seemed exquisitely funny that that particular

186

person, in all probability the pink of respectability, should be in some way connected all unconsciously with your furtive goings on. Or alternatively, in a spirit of bravado you chose one that was near your own, and got a sort of kick out of the quite imaginary risk you were running. That seemed sound psychology, anyhow.

We are getting on, Anne thought, as she came round to her starting point for the third time. Now let's see how it works out. (*a.*) The joke was that they knew blind Mrs. Peabody, and thought it was a real stroke of wit to put her flat, of all places, in a hotel register. If that's the right answer, I'm sunk. I simply can't face the prospect of rummaging into Mrs. Peabody's private life and trying to find out which of her acquaintances might possibly play a trick like that on her. (*b.*) The joke was that the address was as near as possible the true one. Fifteen—Parbury—Gardens. Three ingredients. And to make a really good joke of it, two of them should be genuine and one only false. So you get—Fifteen, Parbury Place, or Terrace, or Street, or whatever it may be. Or Fifteen, Something-or-other Gardens, or finally, Umpteen, Parbury Gardens.

She pondered the alternatives gravely. Between three such crass imbecilities, which to choose? On due consideration, she struck out the second. To start with, among all the scores of "gardens" in London, it would obviously be hopeless to try to find the right one. In the second place, the name of the gardens was the really essential part of the address. Change that, and you change its identity. And with the identity, the whole feeble joke disappeared. Surely the most cretinous nit-wit could not possibly have thought it funny, or risky, to say, Fifteen, Parbury Gardens, when the real address was Fifteen, Daylesford Gardens, for instance! Remained the other two possibilities. More from laziness than from any rational motive, she preferred the theory of Fifteen, Parbury Something. There could not be more than a limited number of streets in London called after Parbury, whoever he or it might be, and there were, she had noticed, one hundred and ten flats in the gardens. Following the line of least resistance, therefore, instead of completing her third circuit of the square, she turned down a side street to where she had noticed the post office.

The lady behind the grill seemed deeply incensed when Anne asked if she could see a Directory. Such things, apparently, were unknown in post offices. From her expression it might be gathered that it was more than a little indelicate to mention them. She did, however, go so far as to admit that improprieties of this nature could be seen in the local public library; and when Anne asked where that was to be found, she ejaculated: "Turn-to-y'r-right-at-bottom-of-th'-street-'n-'s-on-y'r-left," with a speed that showed how often she must have given the direction to other seekers after the forbidden fruit.

Five minutes later, Anne was in the public library with the Directory open before her. It did not need more than a glance to explode her theory. Parbury Gardens was positively the only Parbury in London, the county suburbs included. There was, it was true, one other thoroughfare with a name that closely resembled it, Parberry Street. But Parberry Street, after inspection, proved to be in the Isle of Dogs, and she felt quite positive in her mind that wherever the Joneses came from, it was not the Isle of Dogs. So that was that! It really simplifies matters a lot, she thought, exhaustion making her positively lightheaded. The answer is simply Something, Parbury Gardens. Somewhere in those flats lives or has lived Mr. M. Jones—or Mrs. Jones. Mrs. Jones, I think. So-called. I don't know why, but I'm sure the address he chose to fake was hers and not his. Positive. Woman's instinct and all that. And only a hundred and ten numbers to choose from. Hooray!

She set herself to read, slowly and methodically, the names of all the inhabitants of the flats as recorded in the Directory. Not one of them conveyed anything to her whatever, and there was not the smallest reason to suppose that any of them would. None the less, she ploughed grimly on, and had almost come to the end, to No. 87, to be precise, when a round-shouldered, spectacled young man approached her and said mournfully, "The library is closing now, Madame."

Anne abandoned the book and hurried out into the sun again. She was astonished to see by the clock in the post office window that it was already six o'clock. She must have been very much longer in the library than she had imagined. She had had no tea, and was ready to drop from fatigue. All the same, her legs carried her back, seemingly of their own accord, back to Parbury Gardens, there to take up again her circumambulation of the square with the persistence and much about the enthusiasm of a convict in the exercise ground of a prison.

Fifteen, her thoughts ran. We've got down to that now, simply the bare numeral. Why choose fifteen, of all the numbers going? Because the proper number was five? Or twenty-five? Or for that matter, any sort of five, up to a hundred and five? Pity they didn't go up to a hundred and fifteen. That would have been a sure guess. Think of a number and double it. That gave you thirty. She shook her head, gravely. Somehow she did not fancy thirty. Of course, there were lots of things you could do with numbers. Add, subtract, divide, transpose. . . . Transpose. *Transpose!* She stood still, staring across the railings at the spot where the perambulator had been and was no longer, while a wholly irrational feeling of certainty flooded in upon her. In that moment, she was convinced that she had solved the problem of the Joneses' address in the register at Pendlebury.

Invisible trumpeters blew a triumphal march before her as she walked over to the entrance from which access was gained to number Fifty-one. Their music flagged a little when she realized that it was the top flat of all and that there was no lift. It had ceased altogether long before she had dragged herself up the long flight of stairs. The name, she had noticed before beginning her climb, was Miss Frances Fothergill. It was repeated on a rather dingy visiting card on the flat door itself. The door itself had a slightly rakish air, with its pale green paint that must have once been jaunty and was beginning to flake off where hearty Bohemian boots had kicked it. Just below the card was the knob of a bell. A decidedly violent bell. The kind that rings just inside the door and makes enough noise to wake the dead. Anne rang it three times before she gave it up.

It seemed almost more exhausting climbing down the stairs than it had been going up. It was like that in the Alps, she remembered, seeing again an endless zigzag path winding down through the woods from the hut to the valley below. She reached the ground floor at last and came out into the open air, her eyes momentarily dazzled by the sunlight. As she did so, she was aware of a strong scent of frangi-pani, a blurred vision of lipstick and silver fox, and a high-pitched voice saying: "Oo! Excuse me! But it's Miss Dickinson, isn't it?"

Anne prided herself on her memory for faces, but she had to blink two or three times before she recognized her. Then something familiar in the tilt of her nose and her odd, angular smile enabled her to place her.

Miss Fothergill—and though Anne had never heard her name, she was quite certain she was Miss Fothergill—was the assistant who had more than once sold shoes to her in one of the big shops. It was not surprising that recognition was difficult, for dressed for the street and with her full war-paint on, this glamorous creature was altogether different from the quiet young woman whom she remembered flitting about the shoe department of Peter Harker's.

"Oo, Miss Dickinson! It's quite a surprise seeing you here, it reely is!" Miss Fothergill was saying.

"Yes," said Anne faintly. "I was looking for a friend, but she doesn't seem to be in."

"It is always like that, isn't it, when you've come a long way? So provoking, I always think. But won't you come up to my place and have a cup of tea?"

"No, thank you very much."

"Oo, but do, Miss Dickinson. You'll excuse me saying so, but you look quite done up, you do reely. It'll be no trouble at all to me, honest it won't. I always have a cup meself when I come home. It does pull you together ever so. I've got the kettle and all ready and waiting on the ring. Do come up just a minute, Miss Dickinson, it'll do you good."

Anne did not feel equal to resisting. She allowed herself to be led once more up the stairs (with many apologies for their length and steepness) and through the battered green door into the flat beyond.

"I'm afraid it *is* in rather a pickle," said Miss Fothergill with a giggle, as Anne sank gratefully on to the shabby divan which almost filled the untidy little room. "If you'll excuse me, I'll go and get the tea. I won't be half a jiffy. Do put your feet up, Miss Dickinson, if you're feeling tired. And I expect you'd like to take your shoes off a bit," she added with a professional glance at Anne's footwear.

She disappeared into the kitchenette beyond and presently came back with a tray.

"I reely must apologize for the service," she giggled. "But I never seem to be able to get them matched up somehow. You know how it is when a cup gets broken and you've only just time to pop round to Woolworth's. Do you take sugar, Miss Dickinson?"

Anne gulped her tea gratefully. It was not Peter Harker's best brand by a long way, but it was warm and invigorating. She refused the solitary slice of cake which Miss Fothergill pressed upon her.

"Oo, but do, Miss Dickinson," she persisted. "I don't want it meself, honest I don't. I never eat anything with my tea. And it's lucky to take the last bit, they always say, don't they? I know a girl friend of mine told me before she was married she was sure it was all along of her— not that you need bother about that sort of luck now, need you, Miss Dickinson? Oo, perhaps I didn't ought to have said that?"

"That's quite all right," Anne reassured her. "I expect it will be announced any time now."

"I'm sure I hope you'll be ever so happy. I'm sure you ought to be. You know one gets quite interested, if you know what I mean, when any of our customers get married. Any of our regulars, I mean. And of course, we've seen Mr. Johnson in with you lots of times. He's ever so nice, I think."

"Thank you," said Anne. "And now I think I must be going. It was really kind of you to give me tea."

"You're welcome, I'm sure, Miss Dickinson. I dare say we shall be seeing you round our place again soon? There's some lovely new autumn styles we've just got in, you would like them, reely you would. Well, goodbye, Miss Dickinson."

"Goodbye."

Throwing economy to the winds for once, Anne went home by taxi. In spite of Miss Fothergill's tea she felt more tired than ever, but it was the exhaustion of the mind rather than of the body. She leaned back in her seat and tried not to think, but found that she might as well have tried to prevent the taximeter ticking up the fare. But unlike the figures on the meter, her thoughts remained obstinately unprogressive. I've got no proof, she kept saying to herself, no proof about the matter at all. All this juggling with figures seemed very clever at the time, but meeting that girl there may have been just coincidence. May have been—if only I didn't know in my bones that it wasn't!

I liked her, too, she reflected. I can't imagine why, but I positively liked her. She was vulgar and overdressed but she obviously had a kind nature. She "took to me," as she would say. Damn you, Miss Fothergill, why can't I hate you as I should? And where am I going to go for my shoes after this?

And all the time, at the very back of her mind, remained another thought altogether, so very much more disturbing that she preferred not to examine it at all.

17

Mr. Dedman Speaks His Mind

Wednesday, August 30th

Things were moving in the office of Jelks, Jelks, Dedman and Jelks. Clerks came and went with an air of busy purposefulness, even on routine matters. Typewriters clicked and jangled at a speedier tempo. Office gossip was a thing of hurried half-sentences instead of long, delicious confidences. For Dedman, the mainspring of the firm, had returned to work, keyed up to a higher pitch of efficiency by his holiday, and was gathering into his capable hands all the strings that had been allowed to fall slack and tangled in his absence.

By midday he had already cleared away the mass of arrears which had accumulated on his desk and had, in addition, put straight half a dozen minor matters which the junior Jelks, now on his holiday, had left in a state of happy confusion. As the clock struck twelve he finished dictating a letter, nodded dismissal to the typist and pressed the bell on his desk.

To the clerk who answered it he said, "Is Mr. Dickinson here yet?"

"Just arrived, Mr. Dedman. Miss Dickinson is with

him, and another gentleman—Mr. Johnson, I think it is."

"Humph! I only wanted to see Mr. Dickinson. You'd better show them all in, though."

Stephen, Anne, and Martin, ushered into the presence, found themselves confronted by a short, compact man of early middle age, with a pugnacious jaw and a round head covered with close-cropped black hair. He acknowledged their appearance with an awkward bow, plumped back into his chair and plunged immediately into business.

"Unusual, I know, for a solicitor to summon his client in this way," he began, addressing Stephen. "For that matter, you're not my client. Your father's estate is. But you are one of the executors, and I want to get to the bottom of this. While I've been away things have been allowed to slide."

"On the contrary," said Stephen stiffly. "We have all been doing a very considerable amount of work."

"The position now is," went on Mr. Dedman, disregarding the interruption, "you have just four days in which to accept or refuse the Insurance Company's offer. Actually, the time expires on Sunday. Mr. Jelks overlooked that fact when he made the arrangement. Sunday being a *dies non*, I have claimed that it should be extended to the close of business hours on Monday. I have put that to the Company and made them agree to it. After Monday it will be a case of suing on the policy if you're going to get anything. Well?"

"Of course we don't accept," said Stephen.

"Very good. What's your case?"

"What it always has been. That Father was murdered."

"Precisely. Who by?"

"Perhaps," said Stephen, "I had better explain what we have been doing."

"Perhaps you had."

"In the first place, I obtained a report from an inquiry agent—"

"Have you brought it with you?"

"Yes."

Stephen handed it across the desk into Mr. Dedman's strong, hairy hands. It seemed to take him rather less than a minute to read it. When he had done so, he leaned back in his chair, nodded thoughtfully and said, "I presume that you have treated all the people mentioned in this as possible suspects?"

"Yes."

"Have you found any reason to connect any one of them with this alleged crime?"

"Yes."

"Good. Which?"

"Parsons."

"Tell me."

Stephen handed it across the desk into Mr. Dedman's and, with some assistance from Martin, went through with it to the end. Mr. Dedman heard him out without interruption. Towards the end of the recital he closed his eyes, but the impatient drumming of his fingers on the desk proved that he was far from being asleep. When Stephen had finished, he opened his eyes again, and said, "Is that all?"

"Yes."

Mr. Dedman made no further observation for a full half-minute. Then he picked up Elderson's report again, glanced at it and said:

"These other people here—have you any suspicions against any of them?"

"Some of them, yes."

"Which?"

"To begin with, Mr. Carstairs and his wife. Mrs.

Carstairs and her husband, I should say, because she is the one that counts. Actually, he is a parson, though he hasn't a parish." He described his experiences at Brighton and went on: "They are not too well off, I should say, and she works as a secretary to a charitable concern called the Society for the Relief of Distress amongst the Widows of Professional Men. Now it's an odd coincidence, but that Society happens to be the one—"

"The one that your Uncle Arthur's money goes to on your father's death. I know the terms of the will—naturally. Well?"

"Well," Stephen went on. It was somehow difficult to put very much conviction into his theory under Mr. Dedman's cold gaze. "Well, it's a fact that the Society is, or was, rather, in very low water. From what I can gather, Mrs. Carstairs' job was in great jeopardy. If she knew the terms of the will, and after all as secretary she would be almost certain to, she had the strongest possible motive to secure this very large sum of money for the Society."

"I see. Which are your other suspects?"

"The Howard-Blenkinsops. This is really a rather extraordinary story, and rather—rather an unpleasant one. To begin with, their name isn't Howard-Blenkinsop at all, but March. A Mrs. March and her son."

"Is that the Frances March to whom your father paid a weekly allowance up to some twenty years ago?"

"You know about it, then?" Stephen asked in surprise.

"Certainly. All the payments were made through this office, and I came across the receipts in clearing up your father's papers this morning. Nothing very remarkable about it. It happens to scores of our clients. Then the son mentioned here was your father's illegitimate child?"

"No. That's just the point. He wasn't. That son is dead."

197

"Oh? Who told you that?"

"Actually, I wasn't told. My sister and Mr. Johnson were. Perhaps it would be more satisfactory if they gave you the whole story."

"Perhaps it would."

Mr. Dedman turned to the other two and, Anne remaining silent, it was Martin who related the story of the discoveries at Bentby Grange.

"I see," said Mr. Dedman again when he had done, and made no other comment. "There are still four other names on the list. I take it that you do not consider them as probabilities?"

"No," said Stephen. "Vanning we have dealt with already. Mallett was a detective from Scotland Yard on holiday. Davitt turned out to be a perfectly innocent stockbroker's clerk with a passion for literature, and Mr. and Mrs. Jones—"

"Were simply a couple out on the loose." It was Anne who spoke, for the first time since they had come into the room. "I've spoken to Mrs. Jones, and I know."

Mr. Dedman looked at her in astonishment. So did Martin and Stephen. Dedman noted that her remarks seemed to be as surprising to them as they were to him, and the fact afforded him a momentary gleam of amusement.

"Very well," he said, and turned again to Stephen. "As to Davitt, you have seen him, I suppose?"

"No. But I had a long talk with his landlady."

"That was even better, I dare say. Few people have any secrets from their landladies. I certainly had none in my younger days. So that represents the sum of your researches, does it?"

"Yes, it does."

"Then," said Mr. Dedman with a smile that seemed to make his pugnacious jaw look fiercer than ever, "I

198

have only one piece of advice to give you. Accept the company's offer."

It was some time before Stephen found words.

"Do you mean to say you really think—" he began.

"Accept the company's offer!" repeated Mr. Dedman in louder tones. "And think yourselves lucky. It's more than you deserve, anyway."

While his visitors remained in stunned silence at the undisguised rudeness with which he spoke, Mr. Dedman pushed his chair back from the desk, clasped his hands and crossed his legs. Had any of his staff been present they would have readily interpreted the movements as signs that he was about to "let himself go." And they would not have been wrong.

"You people," he began, "took upon yourselves to prove that the late Mr. Dickinson was murdered. I dare say he was. Far more people are murdered every year than the average person suspects. In any case, from my knowledge of him, I should not say that he would have committed suicide—in the first year of a life policy, at any rate. He knew that much about insurance, I have no doubt. Having adopted that course, you have gone about it in a way that I can only truthfully describe as imbecile. Your object was, or should have been, to collect evidence, *evidence*, that would convince a Court of law that the probability of his having been murdered was substantially higher than the probability of his having died by his own hand. By what you have done, and by what you have failed to do, you have made it virtually impossible to do anything of the kind."

He paused to take breath. Martin opened his mouth to say something but Mr. Dedman forestalled him.

"I gather from what you have told me," he went on, "that you have come to the conclusion that Parsons in all probability poisoned Mr. Dickinson by mistake in an attempt to rid himself of a blackmailer whom we have agreed to call Vanning. I dare say you are right. Speaking between these four walls, as an ordinary individual, I consider it quite possible that he did kill your father, in the way that you have suggested. But what have you done? You took no advice—you made no inquiries—you simply walked in on this wretched Parsons creature and killed him. And with him you killed whatever chance you ever had of proving your case. Do you imagine that it will be possible now to prove that Vanning ever had a penny from him—the very first step in your case? Of course, as the result of his death, all Parsons' defalcations will come out—quite a sufficient motive for suicide without adding blackmail and murder to it. Can you visualize what sort of case you've got left now? I can, and I've been in charge of all the litigation in this office for fifteen years and I know what I'm talking about. You'll be reduced to accusing a dead man of murder. That will be bad enough—'blackening the memory of the deceased,' and so forth. But you'll have to do more than that—you'll have to accuse another man of blackmail, a man very much alive and able to defend himself, without a shred of evidence to support you. You'll simply be laughed out of Court, if you ever get there—which you won't, so long as I'm solicitor to the estate. With Parsons alive, with a charge of embezzlement pending against him, it might have been possible to do something. Very carefully handled, I can visualize negotiations with the Company coming to a successful conclusion. As it is—the thing is a wash-out."

He slapped his hand on the desk to emphasize his words.

"Then, the Carstairs. Your theory there, I gather, is that this parson and his wife, or the wife without the parson, encountering Mr. Dickinson accidentally in this hotel, seized the opportunity to murder him for the good of this charity and more particularly of its secretary. Well, I'll make you a present of this—the S.R.D.W.P.M. is not one of the charities that solicitors of good standing care to advise their clients to remember in their wills. What your Uncle Arthur's motives were, I don't know. His will was not drawn up in this office. I had occasion to look at the Society's accounts some time ago, and I didn't like them. I estimated that approximately thirty per cent of the money contributed by the public reaches the widows of professional men. The rest goes into the pockets of the whole-time salaried organizers—people like Mrs. Carstairs. But because the woman's a parasite on public benevolence, does that prove that she's a murderess? Of course the Society was hard up. That sort of concern always is. Of course the falling in of the reversion was a very useful windfall. But so far, all you've got is the word of Mr. Carstairs—of all people!—to support your extraordinary theory. And has it occurred to you that if this so-called charity was really in such desperate straits, they could have sold the reversion to the bequest, not for the whole amount, of course, but for a good round sum? A much safer method of raising the wind than murder, I can assure you. The whole idea is simply too preposterous for words.

"But what I simply cannot forgive you," Mr. Dedman proceeded with unabated vigour, "is the way you have handled the March business. Here you've got the almost ideal suspect. A discarded mistress, with a fortune in prospect! And has it occurred to you also that she was the only person in the hotel who would have been in the least likely to penetrate into your father's room with his knowledge and consent?"

"But," Martin protested. "She didn't even know who Mr. Dickinson was until after he was dead!"

"So she told her employer. Or rather, so her employer told you she had told her. And on that third-hand evidence you believed it! Well, it may have been so. I'm not suggesting that it isn't possible. I'm looking at the possibility of using facts to persuade the Insurance Company to cough up the policy moneys. If you had gone to them and said: 'You are proposing to rely on suicide as a defence to this action. We can prove the presence in this hotel of a woman with the opportunity of murdering the deceased, and an overwhelming motive for doing so. Now what about it?' If you had said that— I think they would have been ready to discuss matters with you."

"But we can still say that to the insurance people," Stephen put in.

Anne said: "But Mr. Dedman, I believe what Mrs. Howard-Blenkinsop told me. You don't want us to accuse an innocent person, do you?"

The solicitor disregarded Anne, and answered Stephen.

"Of course you can," he said. "But do you think they are going to listen to you after next Monday? And don't forget, after the time limit for taking their offer has expired, you'll have nothing to fall back on. It'll be all or nothing then, with tremendously heavy litigation in front of you."

"I can approach the insurance people tomorrow," Stephen objected. "Today, for that matter."

"Do, by all means, and see what sort of answer you get. They will say: 'Indeed? And who was this Mrs. March? We have a list of people staying in the hotel and her name doesn't appear there.' What's your answer? 'Well, it must have been Mrs. March, because Mrs. Howard-Blenkinsop told me so.' 'Quite so,' they'll say. 'And how can you produce Mrs. March?' And you'll be reduced to saying: 'As a matter of fact, Mrs. March isn't here. I don't know where she is, but I believe she's abroad.' Then the Insurance Company will look down its collective nose and inform you that it doesn't believe a word you are saying and the offer remains open till Monday, good morning. Well, you can take the risk if you like, but if you do, you do it against my advice, that's all.

"Incidentally," he added, by way of afterthought, "have you troubled to test in any way the truth of the assertion that Mrs. March's eldest son is dead? No? I thought not. For all you know this rather remarkable cook may have invented his death as an excuse for getting a couple of day's holiday out of her employer. He may be alive still. He might have been one of the waiters at Pendlebury Old Hall. He might—oh, well, there it is," he concluded pettishly. "I'm afraid, taking it altogether, I can't congratulate you on your efforts at detection. And my advice remains as I have stated."

Mr. Dedman completed his tirade, handed Elderson's report back across the desk to Stephen and at the same instant made it clear in some indefinable but unmistakable way that he had lost all interest in the subject. So much so that when a moment later they rose to go he sounded genuinely surprised to see them there at all. It was Anne who led the retreat. Stephen seemed capable of sitting sulkily in his chair forever, and Martin was always unable to take a hint.

"Thank you so much, Mr. Dedman, for taking such trouble about our affairs," she said in a voice of apparently sincere gratitude. "You have put everything very clearly. We will let you know what we want done in good time."

She went out of the room, the men following meekly in her trail. Mr. Dedman gave her his jerky little bow as she went. Before she was out of the office he was dictating like mad. The letter was on a totally different subject. A fresh point had occurred to him while Stephen had been talking about Parsons. The ability to think of two things at once was what had made it possible for Dedman to get through approximately twenty-four hours of work in a normal day. It had never occurred to him to wonder why he was not popular in the office. Even he could not think of three things at once.

18

An Inspector with Indigestion

It would be inaccurate to say that Inspector Mallett had forgotten his interview with Stephen Dickinson. It was never safe to assert that the inspector had forgotten anything. But it was certainly the fact that since the interview had taken place he had scarcely given the matter a further thought. It was only an accident that brought it to his attention again—an accident that was to have important consequences. Admittedly it was a very rare and therefore unexpected occurrence, and as such worthy of record for its own sake. To Mallett at the time it seemed positively overwhelming.

The truth was that on this particular morning he, of all people in the world, was suffering from an acute attack of indigestion. So unfamiliar to him were the symptoms that he actually spent some time wondering what was the matter with him. He spent a good deal longer speculating in vain what could have caused the trouble. He ran over in his mind the gigantic meals which he had consumed during the past day and could find no solution. There had been nothing out of the ordinary in any of them, for Mallett, incontestably the heartiest trenchman of the force, liked his food plain and plentiful. True, the exigencies of the service had compelled him to lunch, comparatively sparingly, at noon and to postpone his enormous supper till two in the morning. But that was nothing out of the ordinary, and he had dispatched his usual breakfast at seven-thirty without a qualm. But there it was—the odious, inescapable fact that he was now reduced to as pitiful a condition as any dyspeptic that ever swelled the profits of the pill manufacturers.

By half-past ten, he could stand it no longer. Something would have to be done to stay the griping pain which was making existence unbearable and work impossible. He was, naturally, completely ignorant of the proper treatment of a malady with which he was so utterly unacquainted; and his first instinct was to turn to someone else for help. At this crisis, his mind went to one Sergeant Weekes, whose indigestion was almost as celebrated in New Scotland Yard as was Mallett's own appetite. Weekes was a man who never went anywhere without a little box of wonder-working tablets, changing in character according to the season of the year or the vagaries of his complaint, but invariably described by their owner in confidential tones as, "The only thing that keeps me going, old man." The inspector had often laughed at poor Weekes with all the unconscious cruelty of ignorance. Now he put his pride in his pocket and, bent double with pain, made his way to the other's room in search of advice and assistance.

Thus it came about that the inspector was at Weekes's elbow at the precise moment when a message was put through to the sergeant from the borough police at Midchester. If Mallett had been slightly more or slightly less stoical in his attitude to pain he would not have been there to hear it. Indeed, if the message had come through as little as two minutes earlier his intense preoccupation with his own affairs would probably not have allowed him to give it any attention. But at the critical moment it so happened that one of the famous tablets had been administered just long enough to secure, if not the instant relief claimed for them on the label, at least an intermission from agony sufficient to permit him to be conscious of what was going on around him.

The telephone conversation, from the London end at least, was not particularly interesting at first. It consisted mainly of the word, "Yes," several times repeated, and varied at intervals—for the sergeant prided himself on being up to date—by "O.K." Meanwhile he was jotting down notes in an illegible shorthand of his own devising on a pad. Near the end of the call, Weekes paused in his hieroglyphics and said: "Just a minute, old man. Will you repeat the names? I want to get them O.K."

The voice at the other end evidently complied and the sergeant confirmed, writing as he spoke, in long-hand capitals this time: "Stephen Dickinson and Martin Johnson. Yes, thanks, old man, I've got the descriptions. We'll let you know what we can do. Yes. . . . Yes. . . . O.K. . . . 'Bye."

He hung up and turned to the inspector with a grin.

"Feeling better?" he asked. "They're pretty wonderful, these little fellows, aren't they? They say it's the charcoal in them that does the good work. Now, if you keep quiet for half an hour or so, you'll be as right as rain, I give you my word. Of course, a big man like yourself, it might take a bit longer. Perhaps you'd like to take another one away with you, just in case. Might come in handy after lunch." He looked at Mallett severely. "That is, if you have any lunch."

"Thanks," said the inspector. "I am much better already. As to lunch—we'll see. But tell me, what was that matter you were discussing on the telephone?"

"Witnesses wanted for an inquest on one Parsons at Midchester," said Weekes. "It seems the coroner there is getting all het up about it."

"And one of them is called Dickinson, I gather."

"That's right. Stephen Dickinson of London. Useful, ain't it?"

"It may be. I'd like to hear the description they give of him."

Wondering at this display of interest in Midland inquests, the sergeant read from his notes a description which, vague though it was, was perfectly recognizable.

"The other individual is named Martin Johnson," he went on.

"I don't know him," said Mallett. "But Stephen Dickinson I do know. This may be interesting. What has he to do with the late Mr. Parsons at Midchester?"

"That's just what the Borough Force there would like to know. It seems that these two young men spent the night in Midchester, two nights ago. They made an appointment to see Parsons next day on the telephone. They didn't give no names, but they were traced through the hotel afterwards. The phone call was made from the hotel, see?"

"I see. Go on."

"Well, this man Parsons was an official of the local Gas Company, and quite an important figure in the town, see? He saw these two. He wasn't in the room with them above five minutes, and then off they went. And an hour later he's found in his room with his head blown to bits and a letter to explain that he's been robbing the Gas Company right and left for donkey's years."

"Very interesting. Very interesting indeed."

"D'you think so? Anyhow, the coroner seems to want to get hold of this couple. Bit of luck if you know one of them. I don't see that there's much chance of tracing them otherwise."

"Stephen Dickinson," said Mallett, "lives at 67 Plane Street, Hampstead."

"That's all right, then. I'll notify the station there, and they can serve the witness summons on him."

Mallett took two steps towards the door and then turned.

"On the whole," he said, "I think I'll go round and see Mr. Dickinson myself about the matter. There's always a chance I may be mistaken."

"Go round yourself?" said the sergeant in surprise.

"Yes. This Parsons business may be important. When is the inquest, by the way?"

"It's been adjourned till today week."

"Plenty of time, then. I'll let you know if this is the right man and anything I can find out about Mr. Johnson. Meanwhile, you needn't do anything about the Midchester police until you hear from me. Thanks for the pill."

And the inspector returned to his room, leaving behind him a sadly puzzled Sergeant Weekes.

Back at his desk once more, Mallett pulled out the file labelled "*Re* Dickinson," which had reposed there since his unconventional talk with Stephen nearly a fortnight before. During the interval it had received one addition only; namely, from the Markshire police to the letter which he had written on the same day. The only matter of interest which this letter contained was a list of the residents at the hotel on the night of Mr. Dickinson's death and a note of the times of their arrivals and departures. This he examined afresh with rather more attention than he had done when he first received it. He ran his broad forefinger down the list until it reached the name of Parsons.

"That'll be him," he said to himself. "Well, it seems simple enough. The boy sets to work to trace all the possible people who could have killed his father, and in due course goes to see Parsons. Parsons has a guilty conscience, thinks he's come after him in connexion with his embezzlements, loses his head and kills himself. I'm afraid young Dickinson will find himself in an awkward position when he has to explain all that at the inquest, though. Not to mention Mr. Martin Johnson. I haven't heard of him before. Friend of the family, I suppose."

In the ordinary way he might well, at this point, have put the matter from his mind altogether, but whether it was the after effect of indigestion or some other cause, his thoughts continued obstinately to revolve round the question. He remained for some time brooding over the list of names, trying to fit them to the faces which he dimly remembered having seen at the hotel.

"But *did* Parsons kill himself simply for fear of his thefts being exposed?" he murmured. "The confession only relates to that, it's true, but perhaps that's only natural. Was there something else which the lad has found out—some connexion between him and his father, for instance? Well, he'll be able to tell me that. It can't have been a very obvious one, or he'd have gone for him straight away, instead of waiting for nearly two weeks. Parsons' death has made it a good deal harder to prove the case, unless he's left something tangible behind him in the way of papers. It might be worth while asking the Midchester police. . . ."

Almost without realizing it, the inspector had completely changed his attitude of mind towards the riddle of

Leonard Dickinson's death. His talk with Stephen must have impressed him far more deeply than he had known at the time, for now that his attention was once more focused on the problem he found himself accepting almost as a matter of course the theory which he had then refused to entertain.

"Let me see, now. . . ." Mallett tilted his chair back and closed his eyes. He saw once more the face of old Mr. Dickinson, heard his low, depressed tones. He reviewed again the short and apparently conclusive evidence at the inquest. There was nothing new in what he remembered, but this time he looked at it from a different angle altogether.

"But . . ." he added. "*But* . . . there are objections to the son's theory all the same. Or if not objections, limitations. If the old man was murdered in this particular place, in this particular way, that implies two or three things." He enumerated them to himself. "Now, if I had been conducting this investigation in his place, I should have gone on those lines, in any case. It would have narrowed things down considerably. But I wasn't conducting this investigation," he concluded with a sigh.

Then Mallett performed a feat which was quite usual for him, but of which he was none the less justifiably proud. Taking up his pen, he proceeded to write down from memory the heads of the conversation which he had had with Stephen twelve days before. He had made no notes at the time, and during the interval his brain had been occupied with a dozen other matters, many of them of urgent importance. Nevertheless, when he had done, the salient points of their discussion were recorded on the paper before him, as accurately and completely as though they had been written down contemporaneously.

He contemplated the result with satisfaction. Then he marked with a pencil certain points in it which struck him as important. Finally, he looked from it to the type-written sheet supplied by the Markshire police and back again, tugging thoughtfully at the ends of his moustache. At last, he pulled himself together.

"This is theorizing without the facts, if you like!" he told himself. "And a most irrational theory at that. All the same, assuming that young Dickinson was right—just assuming. . . . It might be worth looking into. . . . It ought to be worth looking into. . . ."

He put the list into his pocket and returned the file to the drawer with his new page of notes as its only contents.

Despite his airy assurance to Sergeant Weekes that he would look into the matter of Stephen Dickinson himself, it took the inspector some time to persuade the Assistant Commissioner who ruled his days to allow him to leave his regular work in order that he might follow an investigation of his own. But Mallett was a man who had earned the confidence of his superiors and when he had asked for an indulgence in the past it had usually been justified by the event. So it was that on this occasion he found himself free to devote at least the afternoon to an inquiry on his own lines, and thereafter, if it seemed likely to bear fruit, to pursue the matter to a conclusion.

Nothing ever pleased him more than the prospect of working on his own. He came back from seeing the Assistant Commissioner with a broad smile on his face. Sergeant Weekes, whom he encountered on the way, saw in his expression merely another triumph for the tablets.

"They've done the trick, I see," he said.

"Eh?" answered Mallett, absent-mindedly.

"That indigestion of yours—it's gone?"

"Indigestion? Oh, yes, I'd quite forgotten. I had a twinge of something, didn't I? Yes, thanks, it's all right now. I suppose it's because I've been too busy to think about it. Well, I must hurry now, I want to get out to my lunch."

There was, the sergeant reflected gloomily, no such thing as gratitude in the world.

19

Stephen Decides

Thursday, August 31st

"Mind you," Martin was saying, "that solicitor fellow was pretty definite about it. And I'm bound to say, he struck me as a pretty knowing sort of fellow. I mean, he seemed to know what he was talking about."

Stephen groaned.

"I seem to have heard you say that at least half a dozen times since yesterday afternoon," he said.

"We've all said everything over and over again," Anne pointed out. "And we're no nearer deciding anything than we were yesterday. My mind's made up, anyhow. What on earth is the good of beating about the bush any longer?"

"We've got till Monday, anyway," said Martin. "That gives us three clear days. Counting Sunday, of course."

"Your arithmetic is wonderful," Stephen remarked.

"Stop bickering," commanded Anne. "Mother, you're as much concerned in this as any of us. Don't you agree with us? You've heard everything that's been done, and how futile it's all been. Don't you think it would be sheer folly not to take what we can get now, while we can get it, in view of what Mr. Dedman says?"

Mrs. Dickinson had been a more or less silent auditor of the discussion that had raged almost without interruption the whole morning. Appealed to now, she seemed reluctant to speak.

"My dear," she said at last in her low, musical voice, "I gave my opinion about this a long time ago, I have been poor before, and I'm not afraid to be poor again. I don't think that either you or Stephen—particularly Stephen—would enjoy it very much. That is why I left the whole matter in your hands in the first place. Now, I understand, it is a choice between taking a small amount of money at once and gambling on getting a large sum in the future. I know quite well which I should do, if the choice was mine, but then I have never been particularly fond of gambling. You must make up your own minds about this."

"Just a minute," said Martin. "In point of fact, Mrs. Dickinson, you and Steve are the two executors of the will, aren't you?"

"Yes, that is so."

"Well, I may be wrong, but I suppose the executors are the people who will have to make the claim on the insurance chaps, if anybody does. In that case, the people who have to make up their minds about what's to be done are you two, and not us at all."

"And what happens if the executors don't agree?" Stephen asked.

"Heaven knows! I suppose Dedman could tell us."

"I don't think that question will arise," said Mrs. Dickinson. "As I have said, I am not making any decision about this. I shall agree with whatever my fellow executor says."

"Then that settles it!" said Stephen resolutely.

"No, it doesn't!" cried Anne. "Look here, Stephen, I

don't care what the lawyers may say, but we are all in this together. You've simply got to listen to me!"

"I seem to have done quite a lot of that lately," was Stephen's comment.

"You've not heard everything yet, by a long way." She looked at her mother as she spoke.

Mrs. Dickinson accepted the glance as a hint and rose to her feet. "I don't think I can help you any further," she said. "Besides, there are two or three things I must attend to before lunch. Let me know what you have decided and I promise that I shall not quarrel with it."

She went out. The door had hardly closed behind her, and Martin had not had time to begin filling a pipe which automatically appeared in his hand upon her departure, before Anne rounded on Stephen. She stood in the middle of the room, leaning on one arm against a table. Her fingers were trembling slightly and her face had gone quite white.

"Look here!" she began in a low voice. "This thing has got to stop! Do you understand me, Stephen? It's got to stop!"

"You're very earnest, all of a sudden," said Stephen coldly.

"Earnest? My God, can't you understand? Can't you see what a horrible thing we've been meddling with all this time? And now, when there's a chance of getting out of it you still want to go on, all for the sake of—"

"For the sake of twenty-five thousand pounds. I must say, it seems quite a consideration to me."

"Oh, damn the money!" Anne exclaimed bitterly, stamping her foot on the floor. "It's all you ever think about!"

"Very well, damn the money by all means, if you really feel inclined to. But what about you? Who was it who always insisted that Father hadn't killed himself? What about your wonderful notion of putting things right with him by clearing his memory? I must say you are about the last person to—"

"Just as you like. I know I'm responsible for this as much as anybody. I didn't know then just what a thing like this led to, that's all. I do now. And that's why I say we've got to drop it. Lord, what fools we've been with our bungling amateur detection. Here we're been talking of suspects and clues, nosing about ever so pleased with ourselves, and what's been the result?"

"Very little, I admit."

"Little? You've driven one man to his death already, and you call that little? Stephen, I tell you this. Unless we bury the whole of this business as quickly and decently as we can, something perfectly horrible is going to happen. Of that, I feel absolutely certain!"

She turned suddenly to Martin.

"You understand what I'm talking about, don't you, Martin?" she appealed to him. "Don't you see how fearfully important this is for all of us? Please, *please* help me to persuade Stephen to be sensible."

"Just a minute, before you answer that one, Martin." Stephen's voice, with a raw edge to it that told of strained nerves, cut across his sister's plea. "I don't profess to know all about all your affairs, but just tell me this: Are you prepared to marry Anne on what you've got, *plus* her share of the insurance company's offer?"

Martin took two deep puffs at his pipe before he answered.

"No," he said at last. "I'm not."

"Very well, then—"

"I don't care," cried Anne. "I'd rather not be married at all than go on like this!"

There was a long pause before Martin spoke again.

"I think Annie's right," he said.

217

"You mean—" Stephen left his question unfinished.

"I mean that we've done enough harm already. And after all, if I get on, we can always get married some time—if Annie will have me, that is."

Anne said nothing. She was looking at Stephen. Stephen looked at neither of them. He remained for a short time staring straight in front of him, and then said slowly: "I see. Well, I suppose I must agree, then."

"You mean it?" said Anne, all her relief showing in her face.

"Of course I mean it," Stephen answered in an irritated tone. "Otherwise I should not have said it."

"Will you let Mr. Dedman know he's to accept the insurance people's offer?"

"Certainly. I'll do it now, if you like."

The telephone was in the study, where this conference had taken place. Stephen went towards the instrument, and as he put out his hand to take up the receiver the bell began to ring.

"Curse!" he said perfunctorily, and answered the call.

"Yes," he said. "Yes. Speaking. Who? Oh, I see. Yes. I'll hold on. Yes. Yes, I say, this is Mr. Dickinson speaking. What? No, I hadn't seen this morning. I say, I didn't look to see this morning. I say, I didn't look to see this morning. Have they? *What?* But look here, that's impossible! Oh, no, I take your word for it, but . . . Anyhow, that's obviously only a temporary reaction. Oh, you think so, do you? Yes, of course I understand it's pretty serious. I know, I know. But you see, just at the present moment I . . . Well, I shall have to arrange something, that's all. But don't you think you could . . ."

The conversation went on a good deal longer. Various words kept on recurring again and again. "Contango" was one. "Carry over" and "Account" were others. "Margin" and "options" also occurred more than once. At last, the call came to an end. Stephen put down the receiver and turned round to display a very pale face.

"And that," he said, "is that."

"What has happened?" Anne asked him.

"Nothing very much. Simply that I am broke, that's all. Completely and absolutely broke. Unless"—he set his teeth—"unless I can find a very considerable amount of money in a very short space of time."

"Rotten luck," murmured Martin.

"Yes, isn't it? And it's going to be dam' rotten luck for somebody else too, I can tell you that!"

"What do you mean?" said Anne sharply.

"I mean that I'm going on with this show."

"But, Stephen, you can't! Not after what you've just said! You promised—"

"Promised, hell! Can't you understand plain English? I've got to lay my hands on more money than I'm worth by next Monday, or I shall be made bankrupt. That's the long and short of it. And I'm not going to be jockeyed out of the chance of it by you or anyone else. That's final."

"Stephen—you can't—you can't!" Quite suddenly Anne's self-control broke down altogether. Bursting into tears, she made for the door. Martin tried to stop her, but she pushed him on one side and ran from the room.

After she had gone, the two men looked at each other in silence for a moment or two. Then Martin said, "On the whole, I think perhaps I'd better not stay for lunch."

"Perhaps not."

"I'll call round after tea. I dare say a spin in the car then might do her good."

"Yes, do."

In the result, Stephen lunched alone with his

219

mother. Anne remained upstairs in her room. Consequently, she was not present when Inspector Mallett called in the afternoon. It was perhaps just as well.

The inspector was at his most genial during the interview. Sitting in the big arm-chair in the study, he resembled nothing so much as a very large cat, purring contentedly in the sun. Unlike a cat, however, he seemed to be genuinely apologetic for his presence.

"I am really sorry to bother you, Mr. Dickinson," he began. "But somebody had to do it, and in all the circumstances, I thought it had better be me. It all arises out of this event at Midchester. You were at Midchester on Monday night, were you not?"

"Yes, I was."

"I thought it must have been you. You and a Mr. Johnson?"

"Yes, that's my sister's fiancé."

"Your sister's fiancé?" The inspector seemed surprisingly interested in this piece of information. "Your sister's fiancé?" he repeated. "Just so. That would explain it, of course."

"Explain what?" asked Stephen, somewhat provocatively.

"I mean, explain his presence in this affair. I suppose I am right in thinking that your visit to Midchester was in connexion with the inquiries you were proposing to make when we last met?"

"Certainly. And I suppose I am right in thinking that your visit here is in connexion with the same business?"

"Not exactly. Not in the way you might imagine, that is. You see, Mr. Dickinson, as you may know, rather an unfortunate thing happened just after you and Mr. Johnson left Midchester on Tuesday morning, and your names have been associated with it."

Stephen sat bolt upright in his chair.

"Good God!" he said. "Does anybody imagine that Martin and I killed the blighter?"

"No, no!" Mallett assured him with a rumbling laugh. "It's not so bad as that. The position simply is that it has been ascertained that you two had an interview with the deceased shortly before he met his death, and the coroner appears to think that you may be able to throw some light on it."

"I see."

"I learned that inquiries were being made for somebody of your name in London, and thought it would simplify matters if I found out whether you were the individual referred to. Now all I need do is to have the Midchester police notified, and you will get a witness summons in due course. The inquest has been adjourned for a week, I understand."

"I see," said Stephen again. Then he added: "I shall have to go, I suppose?"

"I am afraid so. Indeed, it would be very inadvisable for you not to go. I can see that the position may be a little difficult for you, all the same, and I dare say you might consider the possibility of being legally represented."

"Thank you very much." Stephen paused, and then added: "By the way, Inspector, you haven't told me how it was that you guessed why I went to Midchester."

"Well, it wasn't exactly difficult. You see, after our little talk the other day, I got a friend in the Markshire police to supply me with a list of the people who had been staying at Pendlebury at the same time as your father, and I noticed the name of Parsons on it."

"Then you were interested in the case, after all?"

"To that extent only. And I wouldn't go so far as to call it a case, exactly."

Stephen stroked his chin thoughtfully for a moment

221

or two before he spoke again. Then he said: "Look here, Inspector, I've been a bit of a fool about this Parsons business. How much of a fool I didn't know until it was pointed out to me yesterday. The more I think about it, the more I feel convinced that I was on the right track about Parsons. Is there any chance of the police helping me now to prove what I still believe to be the fact—that Parsons actually murdered my father?"

"Well," said Mallett slowly, "where there has been no crime officially known to the police and where the proposed suspect is dead in any case, there's very little we can do. All the same, in the very special circumstances here, entirely unofficially . . . Perhaps you could tell me just what your theory about Parsons is?"

Stephen plunged once more into the narration of the events which had taken place at Midchester and the theory Martin and he had built up upon their discoveries there. The inspector listened to him with grave attention. At the end of the recital he nodded slowly.

"Well, Mr. Dickinson, your theory is decidedly interesting. I wouldn't put it higher than that, but it is interesting, and if I may say so, ingenious. I see no reason why discreet inquiries should not be made, both in Midchester and London, and if anything comes of them, I shall, of course, let you know."

"If only the time wasn't so desperately short!" Stephen said. "I must, I simply *must*, have something to go upon by Monday at the very latest."

"I shouldn't despair of getting information by Monday," the inspector reassured him. "If there is any information to get, that is. We move pretty quickly in the Force, you know."

Sitting there in his arm-chair, he looked as solid and immovable as the Sphinx.

"As you are so short of time," he went on, "it was perhaps rather unfortunate that you didn't investigate the position of Parsons a little earlier in the day. I suppose that was because he happened to come at the bottom of your list?"

"We left him and Vanning to the end because they seemed the least likely."

"Just so. And before you got to them, I suppose you had sifted out all the other people on this list of mine?"

"Yes."

"Without any results?"

Stephen hesitated. With the recollection of Mr. Dedman's bitter sarcasm fresh in his mind, it was not surprising that he should be unwilling to expose his and Martin's shortcomings in the art of detection to a professional.

"Without any tangible results," he said, at last. "If there had been any, I should not have bothered about Parsons, of course."

"But there were results of a kind?"

"In two cases there was apparently something to go on, but it didn't amount to very much when you examined it afterwards."

Mallett shrugged his shoulders.

"This is your affair, of course, Mr. Dickinson," he said. "But I rather gathered that you would be glad of any help, official or otherwise, that I could give you. Besides, if you have any grounds for suspicion against anybody, I'm not sure that it isn't your duty to reveal them."

So encouraged, Stephen put to the best of his ability the case against Mr. and Mrs. Carstairs and Mrs. March. If he feared a repetition of the contemptuous reception which he had met from Mr. Dedman the day before, he was quickly reassured. The inspector proved to be a courteous and attentive listener, although it was impossible to tell from his face what impression the story was making on him.

"I'm afraid you'll think we have made a bad bungle of the whole affair," Stephen concluded.

"Not at all," Mallett assured him. "Not at all. I think, if I may say so, that you have been remarkably thorough in your investigations, all things considered. I shall remember what you have told me and follow it up so far as I can. There is only one aspect of the case which I am surprised that you have not taken into account," he added.

"What is that?"

"I seem to recollect at our first meeting your being somewhat impressed by one little fact which I brought to your notice. I mean, the curious little incident of the man whom your father thought he recognized while I was talking to him at the hotel. Have you considered that at all?"

"No. I admit I have not."

"Considering it now, do you think that any of the people we have been discussing could be identified with that person?"

"I don't think so."

"There may be nothing in it, of course, though I remember that at the time I first mentioned it to you, you seemed to attach some importance to it."

"I'm afraid I had forgotten all about it until you mentioned it just now."

"We are all of us liable to forget things," said the inspector, with the air of a man who was quite confident that he, personally, never forgot anything. "But it does seem to leave rather a hole in the inquiry so far, doesn't it? If you don't mind taking a word of advice from me, you'll devote a little time to filling that hole—if it can be done."

Stephen nodded thoughtfully. "Yes, I will," he said.

Mallett looked at his watch and rose to his feet.

"This has been a very interesting little talk," he said. "I don't mind telling you, Mr. Dickinson, that this affair has aspects which puzzle me quite a lot—entirely unofficially, of course, but I am puzzled. How far I shall be able to help you, I can't say, naturally. A lot depends on what, if anything, we can find out about Parsons and the gentleman who called himself Vanning. Meanwhile, have you considered the advisability of employing a private inquiry agent? They are not a class of people I care for very much, as a general rule, but there is one I know of who is quite reliable—when he is sober, that is."

"Do you mean Elderson?"

"That's the man. Don't let it get out that I sent you there, though."

"I have been to him already. In fact, it was on his investigation at the hotel that we based everything we have done since."

"Indeed? You sent him down there and he made you a report, I suppose?"

"Yes."

"Would you mind very much if I looked at it for a moment? One never knows, it might give one some ideas."

Stephen fetched it, and Mallett glanced through it. His inspection was a good deal less cursory than Mr. Dedman's had been, but it was none the less quick enough. As he was in the act of handing it back his features were suddenly convulsed in a spasm of pain.

"Is anything the matter?" Stephen asked.

"It's nothing," said the inspector faintly. "A touch of—of indigestion, I'm afraid." (Was it imagination, or did he blush as he made the confession?) "I think I must have eaten something poisonous," he went on.

"You don't look at all well," said Stephen. "Don't you think you should see a doctor?"

"Perhaps I should," said Mallett. "I dare say it's nothing to worry about, but I—I'm not used to this sort of thing. Do you know of any good doctor handy?"

"Our own man is only just down the road. He's pretty useful." He gave the name and address.

"Thank you. I'll look in there on my way. Goodbye."

He shook hands, and then added: "I had quite forgotten—Mr. Johnson will have to get a witness summons too. Will you let me have his address also?"

Stephen wrote it down for him.

"No doubt you will be seeing him soon," Mallett said, "and can let him know what to expect."

"I will, of course. As a matter of fact, I am expecting him here about five o'clock."

"That's all right then. Goodbye once more, Mr. Dickinson."

And with the best speed he could, the inspector made his way down the street to the doctor's house.

Soon after five, Martin's little car clattered up to the front door of the house. Stephen and his mother were finishing tea in the drawing-room.

"I'm afraid Anne won't be able to come out with you after all," said Mrs. Dickinson. "She seems to be in a thoroughly nervous state and I'm keeping her in bed."

"Sorry about that," said Martin. "Bit of a strain and all that, I'm afraid. Perhaps you'll tell her I looked in—if you think she'd like to know, that is. No thanks, I've had tea. I think, if you don't mind, I'll be toddling off now."

Stephen went out with him into the hall, and told him of the forthcoming summons to Midchester. Martin's sole comment was, "Bad show."

"Annie seems dreadfully wrought up about things," he added.

226

"Yes," said Stephen. "Do you know why, exactly?"

"No, I thought perhaps *you* would."

"I should think in some ways you know her better than I do."

"Well, she is sensitive and all that sort of thing," said Martin vaguely.

"You can't think of anything in particular that she should be sensitive about, so far as this show is concerned?"

"No—o, I don't think so. All the same, I can't help thinking it would be a good thing if you could let things drop altogether."

"I can't," said Stephen with an air of finality. "And, as a matter of fact, even if I could, I wouldn't—now."

"Meaning?"

"Meaning that I've just got an entirely new slant on the whole affair that may make all the difference."

"Well, I wish you luck, that's all," said Martin, opening the front door.

"I shall want you to help me, you know, Martin," Stephen told him, following him on to the pavement.

"Me? But I'm with Annie on this, you know."

"I dare say you are. But doesn't it seem to you that the quickest way to put her mind at rest will be to finish the business in the way we've always wanted to?"

" 'M, yes, I suppose so, in a way."

"Anyhow, I can't do this job properly without you. I want your car, at least. You can just be chauffeur if you like. Come round tomorrow morning. It will be the last time, Martin, I promise you that."

"All right, then. Shall I be round about tennish?"

"Ten o'clock will do. So long!"

"So long!"

Stephen turned to go back into the house and Martin settled himself in the driving-seat of his car. On the pavement opposite stood a shabbily dressed man. Martin observed casually that he had not seen him there before, and that he was supporting a tray of bootlaces and collar-studs for sale. He could be excused for not observing that attached to his waist coat was a rather more intricate object which was not for sale.

"Full face *and* profile," murmured the shabby man to himself when he was alone in the street once more. "Good enough, I think."

As he went back to the motorcycle which he had left at the police station, he reflected that in an instant of time, by the pressure of a finger, he had done something permanent and irrevocable. It was like pulling the lever that opens the trapdoor of the scaffold.

He was, for a policeman, a dangerously imaginative man.

20

Return to Pendlebury

Friday, September 1st

"How's Annie this morning?" were Martin's first words when he arrived at Plane Street next day.

"She's better," said Stephen shortly. "Had her breakfast in bed and isn't down yet. We'd better be getting off, hadn't we?"

"You know, Steve, I've a sort of notion you're not very keen on my seeing Annie this morning," Martin remarked, peering doubtfully at him through his thick glasses.

"My good Martin, do you want a repetition of yesterday's scene? Because if you do, I don't."

If Martin objected to being addressed as "My good Martin" by his prospective brother-in-law, he did not show it. He merely blinked at him and said:

"You don't think she'd like my coming out with you on this show?"

"She'd raise hell's delight, I should think."

"In that case," said Martin uncomfortably, "I think perhaps it would be best if I didn't come after all."

"You're coming, all right," answered Stephen in a

tone of such unusual authority that Martin, to his own surprise, found himself submitting quite meekly.

"Where are we going?" he asked when they were settled in the car.

"Oh, go through Hemel Hempstead. I'll explain as we go along."

Martin nodded and said nothing until they had covered some thirty miles. From time to time Stephen gave a direction, but otherwise he remained equally silent.

"Look here," Martin said at last, "I wish you'd tell me where we're going."

"Doesn't the road seem familiar, Martin?"

"I know most of the main roads about London, as a matter of fact. I don't know that there is anything specially familiar about this one. The last time I came down it was the day of your guv'nor's funeral, actually."

"Oh, yes, of course, coming back from Pendlebury. Well, as it's on our way, we might as well look in there."

"At the churchyard, d'you mean?"

"No, I meant at the hotel. (I wish you wouldn't swerve all over the road like that, Martin.) That is, unless you're nervous of going there."

"Why should I be nervous?"

"Why, indeed? After all, if you're investigating a murder, it's the natural thing to go to the place where it was done, isn't it? Are you feeling the heat, by the way?"

"No, why?"

"I thought you were sweating a bit, that's all. As I was going to say, it's an odd thing that all this time we've been hunting all over the country for clues, but none of us has ever thought to look at the hotel itself."

"Why should we? We paid Elderson to do it for us."

"Very true. It struck me at the time as rather odd that you were so keen not to go down there when we were first discussing this business."

"You didn't want to go down there yourself, for the matter of that."

"I had a very good reason. (I wish you'd look where you're going, Martin. You nearly had us into the ditch that time.) Your reason was, so far as I can remember, that you were afraid of being recognized by the people at the hotel—as a result of having been at the funeral."

"Yes. That's absolutely right. And a jolly good reason too."

"Of course, at the funeral you'd be one of the crowd of relations. I shouldn't have thought there was much risk. Anyway, that reason has gone now, hasn't it?"

"Yes, if you say so."

"I tell you another thing that has occurred to me lately, Martin. When you and Anne went off to Lincolnshire, I remember that you were very insistent that she should be the one to interview Mrs. Howard-Blenkinsop and that you should merely drive her down there."

"I don't know what you're driving at. You know as well as I do that I did see Mrs. Howard-Blenkinsop and had a glass of sherry off her."

"I wish you wouldn't turn round to talk to me like that, Martin. It's very dangerous. I can hear you quite well when you're looking ahead, you know. Yes, you talked to Mrs. Howard-Blenkinsop all right, but that was after you knew that she wasn't the woman who stayed in the hotel. It was awfully clever of you, Martin, to spot that so quickly."

"I wish you wouldn't go on saying 'Martin' every other word. It gets on my nerves."

"Never knew you had any, Martin. Sorry, but the name seems to have a fatal fascination for me. By the way, what do you think M stands for?"

"M?"

"Yes, M in M. Jones. In the hotel register, you know."

"How the hell should I know?"

"I just thought you might, that's all. You see, it has just occurred to me (funny what a lot of things keep occurring all of a sudden!) that if you are out on the loose—I think that is the accepted expression, isn't it?—there is always the suitcase problem to be got over."

"Now what on earth—"

"Come, come, Martin, you're not as dense as that, you know. In fact, I've always looked on you as pretty smart. You were fearfully clever at Midchester, I thought. For instance, your notion of having a good look at Parsons at the meeting before you decided that it was safe to go and see him—"

"Safe?"

"But I was forgetting. We were talking about the great suitcase problem, weren't we? What I had in mind was that if your suitcase was marked, say, 'M. J.' in letters large as life, it wouldn't do to go and register as Thomas Smith, for instance. It might make the man who took it up to your room just a bit suspicious. So you'd decide that the J. stood for Jones, just for that night, and M., I suppose, would be Michael or Matthew or Melchisedeck. . . . Do you really want to stop at Pendlebury, Martin?"

"Damn you! Why shouldn't I?"

"Just as you please. I thought perhaps you might be afraid of someone recognizing you—from having seen you at the funeral, of course. And talking of recognition, it is a bit awkward when you are recognized when you're out on the loose, isn't it, Martin?"

Martin did not answer, except by putting his foot down more firmly on the accelerator. The car was travelling at its highest speed now, and in the roar of the air past the windscreen Stephen had to raise his voice to be heard.

"Of course, it would depend on who recognized you, I suppose," he went on. "For a man who is wanting to get married I should think his prospective father-in-law is about the worst person to run into. Especially if it's a father-in-law who doesn't like him in any case."

Stephen put his mouth very close to Martin's ear so that there was no chance of a word being lost. His voice had suddenly dropped entirely the ironic tone which it had held until then.

"You wanted Anne, and you knew your chances of getting her were absolutely gone if he saw you there," he said. "You wanted money, and you thought he had plenty to leave. You knew that life in our family was hell so long as he was alive, anyway. So you took your chance then, you murdering swine! And it's no good your thinking you can serve me the same way you did him. I'm ready for you—there's a gun in my pocket and if you don't do just what I tell you—*Martin!*" His voice rose to a scream as his gaze shifted momentarily to the road ahead. "Look out, for God's sake!"

But Martin was past all heeding. Red-faced, stammering, his wide eyes grotesquely magnified by his thick glasses, he turned to face his accuser. The car swung dangerously on to the offside of the road as it reached a sharp left-hand bend. The heavy lorry which was coming down the steep eastern slope of Pendlebury Hill had no chance whatever of avoiding it. It crashed into the side of the little car and rolled it completely over, a tangled heap of steel and glass.

Mallett's car had left New Scotland Yard at about the same time that Martin's had started from Hampstead. It had to traverse the whole of Central London before getting on to the open road and consequently, in spite of its superior speed, it was some twenty minutes later that it arrived on the scene of the accident. A police constable was taking particulars from the white-faced lorry driver and an ambulance was drawn up by the roadside. As Mallett got out of his car, the first-aid men were lifting two limp bodies on to stretchers. One of them was groaning feebly and turning his heavily bandaged head from side to side. The other was ominously still. The inspector looked at them. His face expressed neither sympathy nor horror, only a mild surprise. He said a word to the driver of the ambulance and went back to his car.

"We'll go on to Pendlebury Old Hall," he said to his driver.

"There's nothing we can do here, I suppose, sir?"

"Nothing at all. It's an unfortunate business, but— perhaps it simplifies things on the whole."

At the hotel he asked for the manager. The man was inclined to be unhelpful at first, but under Mallett's gentle pressure soon became amenable enough. He looked with interest at the photograph which the inspector showed him but shook his head doubtfully.

"I think so, but I couldn't be sure," he said. "Not to swear to, I mean. I dare say some of my staff could, though. Shall I ask Miss Carter?"

"Would you know him again if you saw him?"

"Oh, yes, I'm certain of that. A photograph's one thing but the living face is another."

"Then if you don't mind coming along in my car, we needn't bother Miss Carter. I'm not so sure about the *living* face, though," Mallett added, sardonically.

His premonition was right. At the hospital they were directed not to the accident ward but to the mortuary. They were conducted there by an attendant, who was as cheerful as only those whose daily business is with death and disfigurement can be.

He whistled jauntily as they walked along the echoing corridor, breaking off to observe:

"Funny things, these car crashes! Here's this chap,

234

multiple injuries all over the place. Simply smashed to bits. He might just as well have stopped a charge of H.E. And the other fellow sitting beside him gets away with a couple of scalp wounds and concussion. Dirty work, isn't it? Well, here we are! You'll find his face is O.K. luckily. It's about the only thing that is."

He drew aside the sheet that covered the face of the dead man. The hotel manager craned forward to see. Mallett stood in the background, anxious neither by word nor sign to influence him in any way. In silence they left the mortuary and when they were outside, Mallett said, "Well?"

"That's him, all right," was the answer.

Confident though he had been, the inspector breathed a sigh of relief.

"Thank you for your help," he said. "And now I'll drive you back to your hotel."

"Am I likely to hear any more of this matter?" the manager asked him, as he deposited him at his door. "It's very bad for business, you know."

"You won't ever be troubled with it again," was the confident reply.

"I'm very glad to hear that. But won't you stay to lunch as my guest, Inspector?"

"No, thank you," replied Mallett with great emphasis.

21

Mallet Sums Up

Monday, September 4th

Mallet was about to begin his report on the Dickinson case when the house-telephone rang.

"There's a Mr. Dedman wants to see you," he was told. "He says it is urgent."

The inspector sighed. The file labelled "*Re* Dickinson," now bulging with papers, yawned balefully at him. He was anxious to be rid of it once for all, and he grudged any interruption.

"Ask him if he'll kindly come back tomorrow," he said. "I'm very busy just now."

There was a pause and then the voice said: "The gentleman says he must see you this morning, sir. Tomorrow will be too late. He is most insistent." Then, in an undertone, "He seems perfectly genuine, sir."

"Very well," said Mallett, in a resigned tone. "Tell him to come up."

A moment or two later Mr. Dedman bounced, rather than walked, into the room. He wasted no time in greetings but came straight to the point.

"I'm a busy man, Inspector," he said, "and so, I have

236

no doubt, are you. I shouldn't be here if it wasn't vitally necessary in my clients' interests. My firm are the solicitors to the estate of the late Mr. Leonard Dickinson. The deceased had insured his life for the sum of—"

"Oh, Mr. Dedman, but I know all about that," Mallett murmured.

"You do? Good! Then I needn't waste any time explaining. The point is, that today is the last day of which I can secure any payment from the Company on the basis of suicide. I understand that you have been investigating this case. All I want from you is a clear indication—murder or suicide—which?"

"Oh," said Mallett quietly. "Murder, undoubtedly."

"Excellent! I'm much obliged to you. You shall hear from us if litigation proves necessary." And Mr. Dedman shot out of his chair and made for the door.

"Good Heavens!" said the inspector in astonishment. "Do you really mean to tell me that you don't want to hear any more? Aren't you interested to know who murdered your client?"

"Naturally I am, but that can wait. I'm a solicitor, not a policeman. Besides, they told me downstairs that you were extremely busy."

"I assure you, they told you the truth. All the same, in your own interests, I should advise you to make yourself acquainted with all the facts of the case before you go to see the Insurance Company. There is a little point of law which you might like to consider first."

"A point of law?" echoed Mr. Dedman, sitting down again.

"Precisely. Do you mind telling me, how did the late Mr. Leonard Dickinson dispose of his estate?"

"One half to his widow for life, with remainder to the children in equal shares, the other half divided between the children absolutely."

"And of that estate the insurance moneys form a part?"

"Of course—by far the larger part."

"Is there not a rule of law, Mr. Dedman, that a murderer is not allowed to profit by the will of his victim?"

Mr. Dedman stared at the inspector silent and open-mouthed. His brisk and business-like manner seemed suddenly deflated.

"Inspector," he said at last, "who murdered my client?"

"His son, Stephen."

"Good God!" said Mr. Dedman, and mopped his forehead with his handkerchief. "Good God!" he repeated. "But—but—Are you serious about this, Inspector?"

"Perfectly serious."

"But I tell you, this doesn't make sense! Stephen! Why it was he who was so insistent all along that—"

"That his father had been murdered? Exactly. It is the only case in my experience where a murderer found himself in the position of having to prove that the crime had been committed, in order to attain the result for which he had committed it."

Mr. Dedman looked at his watch, replaced it in his pocket, and then crossed his legs and settled back in his chair.

"Please tell me all about it," he requested, in tones that were for him positively humble.

Mallett was only too glad to comply. If he had a weakness, it was that he loved an audience. The circumstances of the present case had compelled him to work entirely alone, and he was pleased with the opportunity. Preparing a written report was always irksome to him, but he thoroughly enjoyed an exposition by word of mouth.

"Stephen Dickinson," he began, "was an inveterate gambler on the Stock Exchange. He was at all material

238

times, as you lawyers say, hopelessly in debt. He was thoroughly unprincipled, like many gamblers, except, oddly enough, where sex was concerned. I haven't been able to trace that he ever had anything to do with women. In that respect, he seems to have been positively puritan. He was, of course, extremely conceited and entirely selfish. I have yet to meet a murderer who wasn't. In particular, he disliked and despised his father, and having met the old gentleman myself, I can believe that he must have been an extremely tiresome person to live with."

Dedman nodded his emphatic agreement.

"About the middle of the summer," the inspector proceeded, "Stephen, whose financial position began to be really difficult, appears to have first formed the idea of murdering his father. He was, of course, well aware of the existence of the insurance policy which had been taken out after the death of Mr. Arthur Dickinson. He was also familiar with his father's habit of taking Medinal tablets under medical advice."

"How do you fix the date?" Mr. Dedman asked.

"It was about this time, as I learned from the family doctor whom I saw the other day, that the father purported to write to the doctor suggesting that as an experiment he should try taking the drug in powder form. The doctor duly prescribed, and shortly afterwards received a letter saying that the powder did not suit the father, and that he would prefer to continue with the tablets. Both letters were, of course, forgeries, and the son intercepted the prescription and so secured the means of carrying out his design.

"Having done this, he waited until his father went on his annual walking tour before putting his plan into execution. There may have been some reason against attempting the murder in his own home. Perhaps he had some sentimental feeling about it. I don't know. In any

239

case, he decided that it should be done at Pendlebury Old Hall Hotel, where he knew that his father, a creature of habit if ever there was one, would infallibly end his holiday. He was in this difficulty, however, that he did not know precisely on what day his father would arrive there. At the same time, he had to make provision for as conclusive an alibi as possible.

"He got over it in this way: He arranged to go to Switzerland with his sister for the holidays and then at the last moment invented some excuse for not joining her at the time arranged. (We have been to some trouble over the week end to find out from the hotel details as to how his room was cancelled at short notice.) Then he went to stay at Pendlebury until such time as his father should come along. He took the name of Stewart Davitt—the initials were the same as his own, naturally enough, so that he should not be given away by his luggage, which, no doubt, was marked 'S.D.' more or less prominently."

"Talking of initials," said Mr. Dedman, "have you observed—"

"I shall come to that presently," said Mallett. He went on: "He gave an address in Hawk Street, which, I have since ascertained, is in fact a lodging-house and was until the other day the address of a clerk in the office of the stockbrokers through whom he carried on his speculations. He was on close terms of acquaintance with this young man, who has, by the way, since been dismissed by his employers for gambling in shares on his own account. At the hotel, he selected the room next to the one which he knew his father always occupied. (I expected he was familiar, to the point of boredom, with every detail of the old man's life at his beloved Pendlebury.) He made an excuse for keeping out of sight of all the other residents in the hotel, and bided his time.

"In due course, Mr. Dickinson came to the hotel. As he always did, he ordered a cup of tea to be sent up to his room. As he always did, when it arrived, he told the maid to leave it outside until he was ready for it. All that the son had to do was to slip out of the room adjoining, empty his packet of Medinal powder into the tea-pot (the stuff dissolves quite quickly and is almost tasteless, I am told) and slip back again. The father came out, took in the tray, added his usual dose to the already poisoned tea and went to sleep, never to wake up again. Early next morning, having made his arrangements overnight, Stephen Dickinson left the hotel, caught the express to London, took the eight o'clock aeroplane for Zürich, and met his sister in Klosters that afternoon, no doubt telling her that he had travelled out by boat and train in the usual way. He immediately carried her off on a long climbing expedition, sleeping in various mountain huts, until he knew that it would be too late for him to be in time for the inquest or the funeral, at either of which he might be recognized. (The Swiss authorities, by the way, have been very helpful in tracing the guide whom they took with them.)

"So far as he could tell, everything had gone according to plan. His father would be found dead of an overdose of his usual medicine, a sympathetic coroner would find that death was accidental and no questions would ever be asked. And that, no doubt, was what would have happened, but for three unfortunate accidents—firstly, the presence of a remarkably apt quotation by the bedside; secondly, the fact that having just come to the end of one bottle of tablets the deceased had opened another to make up his usual dose; and lastly, the very peculiar manner in which the old gentleman had talked to me on the eve of his death. And the son had put it out of his power to correct these misconceptions at the inquest! Whether he realized at once how fatal a finding of suicide was to his hopes of reaping the reward of his crime, I don't know. At all events, he learned it soon enough. It put him in a very nasty position." Mallett chuckled. "A very nasty position indeed! Having taken the appalling risk of committing murder, he had to take the yet more terrible risk of proving that a murder had been committed—by someone.

"And so Stephen Dickinson, the gambler that he was, decided on the greatest gamble of his life. And before taking any other step, he came round to see—*me*, of all people. I suppose he thought that I might be able to give him some useful facts, that would help him in disproving suicide, but I fancy that his real motive was to see whether he could get away with an interview with me without arousing any suspicion in my mind. If he could do that, no doubt he felt that he would be safe in carrying out the inquiries which he proposed. And he certainly succeeded! I never gave the matter a thought. It wasn't until the other day, when the suicide of that man at Midchester brought the whole affair back into my mind again, that I ever seriously considered the question of whether Mr. Dickinson had been killed and if so, by whom.

"Of course when you come to look into it," the inspector confessed with a shrug of his shoulders, "the whole affair becomes startlingly simple. There is the question of motive for one thing. But over and above that, the principal clue, as you no doubt have realized, Mr. Dedman, is the perfect knowledge that the killer must have had of his victim's habits. Consider: he must have known, in the first place, that he would be at this particular hotel, and sleep in this particular bedroom. He must have known that he was accustomed to this particular drug, and to taking it in this particular way. He must even have been

242

familiar with his insistence that the tea should always be left *outside* the door. Now who on earth could have had such a combination of knowledge except a member of the deceased's own family?"

"Something of that sort had occurred to me," remarked Dedman. "That was why I favored the theory that the murderer had made a mistake and that the deceased had taken the poison intended for someone else."

"Instead of which," Mallett rejoined, "if Vanning—whose real name is Purkis, by the way, a nasty little blackmailer—if he had slept in the room that was originally intended for him, he would have been murdered in place of Mr. Dickinson!

"Well, the rest of the story is no news to you, I think. After his interview with me, young Dickinson spent the next two weeks scouring the country trying to fix the responsibility for his own crime on to the shoulders of some innocent person, aided and abetted by his equally innocent sister and her fiancé. They investigated the antecedents of every person staying in the hotel, except, of course, the mythical Mr. Davitt."

"He reserved the case of Davitt for himself," Mr. Dedman put in. "And invented a purely imaginary interview with an equally imaginary landlady to account for him."

"That is just what I expected. The attempt to find a scapegoat for his own crime was a forlorn hope, of course, but it came perilously near to success twice. The first time, was in the case of Parsons."

"I told him that properly handled, the Parsons affair might have produced a favorable settlement from the Insurance Company," said Mr. Dedman in vexation. "It was really pitiful to see how he and young Johnson bungled that business! I beg your pardon, Inspector, I was forgetting. Please go on."

"The second time," said Mallett, his moustache points twitching as he tried to suppress a smile, "the result was very nearly more serious than it had been in Parsons' case. I think he was prepared to throw up the sponge after you had pointed out to him that he had failed to prove Parsons' guilt; but the news that his last speculation had ruined him drove him to make one last despairing effort. And I am afraid I was really responsible. As a last resort, he tried to put the guilt upon Martin Johnson. You see, Johnson really had something to hide. He was no murderer, but he did happen to be in the hotel on the night of the murder, and he was almost recognized there by Mr. Dickinson. Incidentally, Mr. Dickinson was talking to me at the time, and I remember noticing that immediately afterwards he suddenly switched the conversation to his daughter, who had not been mentioned before. I saw the significance of that only when I had learned that Johnson was his daughter's fiancé."

"I knew it!" exclaimed Mr. Dedman. "Jones!"

"Exactly. The suitcase point over again."

"But not that point only. I knew it as soon as I saw Miss Dickinson's face when the name of Jones was mentioned in my office."

"She knew that he had been there, gallivanting with another young lady of his choice?"

"Undoubtedly. And I am very much afraid she knows a good deal more than that."

"I am sorry to hear it. So far as Stephen Dickinson is concerned, he does not seem to have guessed it until at our last meeting I put it into his head. I did it to test his reactions, but I confess that I did not think they would be as violent as they proved to be."

"That is a question that is puzzling me," said Mr. Dedman. "How did young Dickinson hope to be able to represent that Johnson was guilty, in the face of the violent denials he would be sure to make, and what was his object in getting him to drive down to Pendlebury?"

"We can only guess at that," the inspector replied. "But I have not the smallest doubt what the true answer is. He intended to kill Johnson."

"But this is terrible!" said Mr. Dedman.

"Why not? One murder often leads to another, and a pistol was found on him when he was picked up. I think that his design was to kill him, and represent it as suicide brought on by remorse acting on a guilty conscience. The point of taking him to Pendlebury, no doubt, was to give colour to the theory. He would be able to say afterwards that he charged him with the crime and that he had then confessed. It would have been very difficult to disprove. Possibly he did actually go so far as to accuse him. That would account for the erratic driving of the car. Johnson will be able to tell you that when he is better. How is he, by the way?"

"Almost recovered. But he has no recollection of anything that happened for half an hour before the accident. On the whole, I think it is just as well."

"As you say. He seems to have got off very lightly. I never saw a more completely smashed car in my life. But of course the passenger's side took the brunt of the collision."

"And how did you come to be on the spot so very opportunely, Inspector?"

"I was going to the Old Hall myself, to see whether the people there could identify Stephen Dickinson from the photograph which I had taken of him the afternoon before. As it turned out, I was able to get the identification from his body instead, which was much more satisfactory."

The two men sat in silence for a few moments, and then the solicitor rose to his feet.

"Thank you," he said. "I shall be making my claim on the Insurance Company for the full amount of the policy moneys today. So far as Stephen Dickinson's share is concerned, I don't think there will be any difficulty. It will naturally fall into the rest of the estate and be divided between his mother and sister. The one thing that concerns me now is to see that Mrs. Dickinson never learns the truth. Goodbye."

The inspector turned to his writing. For an hour there was no sound in the quiet room except the gentle scratching of his pen on the paper. At last, even that ceased. The record was complete. The file of "*Re Dickinson*" returned for the last time to its drawer in the inspector's desk.

At his mother's insistence, Stephen was buried in Pendlebury churchyard next to his father. There was a full attendance of the family at the funeral. It was observed by all that Uncle George was in far better humour than usual. The reason, as Aunt Lucy could have told them, was that since the settlement with the Insurance Company there was no longer any ground for fearing that he would be called upon to contribute anything to the support of his brother's family.